WHEN THE RING CALLS

Nicola Samuel-Stevens

Book 1 of the KINGSLAND series

Disclaimers

1. This is a work of fiction. Unless otherwise indicated, all the names, characters, businesses, places, events and incidents in this book are either the product of the author's imagination or used in a fictitious manner. Any resemblance to actual persons, living or dead, or actual events is purely coincidental.

2. Everything Christian and Biblical imparted in this book is true. Talk to an adult who holds a position of responsibility in a church if you have any questions about anything you have read. Some things in the Bible are so powerful that they should NOT be used without fully understanding. They should NEVER be used lightly or experimented with, and certainly NEVER without a responsible and knowledgeable ADULT present.

3. All the Bible quotes in this book are taken from different translations and are reproduced under the terms of 'fair use'

ISBN 978-1-304-48858-9

**For Jordan
With love
Always & forever
xxx Mum xxx**

KINGSLAND

To Glorify God
To teach the love and ways of Christian Faith
To show it to be the joy and adventure it truly is
To spread His gospel and advance His Kingdom
To dispel any and all ungodly myths and
practices
To equip all with the knowledge, power and
authority given to us by Jesus, in His name
To stand firm against the Enemy
To live in freedom
To lead a victorious life
To deepen our relationship with God the Father,
Jesus Christ the Son, and the Holy Spirit.
AMEN

CONTENTS

All chapter titles in this story are inspired by
and taken from book titles in the Bible.

*Explanations regarding Christian and Biblical
references and terminology can be found in
alphabetical order at the back in the Appendices.
The references sourced are accurate but by no
means exhaustive.*

WHEN THE KING CALLS

CHAPTER ONE

Darwin's Genesis

"What are you doing?" asked a shy, tentative voice. Hilly opened her eyes, unsure if she had imagined it. She often came to this spot. A small oasis of leafy calm, hidden just behind the bike shed, next to the allotments. No one else ever came here. It was her place of retreat, away from the daily hustle and tussle that was school. Her secret place.

"Were you taking a nap?" the voice asked curiously.

'The hedge, the hedge is talking to me,' Hilly thought wryly, and mumbled, "I know I prayed for a hedge of protection, Lord, but I didn't expect it to speak!"

The voice giggled. It was a sweet, muffled sound as if the owner were trying to stuff it all back in.

"I think you'd better come out," Hilly called kindly, eyeing the laurel hedge with amusement.

"No, I'd rather stay here, if you don't mind." The voice faltered. "But," it said hesitantly, "It was cool, what you just did, for Tom."

"You were there?" asked Hilly.

"Yes!" the voice said vehemently, "Jess is always picking on Tom, it's not his fault that his uniform is too small for him, he's grown a lot in the last two weeks. My mum says that Tom is going to take after his father, who is a walking beanpole." The words seemed to leap out of her mouth, much like first time parachutists from a plane – at first clinging, terrified, then finally euphoric once they were actually out!

The impassioned defence of a friend made Hilly smile. She decided she rather liked this talking hedge, it had chutzpah and a heart!

And it was right, Jess Wilkins was a bully, of that she was in no doubt. But she was also aware of the spiritual influence fuelling his actions and the unfortunate circumstances of his home life. So before stepping in she had asked God the Father for protection, wisdom, and to pour His peace on the unfolding crisis. Then still speaking under her breath, wielding the quiet authority bestowed upon her, she had called, "Jess!" looked directly into his eyes and commanded him to "Stop!" Although she was speaking to him, she was also addressing the Enemy – the Devil. He did not have a choice: fists clenched, he took a faltering step towards her, cussed, turned on his heels and sloped off. Then dispersing the remaining spectators with a swift, "You too!" she had helped Tom to his feet and sent him off to see the school nurse. Thanking the Father, she had headed for her secluded corner, praying for the immediate healing of Tom's bleeding nose in the name of Jesus, the son of God.

"You were very brave," said the hedge.
"Oh, I wasn't brave." Hilly smiled.

"Yes, you were!" rustled the hedge. "I saw you, you looked him straight in the eye and told him to stop! One word! Stop! And he did! You were amazing and sooo cool!" the voice rushed on, another parachute moment in full flight (or perhaps we should say, 'full float'…!)

"Anyway," it continued, "How did you do that? Did you take lessons? Can anyone learn? Was it expensive? I bet it was. Ooooh, would I need to wear some kind of uniform or something, like in Taekwondo? Hiyah!! Cos look, I might be small, but I'm tough!" said the hedge, doing a particularly good impression of some form of martial art. "Hey, you still haven't answered my question!" the voice finished, finally running out of breath.

"Uh, um which one?!" asked Hilly, amused and amazed that anyone could fit that many words in one breath!

"What were you doing, just a minute ago, when you had your eyes closed? Were you napping? Can't say as I blame you mind; you must be shattered after standing up to Jess like that!"

"Oh that, no, I was praying," Hilly said. A silence followed, worthy of whistling wind and tumbleweed. "Hello?!" she called.

"They said you were weird," came the voice, barely above a whisper.

"Thank you!" chuckled Hilly, having heard this sort of comment many times before.

"Thank you? I thought you'd be cross."

"No, no, I do weird, weird is great, thank you!"

"You are definitely weird, weird with a capital WUH!" said the hedge.

"Thank you, thank you again!" Hilly chortled.

"You're welcome," replied the voice, unconvinced. "Weirdo!"

Suddenly the absurdity of the whole conversation had Hilly laughing. Only that very morning had she asked Father God to bring more signs and wonders into her everyday life, but this, this 'verbal herb' was not what she had been expecting! The Lord certainly had a sense of humour!

"What's so funny?" asked the slightly irritated voice.

"Well, this is a first!" Hilly giggled, her mirth rising.

"What is?!"

"It's not every day I get insulted by a shrub!" she roared, flopping onto her back. It wasn't that funny really, Hilly thought, clutching her belly, yet somehow it just was!

Amidst loud rustling and snapping twigs, a small shadow fell across Hilly's face. She opened her eyes to see a petite birdlike girl with bright auburn hair, startling amber eyes, freckles, and a frown, standing over her, tapping her foot. "I am NOT a shrub!" she huffed indignantly.

She reminded Hilly of a furious speckled woodpecker. Her sharp honed features and feathered haircut added to this impression, particularly her slightly pointed nose. But even in her current agitated state, Hilly thought she was wonderful.

Wiping her eyes, Hilly jumped to her feet. "Hi," she grinned, holding out her hand, "I'm Hilly, Hilary Trueman."

The girl looked suspiciously at her, then shook it vigorously once, with a tiny, but surprisingly strong, hand. "Lauren, Lauren Darwin," she said guardedly.

"Woah, that's quite a grip you've got there!" Hilly said, wriggling her crushed fingers.

"Mmm, must be the potatoes," said Lauren absently, not taking her eyes off Hilly.

Blinking, Hilly thought, 'potatoes?' but decided to let that one go for now. "So, are you in the same year as Tom?" she asked.

"Yes, I've just joined, although I've been friends with Tom all my life. We're neighbours, we live right next door to each other."

"Ah, mystery solved, I didn't think I'd seen you before." Hilly smiled.

Lauren relaxed a little, allowing a small smile to flicker across her own lips, and thinking to herself, there was something about this girl she could not quite put her finger on. She looked ordinary enough: brown shoulder length hair, brown smiley eyes, even her skin tone was 'summer holiday' brown and she had an open, friendly smile, but it was not just that... Then realising that she had been staring she replied, "Yeah, I've only been here, two weeks. What year are you in?" she asked Hilly, trying to figure out what it was about her that felt different.

"Year nine."

"Year nine? So, you're only fifteen?" Lauren asked, surprised.

"Fourteen, I'm fifteen in a couple of months. You must be eleven, if you're in Tom's year, year seven?"

"Yeah," said Lauren. Then, taking another breath, she blurted, "Even though you're short, very short actually, I thought you were a lot older, you know, the way you bossed Jess around, I thought you were like, a prefect or something."

"Yeah, I get that a lot." She shrugged self-consciously. "My mum says it's because I've got 'an old head on young shoulders', or something. And the 'short', 'very short' thing, well, that comes from the 'Hobbit' side of the family!" she teased.

"Hobbit?"

"Yeah, complete with hairy feet!"

"Ewww you've got hairy feet?! Gross!" shuddered Lauren, taking a step back.

Restrained laughter bubbled within Hilly. "Oh, but it's not all bad," she continued, her eyes dancing with mischief, "At least I get to have a second breakfast every day!"

"Second breakfast?" Lauren repeated, completely bemused. "What's that got to do with anything? I often have two Weetabix."

Lauren's last comment finished Hilly off, a huge guffaw exploded from deep within, leaving her convulsing in helpless laughter. Between gasping snorts and gurgles, she tried to apologize. "I'm so," *gasp* "sorry," *gurgle*. "You are just," *snort* "so fuuunny!"

Despite herself, Lauren felt a delicious warmth rise up from within, spreading into a huge grin.

"I am?" she asked, both puzzled and flattered. No one had ever said that about her before. She tried it on for size. Yes, that would do nicely. Funny fitted her perfectly.

She watched Hilly trying to regain control and said, "You know, you laugh so much you should be called 'Hilarity' Trueman, not Hilary!"

This set Hilly's giggles off again until, grasping her sides, she wheezed, "Stop! Don't say any more, or I'll wet myself!"

Delighted at Hilly's reaction, she determined there and then that this would be her main goal in life from now on, to make people laugh. Well, that and bagging an A star in art!

Dryly she quipped, "Like I said earlier, 'weirdo'!" Then, rolling her eyes dramatically at Hilly's renewed giggles, she asked, "What planet are you from? Not this one, that's for sure!"

"Nope, you're right," said Hilly, pulling herself together, "I don't belong here. "We are in this world but not of it."

"What?" Lauren asked with a raised brow.

"Or more accurately, "*They are not of the world, even as I am not of the world*' – John 16," Hilly quoted.

"John who? Sixteen? What year is he in?" asked Lauren, completely baffled.

Just then the school bell rang, signalling the end of lunch.

"He's not in a year," said Hilly over her shoulder, "He's in a book – come on, or we'll be late for class."

"Okayyy," Lauren huffed.

12

Ha! thought Hilly – the 'woodpecker's back! "Look, meet me back here, in last break, and I'll tell you all about the book."

"...'Kay, but it better be a good one!" Lauren warned.

"Oh, it is," said Hilly, smiling enigmatically.

* * *

CHAPTER TWO

Lauren's Exodus

"So, come on then, tell us about that book and this 'John' bloke," Lauren urged. "We've only got ten minutes, mind," she said, plonking herself on the grass next to Hilly.

'Us' being the operative word, for hovering uncertainly beside her was Tom, looking a little pale and awkward. He was tall and gangly, with dark brown hair and wide blue eyes.

"Hi Tom, how are you feeling now?" Hilly asked.

"I'm okay," he mumbled, not quite making eye contact.

"Any more trouble from Jess?"

"No." He winced, touching his nose. "Th-thank you, for earlier, for wh-what you did," he stammered.

"No worries." She smiled, taking note of his defeated posture. "You could learn to do it too, you know."

"Really?" he asked, doubt written all over his face.

"How?" asked Lauren, her curiosity ignited.

"Well, it's one of the many things I've learned from reading that book," Hilly enthused. "It contains the knowledge and ability to prepare you to face any challenge and overcome any problem."

"Go on then, we're all ears," said Lauren expectantly.

"Well..." Hilly exhaled, blowing through her lips. "There's so much to tell you, it's hard to explain it all in ten minutes, but in a nutshell, it's about the creation of an entire world, well, universe actually. Ummm...an evil that enters that world, and an enemy that rebels and tries to destroy it – down through many generations. Uhhh there's countless characters, some even having their own chapters; aaaannnd...tons of adventures that include kidnapping, slavery, murder; there are battles, weddings and the dead brought back to life."

"Cool!" said Tom, "Zombies!"

"Ah not quite!" said Hilly, hastily moving on. "It's about a beautiful kingdom full of joy and peace, ruled by an ever-loving King, a Father, who sacrifices His only son to save His people; and the birth of a hero, born to save that world. Ummm...and a comforter, a 'Spirit of Truth' sent to help and guide His people. There's no sickness there, no crying, no death, just happiness." Hilly paused to gather her thoughts and found herself the focus of two very wide sets of eyes, one blue and earnest, the other amber and ambiguous.

"Sounds great!" exclaimed Tom excitedly.

"Mmm," shrugged Lauren, still not entirely convinced.

Holding their gazes, Hilly leaned forward. "This book, it's not just a story," she said quietly. "It's a belief, a way of life. It guides you, empowers you, it protects you, and teaches you everything you'll ever need to know."

"It does?" asked Tom intently.

"How? How can a book do all that?" asked Lauren.

"Because it's not the book itself, but the power of the words written within the book by a mighty, all-knowing, all-loving author. One who I have come to love with all my heart. This book has changed the lives of millions and millions of people. It's full of knowledge and wisdom, advice and some profoundly serious warnings."

Both were now listening, openly intrigued, leaning in.

"This book, the events described, the truths recorded, the miracles performed and the prophecies, that have already come to pass... The supernatural content of this book and the message it contains... Well, it's been the cause of controversy and turmoil, love and hope throughout the ages. The cause of terrible, terrible things done in its name. It has divided nations, it has torn down cities, it has ripped families apart. It has been the cause of dreadful wars – not something we like to dwell on. And yet, this book, and the truth it contains, is the only thing that can save humankind. It is the only thing that gives us hope and the promise of a better, everlasting, never-ending future."

Tom and Lauren exchanged looks. "Ffft, you take it all very seriously, don't you?!" Lauren quipped. "Do you belong to some 'fan club', or something?"

"I do." Hilly smiled wryly.

"I knew it!" she declared gleefully. "Okay, you've got me, I'm interested. What's this book called? And how does this 'John' bloke fit in?"

16

Smiling, Hilly said "'John' is a fisherman and one of twelve very important men in the book."

"And the book?" Lauren pressed.

"The Bible," Hilly said simply.

"Woah, and I thought 'Star Wars' was intense!" Tom exclaimed.

Lauren stared open mouthed, incredulous, before exploding, "THE BIBLE?!" She elbowed Tom in the ribs and gave him a 'shut up Tom' look. "You've got to be kidding me!" she continued. "I've just wasted my last break, listening to a bunch of stuff from the Bible?!"

"Yep!" Hilly smiled. "Amazing, isn't it?"

"I could think of a few things to call it, 'amazing' isn't one of 'em," Lauren grumbled, now in full 'woodpecker' mode. "Anyway, I don't believe all *that* happened in the Bible."

"Yeah, it did." Hilly nodded.

"What, murders and kidnapping?" Lauren scoffed. "I thought it was just about Christmas, and the Nativity and baby Jesus!"

"Well, yeah! That and other things," Hilly affirmed.

"Who was kidnapped?" asked Tom curiously.

"There were a few, but Joseph, son of Jacob, not Joseph, husband of Mary from the nativity, was one of them. You know, the one who had dreams and wore a robe of many colours."

They both looked blankly at her, Lauren's cheeks pink with rising irritation. Something had definitely been stirred within her.

Then Tom's expression shifted. "Are you talking about the 'Joseph' who had an 'amazing technicolour dreamcoat'?"

"One and the same," Hilly said.

"Hang on, I thought that was a musical?" Lauren challenged.

"It is, but it's taken from the Bible, from the story of Joseph's life, found in Genesis 37," Hilly explained.

"Flippin' 'eck, you'll be telling me 'Phantom of the bloomin' Opera's from the Bible next!" Lauren complained.

Hilly giggled. "No, but it's by the same composer – Andrew Lloyd Webber!"

Lauren snorted, rolling her eyes. "Well, I've heard enough of this," she said, standing up. "Come on Tom, we've got chemistry next."

"Yeah, okay," he said dejectedly. "Anyway, how would any of this stop Jess Wilkins from picking on me?"

"Because the Bible will give you the skills and courage to stand strong against Jess. Like I did," Hilly assured him.

"What, like musicals?! What ya gonna do, sing to him?!" Lauren scoffed, her feathers decidedly ruffled.

Hilly smiled. "Well now that you mention it, 'Worship', which does include singing, is a very powerful weapon."

"Right! I'm out of here!" Lauren declared. "Tom!" she barked over her shoulder, marching off towards the classrooms, her receding remarks pecking the air as if it were a tree. "I! Don't! Believe! In all that stuff…! Anyway, it's boring…! Next she'll be saying 'Jesus loves me!'" she trilled.

18

Tom followed in her wake, head down, shoulders slumped.

"Well, that went well, Lord." Hilly grimaced. "Certainly rankled the enemy! I sure hope I heard you right, Father."

Then 'God's peace' settled upon her, and she headed off to her next lesson, fighting the mischievous urge to run after Lauren singing 'Yes Jesus loves you' and giggling at what she imagined would be her horrified reaction! "You know Lord, she really is like a feisty woodpecker!" giggled Hilly.

* * *

CHAPTER THREE

Levi's Tuchus

"Levi Silverberg, get your tuchus back inside and finish your homework!" shrilled his mother. "No buts. Biology and then bedroom – it needs tidying. Now!"

Lauren often wondered if Levi Silverberg ever got to take his 'tuchus' out. She could hear him riding around in his backyard and imagined it to be some super-duper mountain bike or something – but he never seemed to get very far before he was hauled back in. Of course, she had never set eyes on Levi Silverberg or his mum, but she often heard them in their garden over the wall, as she sat peeling potatoes in the rear of her dad's fish and chip shop 'The Chirpy Chippy'.

Her parents had moved to Kingsland just after she was born, inheriting the chip shop and its name – unfortunately.

She felt like she had spent her whole life peeling potatoes, her hands covered in mud and up to her knees in vegetable skins. But it helped her parents, and she was grateful for the pocket money she earned. Her latest save was for a ticket to see 'Cats' when it came to Kingsland in a couple of months.

She loved a trip to the theatre. Especially to Kingsland's theatre. Beginning with the excited walk along the promenade, the anticipation as present as the salty sea to her left, and the fresh grass and bubbling fountain to the right. Oh, and the wonder as she caught her first glimpse of 'The Majestic', its towering white marble columns, and floodlit angels standing guard over shimmering Corinthian pillars flanking two huge ornate gilt doors. Then her barely contained thrill as she climbed the wide sculpted steps into the dazzling mirrored foyer, reflecting an exquisite Lapis Lazuli floor and enormous potted palm trees. But her absolute favourite place was the breathtaking auditorium with its stunning floor-to-ceiling archways of delicately carved art nouveau ladies, each creating a sweeping canopy of feathered fans and bangled hands, looking for all the world as though they, and only they, held the ceiling aloft. And sitting beneath, cradled in her plush deep blue seat, she would wait for the rich velvet 'stars in a midnight sky' curtains to open and reveal their latest splendours.

Then, afterwards, the delight of the walk back along the beach, toes wiggling in the soft, cool sand, reliving every glorious moment of the show; the strings of colourful twinkling lights looping along the shoreline like an expensive necklace of sparkling gems draped upon the throat of a beautiful lady.

She knew every glorious inch of 'The Majestic' – she had spent a whole summer holiday drawing and painting it for an art project. Lauren was one of the lucky few, who knew exactly what she wanted to be when she left school: a set designer – creating scenery for the theatre, especially for musicals. Musicals were her heart.

She was still recovering from Hilly's surprise revelation that 'Joseph' was inspired by a Bible story; but now she came to think of it, it was obvious really. It even mentioned the Bible in the lyrics!

In fact, truth be told, she had been thinking a lot about everything Hilly had said yesterday and had to confess it had both annoyed and intrigued her. She had never considered the Bible to be anything other than a religious book for religious people, whose contents she had never understood. But Hilly had made it sound wonderful, exciting, mysterious. Like she knew the book personally. Then Lauren blushed at the memory of how rudely she had reacted when Hilly had revealed its title. Even Tom had been surprised by her behaviour. She still did not quite understand it herself. And she had really liked Hilly, too, but wondered if Hilly would ever speak to her again.

"Hey, Dilly Daydreamer," her dad chided, "Have you finished those spuds yet?!"

"Nearly Dad – only another two ton to go!" she joked.

"Shiver me timbers, wench! Finish 'em quick, or there'll be no supper for 'e tonight, my girl!" he said, putting on his best gnarly pirate voice.

"Yes, Cap'n!" she laughed.

She loved her family – her daft dad, always teasing and cracking jokes. Her equally daft mum, always ready with a hug and some fantastical tale or other. And her older brother Ben, who was not so much daft as downright dangerous! He thought nothing of climbing out of his bedroom window and sneaking off to the garage to tinker with his latest invention – most of which seemed to have a nasty habit of exploding!

Humming happily, she focused on finishing her last few potatoes, lost in imagining what the set for 'Cats' would be like. Ironically, a musical also composed by Andrew Lloyd Webber, Lauren mused.

Just then Tom popped his head around the door. "Hi Lauren, you want a hand?" he asked. Tom was used to pitching in and his efforts were always generously rewarded with as much cod and chips as he could manage!

"Yes, please." Lauren smiled. "There's only a few left to do, then we can go." They were off to the cinema that evening. "Have you decided which film you want to see yet?" she asked.

"I fancy 'Transformers', although 'Batman' looks good too," he said grinning, as she rolled her eyes at his inability to choose.

"Well, I fancy 'Transformers' too," she said, settling the matter. She grinned back at him as he dropped a potato in surprise. "Great!" he said. "But I thought you fancied Batman."

"Fancied Batman?! Who is this 'Batman'?" came her dad's teasing voice from the counter. "And why haven't we been introduced yet?!"

"Dad!" Lauren groaned, embarrassed. "It's a film, not a boy!"

"Remember kiddo, any potential boyfriend has to come through me first!" he continued, attempting to do a very bad James Bond impression, which Lauren found sooo embarrassing!

Tom was laughing. She splashed him with starchy potato water, but it did not stop him. "Go on, Mr. Darwin," he urged, "Say something else!"

"Now then young Thomas, I suggest you take my daughter to the cinema and challenge this 'Batman' – any problems, send him my way, after all, I am licensed to 'grill' you know!"

Both Lauren and Tom were giggling now. "Dad you're crackers!" she laughed, hugging him. "We're all done, see you when we get back!" She grinned, grabbing her jacket, and heading out the door, Tom in tow.

"See you later, Mr. Darwin," he called.

"Bye kids, have fun! Say hi to Mr. Carter for me."

"We will!" they said in unison.

Mr. Carter was the owner of a tiny, one-screen cinema called 'The Green Sardine', that only seated fifty people. It was bijou, antiquated, charmingly shabby and always remarkably busy; and conveniently located just four doors up from 'The Chirpy Chippy'. The lovely old cinema was nestled at the back of a cosy little tearoom that served quaint pots of hot tea, coffee and homemade cakes and buns. It also served enormous milkshakes, to which both Lauren and Tom were rather partial.

Mr. Carter always offered a choice of three films, and they would be shown back-to-back with short intervals in between – just long enough to run out to the loo or squeeze in another milkshake! You could book to see one or stay to see all three. It was enchanting, endearing and somewhat of a curiosity to all who visited. It was as if it had decided to just step aside one day, and slumber peacefully, whilst the rest of the world had marched on. It exuded nostalgia and welcomed you in like an old friend.

Mr. Carter's grandfather had bought the building when it was just an old run-down hardware shop back in 1903. He had furnished it and soon realised his dream to be the proud owner of a 'Motion Picture House'. It had flourished in the era of silent movies, with his talented wife, Lillian playing the piano down at the front, with the famous faces of the day immortalised upon the silver screen above.

It was the first cinema in Kingsland to host a 'talking picture' and the first to boast Technicolor, but once a year, to honour its humble beginnings, it celebrated with a 'Silent Movie Week'. Everyone was encouraged to come dressed up in any style, from any era; which Lauren always thought rather fun, because you could find yourself sitting between Queen Victoria and Charlie Chaplin, or Elvis Presley! Last year a lady sitting at the front, had had to move to the back, as her 60's beehive was combed so high that folks behind her could not see the screen properly!

For that week the current Mr. Carter's wife, Judith, also sat down at the front, playing the piano just like her predecessor, whilst Mr. Carter

Junior Junior spiced things up by creating various sound effects – creaking doors, horses' hooves, bells, horns and so on. Lauren had been to several of these celebrations over the years, they were always a riot and never the same twice. As her nan said, "It's like taking a trip down memory lane in a rocket!"

"That was brilliant!" exclaimed Tom, holding the door open for Lauren.

"I know! I thought it was more exciting than the last one," she agreed, zipping her jacket up against the cold night air.

"I loved the bit where…"

"…You fall flat on your face, Conner!" growled Jess Wilkins, shoving Tom headfirst into the road.

"Aaah!" Tom shouted in shock and pain, as he fell very hard onto the tarmac.

"Tom!" screamed Lauren, running over to help him up. "Keep your hands off him, Jess!"

Jess stuck his foot out and sent Lauren tripping into Tom as he was trying to get to his feet.

"Keep your hands off him, Jess!" he mocked, holding his sides with exaggerated laughter. "Looks like you can't keep your hands off him!"

Landing in a heap of tangled arms, legs and blushes, Lauren shrieked, "I'll get my dad if you don't leave us alone!"

"You'll get your dad?!" bellowed Jess with renewed laughter, tipping the remains of his coke over them both, crushing the tin and kicking it at them.

"You are nothing but a great gormless bully, Jess Wilkins!" shrieked Lauren in helpless fury.

Tom was back on his feet now and pushed Lauren behind him as Jess took a swing at her, catching him full in the stomach. Winded, he doubled over in pain, gasping for breath.

"Don't play the hero, Conner!" said Jess, scornfully, stepping towards them, "Cos a hero, you ain't!"

"Oh, and I suppose you are?!" came a calm retort, the speaker skidding to a halt between them, using himself and his bike as a shield.

"Get out of my way 'Burger', this has got nothing to do with you!" spat Jess.

"Picking on someone half your size, threatening to hit a girl, behaving like a brainless ape – this makes you a hero, does it?" the boy continued, ignoring an unspoken threat from Jess. "Your dad must be so proud."

"You keep my dad out of this, 'Burger'!" warned Jess, fists clenched.

"Why don't *you* keep your dad out of it?" he suggested, eyeing Jess' clenched fists pointedly.

It was as if Jess had received a physical blow. He stumbled backwards, suddenly white as a sheet, eyes wide with pain, his speech incoherent, inarticulate. "Why you…he… never…he didn't…you can't…" He stepped further and further away with each word, raising his arms defensively as if warding off an attack. Finally he ran off down the street, screaming obscenities and threats over his shoulder.

Lauren had been watching this whole exchange with a mixture of awe, confusion and relief. "What just happened?" she asked, bewildered.

"Jess just met his match," breathed Tom, straightening up. "Thank you," he said to their rescuer, nursing his still-aching stomach.

"Yes, thank you," Lauren added quickly, examining their rescuer properly now they were out of danger. He was tall, athletic, tanned, with a mop of dark shiny hair, brown eyes, and a kind face.

"Not a problem." He smiled. "Jess Wilkins and I go way back. He used to go to my school, until he got kicked out. I feel sorry for him really," he said sadly.

"Well, I don't!" exclaimed Tom emphatically, rubbing his stomach. "So far this week that boy has tripped me up, given me a bloody nose, pushed me into the road, punched me in the stomach and called me all sorts of awful names. Not to mention trying to hit Lauren."

"Yeah, I know, he can be a nasty piece of work – but he doesn't know any different."

"What?!" asked Lauren astounded, her woodpecker temperament rising now her shock was subsiding, "Doesn't know any different?!"

"Imagine if what he's been doing to you this week is possibly the reality he faces every single day of his life," the boy said placatingly.

Stunned silence followed this remark, but before anyone could say any more, Lauren's dad came bowling out of the chip shop, concern etched across his face.

"Sweetheart, are you alright? One of the customers just told me. What happened? Are you hurt? Who was it? What about you, Tom? Are you okay? And who are you?" he asked sternly, looking at the boy.

"I'm fine, dad, honest," interrupted Lauren, "Poor Tom's the one who got hurt. It was Jess Wilkins again. He punched Tom in the stomach. And this boy rescued us from him," she said by way of introduction.

"That blasted thug!" he exclaimed angrily. "Tom, let's get you inside and I'll get Mrs. Darwin to take a look at you. Where does this boy live? Someone needs to have a chat with him, or better still his father."

All three children exchanged glances as they followed him back into the shop, but did not say a word.

"Lauren, darling, are you alright?" asked her mum anxiously, coming out from behind the counter.

"I'm okay, mum, it's Tom who's hurt."

"Tom, let me take a look at you, sweetheart," she said kindly.

Whilst Mrs. Darwin fussed over Tom, Mr. Darwin finished serving the last customers of the evening, locked the doors and joined them at the table.

Heaving a sigh of relief, Mrs. Darwin said, "Well I don't think there is any permanent damage, Tom, but if the pain gets worse, or you feel unwell in any way, get your mum to take you to the hospital, okay?"

"Okay, thank you, Mrs. Darwin," he said.

"I don't know what the world's coming to, when a thug like that boy Wilkins, is allowed to roam the streets. He should be behind bars, if you ask me," she exclaimed indignantly. "I'll give your mum a ring, Tom and let her know what's happened."

"Right, if you guys are sure you're okay, I'll get on with the 'clean down',"

Mr. Darwin said, getting to his feet. "Tom, we'll give you a lift home tonight if you can hang on for half an hour or so," he finished kindly.

"Thank you, Mr. Darwin."

"And thank you, young man, for stepping into the fray." He smiled at the boy and extended his hand. "I'm Frank Darwin, Lauren's dad, and that's her mum, Jenny."

"I'm Lee," he said, standing up politely and shaking Mr. Darwin's hand. "Nice to meet you, Mr. Darwin."

"Likewise, Lee. Okay, can I get you kids a drink, while you wait?"

Moments later they were all sat sipping ice cold cokes. "Right, spill the beans," said Tom, uncharacteristically assertive. "What did you mean about Jess Wilkins? Who is doing all those things to him?"

"We think it's his dad," answered Lee.

"Why do you think it's his dad?" asked Tom.

"Because the neighbours have heard them arguing."

"Which neighbours?"

"Several actually."

"Anyone else?" Tom continued intensely.

"The postman."

"Then why haven't they reported it?" Tom demanded incredulously.

"No one is willing to get involved. Except the postman, who knocked on the door, hoping to put a stop to it."

"And did it stop?!" Tom asked loudly, "How do you know all this?!"

Lauren had never seen Tom like this before. She watched him intently over the top of her glass. "Are you alright Tom?"

"Yes, why?" he asked, shortly.

"It's just, you're making me feel like I'm watching an episode of 'Mastermind'!" she teased gently.

Frustrated, he said, "Sorry, I got a bit carried away. It's just that I hate feeling guilty for hating someone who clearly hates me and everyone else and deserves to be hated in return!"

"That's a lot of hate you got there," Lee said dryly.

Grinning sheepishly, Tom shook his head, "I know, but he's such a...urgh! And now I find out I should feel sorry for him instead! And I hate that!" he concluded, exasperated.

"Don't worry Tom, he'll get his comeuppance," Lauren comforted. "Anyway, how do you know all this?" she asked Lee.

"My dad is the postman."

"Oooh!" they breathed in unison.

"Why hasn't something been done to stop it? Social services or something?" asked Lauren.

"Because Jess denies that it's happening. And his dad says it's all a pack of lies made up to make him look bad. And without actual proof, there's nothing they can do."

"That's harsh," said Tom.

"Why would he deny it?" asked Lauren.

"I don't know. Fear, shame, embarrassment? Who knows?" said Lee, shrugging. "It's just all very sad."

"That explains why he acted really strange when you mentioned his dad," said Lauren.

"Yeeaah," Lee said slowly.

"Come on, spill," urged Tom. "You know more than you're telling us."

Lee looked at them both intently, as if trying to decide whether he should share more. "Look, it's not quite as simple as that," he said, "Let's just say that there's a few of us who are trying to help him."

"Help him? How?" asked Tom.

Lee looked reluctant to say any more.

"Maybe we could help him too?" Lauren offered.

"Lauren!" Tom admonished.

"Well, we could…" she said, her eyes quietly pleading.

Sighing, Tom conceded, "Well at least he might stop picking on me then."

"So how are you trying to help him?" Lauren asked.

Lee hesitated, looking intently at them both, then his focus seemed to shift before he made up his mind. "Okay," he said quietly, "We pray for him."

"You pray for him?!" Tom blurted incredulously.

"Yeah," Lee said with confident authority.

"And is it working?!" Tom asked doubtfully.

"Yeah, it is," Lee said.

"Really? How can you tell?! Cos from where I'm sitting, it doesn't look like it's worked at all," Tom grimaced, rubbing his abdomen.

"Well, the last person Jess picked on ended up in A&E, so I'd say this is an improvement," Lee said calmly.

"Oh, well, nothing for me to worry about then!" Tom said, running his fingers through his hair nervously.

Lauren had not spoken for a while, which was most unlike her. She had listened the whole time without once taking her eyes off Lee. She was remembering the way in which he had spoken to Jess, and it reminded her of Hilly. She cleared her throat. "Umm, you don't happen to know Hilly Trueman, do you?"

Lee smiled, surprised. "Yeah, I do, she's a friend of mine, she goes to my church. She's praying for Jess too. Why d'you ask?"

Tom was looking at Lauren like she had suddenly grown a second nose.

"It's just that earlier you spoke to Jess in the same way that Hilly spoke to Jess yesterday, in school," Lauren explained.

"Ohhh," said Tom catching on. "So does this mean you can do the same 'stuff' that she can do?" he asked eagerly.

"Uhh, I guess," said Lee, looking from one to the other. "What do you mean by 'stuff', exactly?"

"You could teach me how to stop Jess picking on me?" said Tom hopefully.

"Oh! Well, umm, like I said before, it's not that simple – there's more to it than that." He noticed Tom's look of disappointment, then added, "But, maybe we could meet up, after school, and I could explain. I only live around the corner," Lee offered.

Tom's eyes were shining. "Great!" he enthused, "You're on!"

"Cool." Lee smiled.

"Does it involve a book?" Lauren asked him warily.

"Huh?"

"Oh, never mind," she mumbled.

"Look, I'd better be heading off home now, but I'll pop round tomorrow," he promised.

"My dad can give you a lift home if you'd like, I'm sure he could fit your bike in the back," Lauren offered.

"No, It's okay, thanks, really. I literally live just around the corner. In fact, my house is right behind your shop."

Suddenly Lauren realized exactly who he was. "You're Levi Silverberg!" she exclaimed, delightedly.

"Yeah, that's right," he answered cautiously.

Tom was giving her that weird stare again.

"It's just I hear your mum calling for you sometimes," she explained.

"Ohhh." He smiled, relaxing.

Then she had another realization. "Oh, so you finally got to take your 'Tuchus' out!" she said, glancing out of the window towards his bike. "I often wondered what it would look like. Can I take a peek? I've never actually seen a 'Tuchus' before!" she said, heading for the door. "What make is it?" She turned to find Lee, pink faced, edging slowly towards the exit, keeping his back firmly to the wall; and Tom, bright red, eyes streaming, with cola jetting out of each nostril.

"Tom!" she cried, "Are you okay?!"

"I'm fine," he choked, wheezing as he grasped his stomach.

"Is it your tummy?! Are you feeling poorly?!" she asked, worried. "Shall I get my mum?"

"No!" He coughed and spluttered, gurgling, and gasping for each breath. Sitting beside him she thumped his back.

Lee hovered by the door. "Uhh, You okay, Tom?"

By now Tom's vocal cords had gone into spasm and squeaked in protest.

"Mmmmm, ooookie, goooooo." He signalled Lee to go. "Gooo! Eeeewww Maaawow." Bizarrely Lee seemed to understand him, waved goodbye, and peddled off quickly.

Tom's choking finally subsided…into paroxysms of helpless laughter.

"Tom! It's not funny, you really had me worried!" Lauren admonished.

"Eeemm sooorreee!" he squeaked, holding his aching stomach again.

"Tom!" she chided, "What's so funny?!"

Clearing his throat, he tried to explain. "Do… do you know what a tuchus is?"

"No. But I would have just seen one if you hadn't been choking!" she snapped, irritated.

This set Tom off again.

"Tom!" she barked, suddenly sensing impending doom.

"Lauren, a tuchus isn't a bike, it's another name for a bum! You just asked to see Lee's bum!" he snorted, choking on his own laughter.

Lauren stared at him, horrified, her cheeks changing colour like traffic lights – red, green and white traffic lights.

"Oh no…" she whispered.

* * *

CHAPTER FOUR

Numbers

Hilly dashed into her maths lesson with only seconds to spare.

"Cutting it a bit fine today, Hilly," remarked Miss Sampson.

"Sorry Miss."

"Right, class, let's get started then. So, continuing on from yesterday, if we applied Pythagoras' Theorem to question number four, how do you think it would solve the problem?"

Hilly's right hand shot up, as her left scrabbled in her bag for her notebook. She had worked hard on this question last night and was keen to solve it.

"Yes Hilly."

Swiftly checking her notes, she answered, "Well, it would give us the length of the third side of the fishpond, which will then tell the builder the size of the wood he needs to finish building it."

"Yes. Which is?" asked Miss Sampson.

"Three metres," Hilly answered.

"Correct! Well done Hilly." She smiled. "Now using the smart board, show us how you used the theorem to arrive at your answer – remember class, always include your calculations, this will demonstrate to the adjudicator how you arrived at your answer – it could be the difference between a pass and a fail…"

The lesson continued on in this vein all morning, giving Hilly no time at all to think about the texts she had received just before class. So when the break bell rang, she swiftly packed her bag and headed off to her secret place.

Sitting cross-legged, she read the first text again, delighting in how the Lord brought people together. No coincidence that Lee should meet Lauren and Tom too, she thought: God's perfect timing. "You are awesome, Lord. You obviously have a pressing purpose for them," she praised under her breath.

However, the second text from Lee had been a bit of a shocker – and the reason she had only just made it to class on time.

'Jess Wilkins in hospital – unconscious.
My dad called ambulance.
Will let you know when I know more.
I've activated the Prayer Burst'

Reading it a second time did nothing to reduce its impact. "'Unconscious'. Lord, what happened?" she asked in shock, getting to her knees. Bowing her head, she began to pray – knowing that everyone alerted on the 'Prayer Burst' – a chain message that alerted folk about situations that needed prayer – would be doing the same. Prayer was the answer to everything. Not for the first time she was reminded of her mum's wise words, "At times like these, use hands and knees, with a grateful heart and a fervent please." This situation definitely called for hands and knees.

"Heavenly Father, I love You and praise Your Holy name.

I thank You for being with me every second of every day.

I thank You that I can talk to You whenever I want.

Lord, You already know what has happened to Jess, I lift him up to You right now, and ask for his full and complete healing, in Jesus' name.

I ask that You send an army of angels to stand guard over him, to protect him from further attack; and I ask for Your perfect peace to rain down upon Jess and his family. Precious Father, speak to his heart – let him feel Your love, set him free from the Enemy's lies. Call him into Your Kingdom, Lord. Amen.

So focused on her prayers, she had not heard the approaching footsteps, or been aware of any scrutiny, until Lauren said, "Uhhhh, sorry to disturb you praying…again! But at least I know what you're doing this time," she said by way of apology, the words skydiving out of her mouth. "Ummm, can we talk to you, please?"

Hilly smiled, "Yes, of course, sit down." She was surprised and delighted to see them again, given Lauren's reaction the previous day.

Tom began to speak before his bottom hit the ground. "We met a friend of yours last night – Lee – and he told us all about Jess Wilkins and his dad. And he said you were trying to help him."

"We've heard that he's been taken to hospital," continued Lauren.

"And we would like to help too," added Tom.

Wow Lord, I did hear you right! Hilly thought to herself. "Okay," she said, smiling, "Lee did text me this morning to say that he'd met you last night. And he asked me to pass on a message to you."

"Oh, cool!" said Tom, pleased.

"He's sorry, but he isn't going to be able to meet you after school tonight," Hilly explained, "He's praying for Jess at the hospital."

"Oh…" Tom's crestfallen expression spoke volumes.

"But he did ask *me* to have a chat with you, instead."

"It's not about the Bible again, is it?" asked Lauren warily.

"Well, it does come into it!" Hilly chuckled.

"Okaaay," Lauren sighed, resigned.

"Look, we don't have enough time now, the bell is about to go. So, meet me back here at lunchtime and I'll explain. Oh, and Lee's asked if we could exchange mobile numbers too."

"Uuum… Lee didn't text you about…anything else…did he?" Lauren asked, blushing.

"No, why?"

"Oh, nothing, just asking," she said, relieved. Doubly relieved now that she would not have to face him after school. She was still mortified that she had actually asked him if she could take a look at his bum!

40

The rest of the morning seemed to drag for Hilly, but she found them waiting impatiently for her at her secret place, and they were not alone.

"Hi Hilly, we hope you don't mind, but we were telling Tom's brother, Mitch, all about you and Lee and Jess Wilkins, and he said he wanted to help too," Lauren explained nervously.

"Hi." He nodded. He was tall and slim like his brother, taller in fact. Dark brown hair just like Tom's, with the same wide-set, innocent blue eyes. She recognized him and smiled. "Hi, year ten basketball team, right?"

"Yeah." He grinned, pleased she had recognized him.

"Okay, tell us about Jess Wilkins," urged Lauren impatiently.

"Well, Lee's sent me a couple more texts now – apparently Lee's dad found Jess unconscious on his doorstep this morning and called an ambulance. He's in intensive care in Kingsland General. They can't find his dad or his little sister Ruby, anywhere. The police are out looking for them."

"That's awful," Lauren said sadly. "No wonder Lee felt sorry for him."

"We all do," said Hilly, "Ever since Jess' mum died, his dad has not been the same. He drinks and disappears for days on end, then rolls home drunk and takes it out on Jess and Ruby."

"When did his mum die?" asked Tom.

"About two years ago, breast cancer, I believe," Hilly answered.

"Right, so, what are we gonna do about it?" pushed Lauren.

"Well, Lee, myself and other members of our church, have been praying for him and his family."

"Not wishing to be disrespectful, but that doesn't seem to have worked," Mitch quietly pointed out.

"Yeah, I guess it must seem like that," Hilly replied, "But it goes deeper than that, it's not that simple."

"That's just what Lee said last night," complained Tom, frustrated. "Why isn't it simple? Explain!"

Hilly looked thoughtfully at them. What Tom was asking required a huge amount of explanation – especially since he was obviously searching for the deeper answers. Surprisingly Hilly felt a peace about what she would have to impart to them in such a short space of time. "Okay… But I think I need to start with some real basics, in order for you to fully understand everything. If I jump in with what we are doing right now and why, without explaining the basics, you are likely to think I've completely lost the plot, because you haven't been on the same journey – you haven't studied the same information or encountered the same experiences. It would be like me asking you to understand how to work out what 10+10 is, without explaining how to work out what 1+1 is first." she said. "Does that make sense?"

They nodded.

"Okay. So, if I tell you stuff you already know, just bear with me. It just makes it easier to explain it in this way. Okay, umm….I am a 'Christian', which is my faith, some call it my religion. There is an important difference. At a very, very uncomplicated level, I would describe *religion* as a belief *in* **God** and *faith* as a relationship *with* **God**. Or to put it another way, *religion* is like, *knowing* 'The Lord's Prayer' *off by heart*; but *faith* is like *knowing in your heart* that the Lord hears your prayers and will answer them. They aren't meant to be practiced separately but sadly, sometimes they are. I am called a Christian because I am a follower or disciple of Jesus Christ – hence 'Christ-ian' – Christian. Jesus Christ is the son of God. The God who created everything. The world, the universe, the first man Adam, the first woman Eve: you name it He created it, including angels. One such angel – Lucifer, an especially important angel – rebelled against God. He had grown proud and wanted to be treated like God himself. God threw him out of Heaven – Heaven is the place where God lives – and Lucifer was exiled, taking a third of all the other angels with him. This is how evil, and sin first entered the world. He and the fallen angels now reside in a place called Hell. Are you with me so far?" she asked, taking a breath.

And was rewarded with three riveted nods.

"Carrying on then… In revenge, Lucifer, also known as Satan, the Devil, Beelzebub, the Enemy, amongst other names, seeks to annihilate everything that God created. That includes you and me. His only aim in life is to lie, steal and kill. And what he does is not always obvious – he is subtle – he will whisper lies, steal your joy, kill relationships. Anything to stop you and me from fulfilling God's plan for our lives. Our names are written in 'God's Book of Life'. He knew us before we were even made in our mother's womb. We are all created, by Him, with a purpose and He loves us all. And the Enemy is jealous, doesn't like it. He has already been defeated and the time will come when he will be thrown into a fiery pit, by the Archangel Michael. He knows this but roams the earth, roaring, trying to take as many of us as he can with him into Hell. For he knows that God loves us all and doesn't want to lose even one of us."

"Woah," breathed Tom, "It's like... war."

"That's *exactly* what it is," agreed Hilly. "But don't worry, Tom, he has neither the power, nor the army to defeat God. And *'If God is for us, who can be against us?'*" she quoted. "And He is, Tom, God is for us – big time!" She smiled. *"'No harm will overtake you, no disaster will come near your tent. For He will command His angels concerning you, to guard you in all your ways; they will lift you up in their hands, so that you will not strike your foot against a stone.'"*

"That's…amazing," swallowed Lauren, blinking back tears.

"Yeah…" agreed Tom, clearly moved.

"Powerful," nodded Mitch, clearing his throat.

Hilly could see that they had all been touched by the Holy Spirit – the very Spirit of God.

44

"*Faith comes by hearing, and hearing by the word of God.*" She smiled softly.

"Meaning?" asked Tom, awed.

"Meaning that faith – the belief in God and His son Jesus Christ, and the Holy Spirit – comes by hearing about them and hearing about them from the word of God – the Bible. Which is what I've just spoken."

"Okay, I get 'all this'," said Mitch. "But how is 'all this' actually connected to Jess Wilkins?"

"Right, I'll come back to that. Uhhh, let me see, where did I get to?" Hilly pondered, retracing her thoughts. "Okay, so, we now know about the Enemy and the agenda of the Enemy... Moving on... When God created us, He gave us free will. He could have created us to love, worship and obey Him automatically, but He didn't – He gave us a choice.

And the Enemy exploited that choice by tempting Eve to disobey God's commands in the Garden of Eden, where she and Adam lived at first. God had invited them to eat fruit from any tree in the garden except the tree in the middle – the 'Tree of Knowledge of Good and Evil'. The Enemy, in the guise of a snake, deliberately set out to deceive Eve, leading her to rebel against God's instructions; and consequently, causing Adam to do the same. God then banished them both from Eden. This is known as 'The Fall'.

And we – the human race – down through countless generations, continue to struggle with the same dilemma here on Earth.

Unfortunately, due to 'The Fall', Earth is currently the domain of the Enemy – but not forever. Whilst Heaven still belongs to God, in between Heaven and Earth, all around us, there is a 'Spiritual Realm' – usually not seen – where a battle continually rages between God's angels and the Enemy's – also known as demons or spirits."

Laurens' eyes were like saucers. "No way!" she gasped. "Is this really true?"

"Yes, it can all be found in the Bible," Hilly assured her. "There are Seraphim, Cherubim and Thrones; Principalities, Powers, Rulers, Archangels and Angels. Which is why we are warned that '*We do not wrestle against flesh and blood, but against principalities, against powers, against the rulers of the darkness of this age, against spiritual hosts of wickedness in the heavenly places*'. Because of this knowledge, we know that we aren't battling against one another, *per se*, but beings in the heavenly realm that influence us."

"This is incredible," said Mitch, "I study religious education, you know, R.E., and I don't know half of this."

"Yeah, well, my dad says not everyone is willing to teach everything in the Bible – just the safe bits! You'd be surprised how many 'Christians' wander around completely oblivious," Hilly stated. "Which is exactly what the enemy wants, of course. Because the minute you become aware, you become a threat. But '*Obey God, resist the Devil and he will flee. Draw near to God and He will draw near to you*'." She smiled.

Again, Lauren's eyes welled up – she felt a strange tug, deep within her, like something was missing – it reminded her of the time she had gone away on a school trip and had been horribly homesick.

"So, when does Jesus come into this?" asked Tom.

"Right about now," Hilly grinned. "Continuing on then… We, the human race, fell so far and so badly into sin and evil (and not for the first time either!); *that God, who loved us so much, sacrificed His only son to save us. Jesus Christ was born into this world to be our Saviour. 'He died for us and rose again'*. And *'through Him we receive our salvation'* – our redemption and eternal life after death. But through Christ eternal life can start now, living from Heaven can start now, not just when we die."

"And, my understanding is, that, by dying for us, Jesus took all our sin upon himself, so we would be forgiven and set free?" Mitch enquired.

"Correct." Hilly smiled. "When Jesus died, He redeemed us from the power of sin."

My nan's a Christian," Tom declared suddenly. "She always cries when Jesus dies…" he said sadly. Then looking around at all their surprised faces, "You know, in films…" he explained, suddenly flustered.

"Me too, Tom," Hilly said gently. "But He rose again, Tom. Jesus is alive! He is as alive today as He was back then and will be tomorrow!" she assured Him, her eyes glowing. "And even when He ascended into Heaven, He didn't leave us alone, Tom. He asked His Father – God, to send us a 'Helper', so we wouldn't be on our own ever again."

"A helper?" asked Lauren, her voice hushed.

"Yes, a 'Helper'. 'The Spirit of Truth'. 'The Holy Spirit'," explained Hilly.

"He is the Spirit of God, our guide our comforter – and so much more." She smiled happily.

Silence embraced them – the wonder of all they had just learnt slowly seeping in through the cracks in their defence.

Until Mitch, clearing his throat, said, "So…so…that's 'The Trinity' – 'Father God', 'Jesus Christ' and 'the Holy Spirit'. Argh! I think I answered that one wrong in my last exam – I missed out the 'Holy Spirit'," he finished glumly.

"Don't worry, Mitch, It's a common mistake," encouraged Hilly, "and you won't make it again!" She grinned.

"No!" he said wryly.

"Well, what was your answer, then?" asked Tom, curious.

"'God' and 'The Father' and 'Jesus Christ'," Mitch answered. "I didn't realize that 'God' and 'The Father' were the same."

"Well, not wishing to confuse you any further, but actually 'God the Father', 'Jesus Christ' and 'The Holy Spirit' are one and the same!"

"Gimme a break!" groaned Lauren, "I was just beginning to think I understood it all."

"I know! It's a lot to take in, in one go," empathized Hilly, "But don't worry, Lauren. God doesn't need you to understand Him, it's more important to Him that you love Him and believe in Him."

"Easy for you to say!" she grumbled.

Giggling, Hilly went on, "So, being a follower of Christ, we are called to keep God's commandments, of which there are ten – and we are especially called to keep the one that Jesus Christ Himself taught – which is to '*Love your neighbour as yourself*'. And *this* is why, despite Jess Wilkins' behaviour, we're doing all we can to help him and forgive him. That and knowing who *the real* enemy is. Where *the real* attack is coming from."

"I understand that," said Tom sighing, "And I do want to help, honest I do…but…it's haaard…"

"Yeah, it is," Hilly agreed, "and we couldn't do it without God's help, His grace and mercy. But '*With God we can do all things*.'"

"And it shows the kind of person you are, Tom, that you're even willing to try after what Jess did to you," said Lauren, giving him a hug.

"Yeah, it does, Tom," said his brother, slapping him on the back. "My bro the hero!" he teased.

"Shut up, Mitch!" he laughed, shoving him playfully.

"Well, it might also help you to remember, Tom, that although *we* do have a choice in how *we* behave, the Enemy will use any opportunity to lie, steal and kill."

"So, you're saying that Jess' actions might have been made worse by the Enemy?" asked Mitch soberly.

"I'd say that was a very strong possibility." Hilly nodded.

"And what about his dad?" asked Lauren, "Him too?"

Hilly nodded again. "But, remember, the Enemy is already defeated. 'He is trampled beneath our feet'; and although it is wise to be aware of the Enemy and his ploys, it is wiser still to *keep our eyes on the Lord*. Look to him for the answers. Don't even give the Enemy the time of day."

"So how do we do that?" asked Tom earnestly.

"Well, there are a number of ways: praying is of utmost importance; reading the Bible, learning and speaking the Word of God is essential; worshiping God is crucial; understanding and wielding the power of Jesus' name is vital; understanding and applying the power of Jesus' blood, shed by Him, for us, on the cross, is paramount; and wearing The Armour of God is imperative."

"Gosh, it all sounds a little full on!" remarked Lauren, frowning.

"When you hear it all for the first time, it can feel a little overwhelming, not real somehow," agreed Hilly. "But after a while, it feels right. And how you're living now, doesn't feel real anymore."

"What's 'The Armour of God'?" asked Tom.

"It's armour that protects us against the Enemy's schemes and the forces of evil, in the heavenly realms. It's God's spiritual armour, His spiritual protection. It's invisible to the naked eye.

"You're pulling my leg!" Snorted Lauren.

"No," grinned Hilly, "The Apostle Paul describes it as 'The Belt of Truth', 'The Breastplate of Righteousness', 'The Shoes of Peace', 'The Shield of Faith', 'The Helmet of Salvation' and 'The Sword of the Spirit'.

"Sounds cool!" said Tom, his eyes shining. "But what is it, exactly?"

"Well, 'The Belt of Truth' stands for the truth of God and His Word. Not my truth or your truth, or the world's truth, but His truth and His alone.

Wearing it is a constant reminder to me that I must always tell the truth and be true to God."

"I think that would be very important," commented Mitch. "What about 'The Breastplate'?"

"'The Breastplate of Righteousness'. God says we are 'righteous' when we turn *away* from sin and turn *to* Jesus. Being righteous means being right with God through our faith in Jesus. Being morally good and honest and trustworthy. Keeping our hearts pure. So, protecting our heart is especially important. 'The Breastplate of Righteousness' protects our heart for God."

"My nan said I should always protect my heart because *'everything I do flows from there'*," quoted Tom.

"Yes, she's right Tom. The Bible tells us to guard our hearts for that very reason," smiled Hilly.

"What about the Shoes?" asked Lauren.

"'The Shoes of Peace' represent being prepared and ready to *take* the truth of our Salvation in Jesus, and the Word of God to others. To take 'The Gospel' – 'The Truth' of God's Word and 'The Peace' of Jesus and spread the 'Good News'. I personally like to think of it as *always* living in God's Way, 'living ready', so we are *always* 'walking the walk and talking the talk'," explained Hilly.

"Living by example?" asked Mitch.

"Yes, definitely, always being prepared ourselves."

"And the 'Shield'?" asked Tom.

"'The Shield of Faith'. Faith is **believing** *every promise of God*. The Enemy wants us to **doubt** *every promise of God,* weaken our faith by shooting fiery arrows of lies and deceit and doubt at us. So, having a strong faith acts like a shield and defends us against the Enemy. The Bible describes faith as *'the substance of things hoped for, and the evidence of things not seen'*. Another way to put it is, 'Faith is the *existence* of things hoped for and the *proof* of things not seen'. Which I always find really exciting," said Hilly.

"The Enemy is such a big pile of poop!" declared Tom vehemently.

"Couldn't have put it better myself Tom!" agreed Hilly.

"I've studied the helmet – 'The Helmet of Salvation'," said Mitch, "I understand by accepting Jesus as our Lord and Saviour, He delivers us from sin and the consequences of sin and protects us from any harm of the Enemy by guarding our minds against his attacks."

"Yes, exactly!" confirmed Hilly. "When we accept His salvation, we are also accepting His protection. Like a soldier in a physical battle needs to protect his head from injury by wearing a helmet, the helmet of our salvation protects us from injury when we enter into a spiritual battle. We are literally wearing Jesus' protection upon our heads."

"And what about 'The Sword'?" asked Tom eagerly.

"The 'Sword of the Spirit' represents 'The Word of God'. We can use God's word to declare and proclaim good things, but we can also wield it as a weapon against the Enemy. We will struggle to fight victoriously if we lack knowledge of 'The Word of God'. My dad actually visualizes his armour and draws his sword when he's doing battle – he's even named it – Vainglorious!" Hilly shared.

"Wow! I love that name!" stated Tom, "Can't wait to put mine on!"

"That's such a lot to remember," sighed Lauren, "How am I going to remember it all? How do you remember it all?"

"You will, I promise you," Hilly reassured her, "I've been journeying with the Lord my whole life, and I'm learning new stuff every day."

"I just don't know where to begin," Lauren confessed.

"Well, right now, we can pray. The more we pray and the more who pray, the greater the impact," she added.

"I don't know how to pray." Lauren blushed.

"Don't worry Lauren, praying is just talking to God. Like you're having a chat with him and listening to what He says," encouraged Hilly.

"Besides, I was saying my prayers long before I could talk!" She grinned, bowing her head. The others, unsure of what else to do, followed suit.

"Dear Father, You have listened to our conversation. You say, *Where two or more are gathered in Your name, You are in the midst.* We welcome Your presence and praise Your Holy name, and thank You Lord for all that You are doing in our lives and in the lives of Jess, his dad, and his sister Ruby. We ask in Your son Jesus' precious name that Jess regains consciousness and is fully healed. We ask that his sister Ruby is found safe and sound and that his dad gets the help and healing he needs too. Lord, we know You have a plan and purpose for this entire family, and we ask that You hold them close at this difficult time, and that Jess and his family rest in your protection and safety. Give them Your comfort, Your peace and Your love, Lord. We also ask in Jesus' name, that any assignment of the Enemy concerning this family, be overcome. And Your will be done. In Jesus name. Amen."

She raised her head to find them all watching her closely. Mitch's wide blue eyes were full of wonderment. Tom, overwhelmed, swallowed nervously and Lauren muttered in utter astonishment, "I never 'chatted' to anyone like that before, let alone God."

Hilly tucked her hair behind her ear self-consciously and waited, aware of the powerful presence of the Holy Spirit. She had never before been called upon to impart this much information to anyone in such a short period of time. It felt like a 'Crash Course in Christianity.' But His beautiful presence was palpable, and Hilly knew this meeting had been an incredibly significant one, for 'The Kingdom'.

"That was incredible," stated Mitch. "I've never felt anything like that before. It was… well…so peaceful and…thrilling all at the same time," he tried, searching for the words.

"Yeah! Me too!" exclaimed Tom. "I felt like I wanted to laugh *and* cry!"

"I felt like…I was…'home'." Lauren whispered, her voice catching. "You pray good," she added, wiping her eyes on her sleeve.

"What you're all feeling, right now, is the presence of the Holy Spirit," Hilly explained gently. "He is such a beautiful person. He's God's spirit; sent from Him to be with us. Because I'm a Christian, He lives within me, all the time. It's like having a part of God inside my heart. He's my friend, my guide, my protector. I wouldn't be without Him. And He comes to live within every person who becomes Christian."

"How?" asked Lauren, still trying to control her tears.

"You invite Him in."

"How?" breathed Tom, reverently.

"By asking God for forgiveness of any wrongs – 'sins', you might have committed in the past. By believing that Jesus Christ is the Son of God; And that he died to save us from the power of sin and arose again," Hilly explained calmly.

"I do!" declared Tom, fervently, "Nan was right, He is real – I can feel Him," he said, his voice gruff with emotion.

"I'm in too," agreed Mitch, "No way this isn't real."

Lauren was openly weeping. "I don't know why I'm blubbing like this; I've never felt so happy!" she laughed, dashing her tears away.

"Hallelujah! Praise You Lord!" rejoiced Hilly beaming. "You are all being called into God's Kingdom." Lost in the moment, she hugged them all.

Afterwards they sat talking animatedly of what they had just shared, each one not wanting the experience to end, all completely unaware of the jubilant celebration taking place in Heaven!

They discussed their plan to help Jess Wilkins and agreed to meet after school to visit him in hospital. The whole of Hilly's church and her family were keen to help.

Walking back to class, Hilly whispered, **"Our numbers are growing for You and for Jess, Lord! Thank You for the privilege of being a part of Your Kingdom. Give me the strength and discernment to continue Your works, to keep listening and obeying You, to trust You and follow You wherever You lead. Amen."**

* * *

CHAPTER FIVE

Deut – A Romany

He had been on the road for six hours. His neck was stiff, his legs numb, not to mention his rear. He was desperate for the loo and hungry enough to 'eat a horse and chase the rider'! So, to be finally pulling into *this* driveway was an answer to prayers. The warm lights of the house spilled out onto the tarmac, like the warm greeting he knew awaited him inside.

Someone dragged back a curtain and a silhouette waved frantically. Simultaneously the front door flew open, and more silhouettes came pouring out. "Doot! It's Doot! Doot's here!" came a child's excited squeal.

"It's *Uncle* Doot to you Missy-Moo!" he chuckled, swinging her high above him as she threw herself into his arms. "Hello sweetheart." He grinned, hugging her close as she peppered him with tiny little kisses.

"I did miss you Uncle Doot!" she said, her little cheeks pink with excitement.

"And I missed you too, darling," he said, smiling into her pretty brown eyes and marvelling at how much she had grown in just three months. "I declare you are at least two inches taller than when I last saw you and your hair is curlier!" She squealed in delight.

"Deut, glad you're home, man," said a deep masculine voice, and he was instantly trapped in a hug huge enough to satisfy a bear. The man, Nigerian-born, and London-bred resembled a great brown grizzly himself. Standing at six feet five inches, he towered over Deut.

"Me too, brother, me too!" he chuckled as all the air whooshed out of his lungs.

"Make room for Mumma!" demanded a voice warm as sunshine. Miriam, a tiny powerhouse of a woman; wife, mother, and the gentle heart of the family, came rushing out of the door to join them.

"And me!" sang another.

"Don't forget me, Uncle Deut!" came yet another.

"Or me!" said the last one, squirming his way in.

Cocooned in this smiling huddle of hugs, he knew he was finally home.

"Well, let's get you inside, your room's all ready for you and your timing is impeccable, Deut, we were just about to say grace!" laughed 'Mumma', taking note of his tired, drawn face.

"Oh, tell me you've made your dumplings, Miri!" he begged hungrily.

"They're waiting on the table!" she laughed.

"Ohh!" he groaned, in tortured joy, "I tell you something, Jed, if you hadn't already married this woman, I'd have carried her off myself in my granddaddy's Vardo!"

"Oooh, what colour, Deut? Canary yellow like Mr. Toad's?!" giggled Miri, mischievously.

"Nope, it was a traditional gypsy caravan in red, green and gold – beautiful – fit for a queen!"

He laughed. "And drawn by Goliath, our Shire horse."

"Aww, well, if it wasn't canary yellow I'd have had to decline." She giggled, then said in mock sadness, "But Goliath on the other hand…!"

"Ahh, you're breaking my heart, Miri!" Deut declared, clutching his chest dramatically, grinning broadly at this tiny woman who could light up a room by merely stepping into it.

"I'd give it up, Uncle Deut, if I were you!" giggled Hilly, "Daddy had a canary yellow Mustang with 122 horsepower!"

"Oh, I think I married the right man!" Miri giggled, slipping her arm around her husband's expansive waist.

"Praise God!" Jed guffawed loudly, slapping Deut on the back.

"Do you know, I remember that Mustang!" Deut grinned, realizing just how much he had missed them and their light-hearted banter. "Kids, remind me to tell you about the time your dad and I drove to Exeter in it!"

"I think that story can wait until after dinner!" interjected Jed swiftly.

"I think I'd like to hear about that now!" said Miri, innocently.

"Aww, now you've done it Deut!" grimaced Jed in mock dread.

Dinner was a loud chaos of "Pass the dumplings, please" and "More potato, anyone?" and "Missy, don't play with your food darling!"

Until Cam – Cameron – Hilly's older brother said, "Tell us about China, Uncle Deut."

The table gradually grew quiet as Deut began to speak of his latest trip, his voice taking on the cadence of a natural storyteller.

"It took longer than I expected. All roads into Beijing are jam packed with traffic. I've never seen so many cars or people in one place. I got lost a couple of times. But I eventually found my contact in Fengtai, at an internet cafe, as arranged.

"His name was Gen, and he was only eleven years old and stood all of three feet high. He was the skinniest little squirt with the biggest smile I've ever seen!" Deut grinned. "But he escorted me around that district like a true professional. We spent the first six hours exploring the area. Basically, I did what I always do – I took photos. They do have some absolutely beautiful architecture there, I'll show you the pics later.

"I met some amazing locals. Oh! Remind me to tell you about the man with the singing parrot!

"But I also managed to observe some of their really unusual customs – which should keep my publisher very happy!" He grinned again. "In fact, just writing about their traditions would take up a whole book in itself! It was intriguing to explore what made Fengtai different from its neighbouring districts like Haidian and Chaoyang. And I tasted some of the local cuisine, which was mouth-watering!"

Miri's eyes lit up. "Anything for me, Deut?" she asked hopefully.

"As always, Miri, I managed to get you a couple of recipes – one for spicy fried chicken you will adore!" He winked.

"Oooh, I can't wait!" She clapped delightedly.

"Bang goes my waistline again!" grinned Jed, slapping his belly.

Everyone laughed, Jed's appetite was legendary.

"As planned," Deut continued, "I collected as much information for my travel guide as possible. And dropped off the Bibles."

"How many this time Uncle Deut?" asked Cam excitedly.

"Ohhh, 230 this time Cam, all translated into Mandarin."

"Bullseye!" celebrated Cam, punching the air in triumph. As far as he was concerned, each Bible delivered was a direct hit against the Enemy.

"Yep Bullseye, Cam!" agreed Deut, high-fiving him like always. But both Jed and Miri sensed that his heart was not really in the celebration this time.

"We were followed," continued Deut. "None too subtly, for the first five hours, by their local law enforcement – 'The People's Armed Police' – intimidating, I can tell you, and a little unnerving if I'm honest. But the Lord was with me every step of the way."

"AMEN!" declared several voices in unison.

"And they were eventually satisfied that I was there to do what I'd said I was there to do, and left me alone. But not until after I'd signed a couple of copies of my latest travel guide!" He grinned wryly. "One of them even recognized me and took a selfie of us sitting together, inside my van!" He laughed. "Little did he know what he was sitting on!"

"The Lord says we are to stand on His word – but I guess sitting on it still counts!" Jed roared.

There was more laughter, and Deut looked around at the happy smiling faces, praising God for getting him home safely.

"So, what happened next?" prompted Dunc – Duncan – Hilly's younger brother.

"An hour later, Gen took me to meet his pastor, Pastor Ling. They meet every night at Pastor Ling's despatch factory. It's a bit like 'Amazon', so it's on the go 24/7, which gives them a legitimate reason to have people coming and going all hours of the day and night. They have an incredible system in place. There are five roads into the factory, and they have someone on look out, on every road, every hour, every day, acting as an early warning. Pastor Ling has old tunnels and cellars beneath his factory that he uses for storage. It's like a rabbit warren down there. One of the larger rooms has been dedicated as their church. It's half a mile underground, hidden behind old crates and boxes and an ingenious fake stone wall that slides to allow entry."

"Wow, that sounds amazing. I wish I could have seen it," Cam chipped in.

"It was something to behold, Cam, that's for sure – but I didn't dare take any photos in case they got into the wrong hands. It just made me appreciate again how blessed we are to be able to worship the Lord openly in this country."

"AMEN to that!" they all agreed again.

"The church itself was very rustic, people sitting on crates and broken chairs, even a broken ladder. But the presence of the Lord was so tangible, I could hardly stand up," shared Deut with awe in his voice.

"They only allow one hundred Christians to attend at each service – that is the amount they know they could evacuate or conceal safely, should there be a raid..."

"You look sad, Uncle Deut," said Missy, climbing into his lap.

"Oh, I'm just tired Missy-Moo," he said, kissing her little hand as she stroked his face in concern.

"Well, there's plenty of time to hear about the rest of Uncle Deut's trip, tomorrow. I think it's time to clear up and head off to bed," said Miri. "It's getting very late!"

"Aww, do we have to?" yawned Missy.

"Yeah, I don't see why we have to go to bed right now," agreed Dunc.

"Dear Lord, I pray that you remove any plugs from their ears or scales from their eyes so that they may *hear* You and me clearly and *see* their way to doing as You command, and I tell 'em!" prayed Miri, over-exaggerating.

"Amen!" agreed Jed, smiling at the mischief in his wife's eyes. Even after twenty years, she still managed to make him laugh.

Giggling at their mum's antics, Hilly and Cam began to clear away the table.

"Daaaad," complained Dunc again.

"You heard your mother, Dunc. Time for bed. Besides, it is later than you think young man."

"Yeah Dunc, we didn't sit down to dinner until Uncle Deut arrived, and that was late," reasoned Cam, trying to mollify his brother.

"Yeah, sorry about that Miri," Deut said, grimacing.

"Don't you bother yourself a bit about that, Deut. Anyway, I put it all down to your wanderlust, you can't help yourself, it's in your Romany blood!" she teased, playfully throwing a cushion at him.

"Actually, this time I'd put it down to the roadworks on the M5, Miri!" he chuckled wryly, lobbing it back. "Hey Dunc, how would you and Cam like to camp out in my van tonight?" he asked, getting an approving wink from Jed.

"Oh, can we, Mum? Can we, Dad?" they both asked in unison.

"Weeell…" said Miri, pretending to think. "What do you think Jed?"

"I think that sounds doable, provided you are both in bed within the next five minutes!" he ordered.

You could almost see the dust settle behind them as they scrambled for the door!

Laughing, Deut followed them out.

"Well, that sorted that!" said Miri, grinning and dusting her hands off. Then she paused, checking if they were now alone. Only Missy remained, having immediately fallen asleep in an armchair. "Jed, do you think Deut's okay?" she said, her tone suddenly serious. "He seems preoccupied," she added, keeping her voice just above a whisper. "He's laughing in all the right places, but…he looks terrible…I can't put my finger on it, but something's not right…it's been playing on my heart all evening – and he looks so drawn," she finished.

"Ummm, there's definitely something he's not telling us, I can feel it in my spirit," he agreed, "And when I hugged him earlier he was all skin and bones."

Hilly re-entered the room, her arms full of schoolbooks. "The table's cleared, dishwasher's packed and the leftovers are in the fridge." She yawned.

"Thank you, sweetheart. Now off to bed with you. No more schoolwork tonight – straight to sleep."

"Believe me mum, I couldn't even if I wanted to." She yawned again, heading for the stairs.

"Night, night, darling. God bless, sweet dreams," Miri said, planting a kiss on her forehead.

"Night Mum, night Dad – love you." Hilly yawned again.

"Night darling. May God stand an angel to watch over you." Jed smiled, resting his hand briefly upon her head.

Missy stirred sleepily. "Come on pumpkin, let's get you to bed too," said Jed, gently picking her up from the armchair, indicating to Miri that they would finish their conversation later.

As soon as Hilly's head hit the pillow, she was wide awake. She had not meant to overhear her parents' whispered conversation, but she had. And now she was alone, it came back to her, their voices echoing round and round inside her head… "There's definitely something he's not telling us… He looks terrible… Something he's not telling us… He looks so drawn…"

Finally abandoning all hope of sleep, she sat up. She had never seen her parents so concerned about Uncle Deut before. They had been friends long before she was born. He had been best man at their wedding, and as far as her parents were concerned, Deut was family.

Her dad had often reminisced about how they'd met when Deut and his family had arrived in town with a travelling fairground, one summer. He was just a boy – full of wit and mischief. He and his grandfather, Vernon Jones, had come to a morning service at Kingsland Pentecostal. They'd hit it off straight away and had been best buddies ever since. For years Deut had visited whenever he was in the area, eventually agreeing to stay with Jed and his parents in his early twenties, after his grandad had passed away and Jed had noticed that something within Deut had passed away with him. But surrounded by such a loving, close-knit family, Deut had gradually recovered. He had remained close to them all ever since.

Deut – short for Deuteronomy Moses Jones, was slight of frame, intelligent, quick witted and had a dazzling smile and dark brown eyes that danced with mischief. After only a few settled years with Jed's family, he had taken to the road again; this time not due to the call of his Romany-gypsy heritage, but due to the call the Lord had placed upon his life. He knew he was to spread the word of God – not only

66

evangelizing, but smuggling Bibles into countries and regions otherwise closed to Christians. His camper van – 'The Trusty Steed' – was full of compartments filled to the brim with books. The secret ones held Bibles. The decoy cupboards held Deut's own book – 'The Travels of Deut: A Romany'. It had started out as a cover identity – giving him a legitimate reason for travelling the globe – tracing his roots back 1500 years to Rajasthan. But it had proven to be an unexpected success, making Deut a household name and bringing in a small fortune in royalties – with which he had bought more Bibles – and written more travel books – ploughing it all back into the Kingdom. The Lord had blessed Deut and his works, *'Exceedingly, abundantly, above all he could ask or imagine.'*

He always seemed to have such an exciting life, mused Hilly. Full of adventure, beautiful places, and interesting people. She had never stopped to think about the dangers he faced or the risks he took smuggling Bibles to persecuted Christians. Bowing her head, she began to pray.

"Dear Father God, I thank you with all my heart for Uncle Deut and the work he does for Your Kingdom. I lift him up to You and ask that Your peace and protection surround him every second of every day. I ask that whatever might have upset or unsettled him, be removed, never to return or be replaced, and Your peace to fill him, in the mighty name of Your Son, Jesus Christ of Nazareth. I also ask that any worry be removed from my parents,

and that everyone in this family sleeps peacefully tonight and awakes refreshed and ready to do Your will in the morning. Amen."

She immediately felt a warm calm descend upon her as her mind stilled and her heart slowed and she drifted off to sleep, whispering…

"With His love He will calm all your fears. He will rejoice over you with joyful songs."

***

"Well, the van's secured, the boys are bunked down for the night, and all's quiet in Kingsland," said Deut cheerfully, joining Jed and Miri in the kitchen.

"Thanks, Deut, that was a master manoeuvre on your part!" said Miri, handing him a hot chocolate. "Dunc is going through an 'I don't need to go to bed' phase, at the moment. Unfortunately, we are *all* suffering the consequences," she said yawning.

"Oh? Is there something on his mind?" asked Deut, concerned.

"There is," said Jed quietly, "But he's keeping it to himself at the moment. We've covered him in prayer and the Lord has instructed us both to give him time – so he'll tell us when he's ready."

"Maybe it's something he just has to figure out for himself," nodded Deut, suddenly lost in thought.

"Mmmm," agreed Jed, exchanging glances with Miri.

"This hot chocolate's gooood, Miri, thank you." Deut slurped noisily, his mind back in the room again.

"Oh, don't thank me, thank our corner shop!" she laughed. "The cheapest and the best! Homemade shortbread anyone?"

Suddenly Deut's mobile bleeped. He snatched it out of his pocket, spilling hot chocolate all over his jeans.

Miri took the mug from his hand as she saw the colour drain from his already gaunt face. "Deut?"

"Deut, you okay, man?" asked Jed quietly.

Deut bowed his head, swallowing repeatedly, as he fought to gain control of his speech. Shaking his head, he let out a shuddering breath.

"I didn't want…to say anything…in front of the kids…" he juddered out, "But whilst I was in Fengtai, there was a raid on one of the neighbouring churches… It was close to Pastor Ling's factory, about half a mile away. Only tiny in comparison, about thirty members. They gathered in the back of a nursery school, under the guise of running parenting classes." He paused, fighting for control. "They went in with tear gas, and automatic rifles. They killed every man, woman and child…" he choked out, his voice breaking, "Including a seven-week-old baby."

"Oh, dear Lord forgive them," exclaimed Miri, horrified.

Tears spilled down Deut's face. Jed laid a comforting hand on his shoulder.

"They said it was a gas explosion. But it wasn't," Deut went on, wiping his face. "Do you remember Gen, my guide? His mother and older sister were attending – she had just had a baby and ironically they were actually holding parenting classes that night."

"Oh, no, no, no," moaned Miri.

"They arrested Gen the following morning. They 'questioned him'," ground out Deut angrily, "Fracturing his skull, his arm, and ribs, then they dumped him. Pastor Ling and I found him and took him to hospital. He's been in a coma for weeks. That text was from my contact – Gen's gone home to be with the Lord…" wept Deut brokenly, "He was only eleven."

"Oh, Father forgive them," prayed Jed with commanding authority. **"We come before You now, Lord, filled with righteous anger and piercing sorrow. And ask You to strengthen and comfort all concerned. We know Your word says *"Evildoers do not understand what is right, but those who seek the Lord understand fully."* We ask, Lord, that those who have done this evil will repent of their ways and seek You – understanding fully what is right."**

Miri joined in. **"Lord, Your word says *"He reveals the deep things of darkness and brings utter darkness into the light."* We ask that You fill Fengtai and the whole of China with Your light, Your 'Shekinah Glory'; bringing peace, repentance, forgiveness, and salvation. For You also say *"Do not take revenge, my dear*** *friends, but leave room for God's wrath,"* for it is written: *"It is mine to avenge; I will repay."* We ask Lord, that Your justice be done, Your peace reign and Your love prevail."

"Maintain love...maintain love and justice, and wait for your God always," whispered Deut, quoting part of Hosea 12:6. *"We are hard pressed on every side, but not crushed; perplexed but not in despair; persecuted, but not abandoned; struck down, but not destroyed.* 2 Corinthians 4:8-9," he prayed triumphantly. *"For the Lord, your God will be with you wherever you go.* Joshua 1: 9-10," he continued, getting to his feet. "Oh Lord, we lift up Gen, his family and all who have suffered, and we find comfort knowing that they are with You, in your embrace, safe and loved in your heavenly Kingdom. Bring Your peace and comfort to all who are left grieving. Hold them close, precious Father. Let them feel Your love. Bring hope where there is none."

Arms encircling one another, they prayed 'The Lord's Prayer', the prayer Jesus taught his disciples to pray:

"Our Father, who art in Heaven
Hallowed be Thy Name
Thy Kingdom come
Thy Will be done
On Earth as it is in Heaven
Give us this day our daily bread
Forgive us our trespasses

As we forgive those who trespass against us
Lead us not into temptation
But deliver us from evil
For thine is The Kingdom
The Power and The Glory
Forever and ever
AMEN"

Miri lifted her voice softly and began to worship God in song.

Father God, Abba dear,
Take all our pain and our fears,
And the loss and the tears,
The anger, the grief, and the jeers,
Take our hurt, take our hearts,
The wounds of a fiery dart,
You are meek, You are mild,
And you comfort us like a child…

Jed also began singing in his deep baritone. Deut, adding his rich tenor, joined them. Bonded in praise. And united in worship.

For they knew that prayer and worship are two of the most powerful weapons against the Enemy. Especially in times of hardship and pain, when it feels like the very last thing you want to do. They knew it was *THE* most effective way to fight the Enemy. He cannot withstand the power and authority of prayer and worship.

They prayed and worshipped well into the night. Led by the Holy Spirit; speaking with God; taking solace from Lord Jesus, until they retired to bed, finding comfort in knowing that

'*The lowly He sets on high, and those who mourn are lifted to safety*'. Knowing that good would prevail. Knowing that '*Weeping may endure for a night, but joy comes in the morning*'.

* * *

CHAPTER SIX

Cousin Joshua

"Any change?" asked Tom, joining them.

"None," answered Hilly. "We have to wait out here, until they let us in."

"He's been unconscious for at least ten hours now…" Mitch stated, checking his watch.

"They told my dad they're keeping him sedated, until the swelling inside his head subsides," she replied, "But we're still allowed in to visit him."

"This place gives me the heebie jeebies." Lauren shuddered.

"Why?" asked Hilly, surprised.

"Why? Duh, It's full of people, who are dead, dying or desperately ill," she declared, shuddering again.

"Sssh, keep your voice down! Anyway, I prefer healing, healthier and heading home!" said Hilly, giving Lauren a playful nudge.

"Okaaay, 'Florence bloomin' Nightingale'!" muttered Lauren, nudging her back.

"Actually though, you don't look very well. Are you feeling okay?" Hilly asked her.

"It's the smell… It makes me feel…urgh…! It's sooo clean!" Lauren moaned.

"It's isopropyl alcohol." Hilly inhaled deeply. "And I *love* that smell!"

"Well, I hate it, it reminds me of the time I had my tonsils out. I ate dry toast and ice cream, and vomited for three whole days!" Lauren paled further at the memory.

"Yuck!" said Tom grimacing.

"Tell me again why we're allowed to visit Jess. Surely it should be next of kin only?" Mitch queried.

"Other than his dad and sister, Jess doesn't have any other next of kin. And as they can't be found at the moment, my dad was granted permission," Hilly explained. "Sister Martin has agreed to dad organizing a visiting rota, so that Jess won't be alone. My mum, dad and uncle Deut, have been here with him this afternoon until 3.00, Lee and my brother Cam were here until 5.00 and we're to stay until 7.00pm and then some other folks from my church will take over."

"Okay, all finished, you can go in and sit with him now," said Sister Martin, holding the door open for them. They filed into the side room, circling the bed.

Jess was unrecognizable, his face battered and bruised. Both eyes were swollen shut, his lips cut and bloodied. He looked frail and small, lost in a sea of white sheets and bleeping machines.

"Oh, my goodness," breathed Lauren.

"I, I don't recognize him," stammered Tom.

"Dad did warn me," whispered Hilly sadly.

They stood united in horrified silence, numbed by what they saw, until Hilly commanded with that quiet authority of hers, "Right, let's pray over him."

Mumbling their assent, they bowed their heads.

"Heavenly Father, we come before You, saddened, shocked and humbled by what we see. We lift Your dear child Jess up to You, Lord, and ask for his full and complete healing, in Your son Jesus' name. We know that *'there is power in the name of Jesus'*. That *'Your name is above all names'*. We know You say, Lord Jesus, that *'Whatever you ask in my name, this I will do, that the Father may be glorified in the Son.'* Therefore, we thank You, precious Lord, that Jess is already healed in Heaven and in the spirit and we ask that he is also healed here on Earth Lord; here on Earth as it is in Heaven. May he be pain free, may all swelling go down and every cut and bruise be completely healed. May his spirit and soul be given new life. Bring him and his life into Godly order, Lord. I also ask Lord that Jess' sister Ruby be found safe and sound. And also, Jess' father. We ask that he return to You Lord. That he be healed of his grief. That he feels Your love; that they all feel Your love, Lord. Bring comfort and protection to this family, in spirit, soul, mind and body. And that any trauma be lifted off them, Lord. That they find solace and peace, in the safety of Your arms. I also ask that all who are here this evening receive Your comfort too, Lord. That any shock be lifted off. That we be filled with Your peace and calm. We ask for Your grace and mercy, Lord. Amen."

"Amen," they all repeated.

"If anyone else wants to say a prayer, please do," Hilly encouraged.

"I, I'd like to," said Tom shyly.

"Go on Tom," Hilly said kindly.

Clearing his throat nervously, Tom began, faltering at first, **"Dear Lord… Dear Lord, I'm not sure what to say…pray…except I want Jess to get better…I want him to know that I…I'm sorry…that his mum died… That I understand now why he's been the way he is, has. Umm, get well soon Jess. Amen."**

"Amen."

Lauren gently touched Jess' arm, and began, her voice barely above a whisper, **"Dear God, I feel so bad for Jess. He must have been so frightened. And lonely. And very sad. I ask that he heals really quickly and never feels like this again. Amen."**

"Amen."

"Lord, I ask that Jess be healed. And if he needs a friend – I'm offering. I hope his sister is found soon. And things with his dad… mend. Amen," prayed Mitch seriously.

"Amen."

During Lauren's prayer Hilly had heard the door quietly open and looked up to see that they had been joined by her brother Cam and Lee Silverberg. They waited until the prayers were finished, then passed on a message.

"Dad said to tell you that he's coming to pick us all up at 7.15," whispered Cam, surprising the others. He gave them all a friendly smile. "Hi, I'm Cam, Hilly's brother." Cam was like an older, taller, male version of Hilly. Brown hair, brown eyes and 'holiday brown' skin, with the same kindness and gentleness radiating from his easy smile.

"And I'm Lee, a friend." He smiled, shaking Mitch's hand. "Hi Tom! Hi Lauren!"

"Hi Lee!" Tom waved, instantly cheering up.

Lauren could not look Lee in the face. Her cheeks suddenly looked sunburned! "Hi..." she mumbled.

"Mum also said, would you all like to join us for dinner this evening?" added Cam. "She said she would be happy to speak to your parents, if you wanted her to. Mum's a bit of a stickler when it comes to safeguarding!" He grinned.

They devoted the rest of their time with Jess to taking it in turns to pray over him. Hilly, Cam and Lee also sang over him, very softly.

I pray for healing, Lord, Lord
I pray for healing, Lord, Lord
I seek Your healing,
Grant him Your healing,
Thank you for healing, Lord,

Heal him, Lord, and he shall be healed
Save him, Lord, and he shall be saved
For You, our Lord, are the one we praise
Praise You, Lord, all of our days

Initially it both surprised and embarrassed the others, but after a while they found it to be incredibly soothing and comforting; seeming to fill them with a certainty that, no matter what, God loved them endlessly.

However, when Hilly began to 'pray in tongues', Cam noticed that both Lauren and Tom stared open-mouthed, somewhat alarmed. Whilst Mitch watched in fascination.

"Don't worry guys, it's nothing to be frightened of," whispered Cam reassuringly. "We will explain it all later." They nodded, but Cam could tell it was not going to be easy.

At 7.15pm sharp, Jed pulled into the car park and found a gaggle of people waiting for him.

"Evening campers!" he called jovially. "Hop in! First stop, corner shop for milk – then back to ours, for a feast! Your cousin Joshua has just arrived too!"

"Fantastic!" exclaimed Cam. "Another chance to thrash him at 'Super Mario'."

"If memory serves me correct, you were the one who was thrashed!" chuckled his dad.

Cam grinned at the memory, "Yeah, but you've gotta admit I gave him a run for his money!"

"That you did son!" Jed winked.

"How long is he home for?" asked Hilly excitedly. Another one to add to our growing numbers, she secretly thrilled.

"I think he's got two weeks half term this time," her dad replied.

"Whoo hoo!" she whooped, "You will LOVE my cousin Joshua! He's eighteen, he lives away

79

at college, he can drive a car, he can speak four languages, he's brilliant at doing accents and impressions! And he has a Labrador called Zebedee, who is adorable!"

"Yeah!" interjected Cam, "You should see Josh imitate my dad!" He laughed.

"Actually, I think he does a better impression of your mother!" grinned Jed. "But don't tell her I said that!" Everyone laughed.

"Dad, this is my friend Lauren," Hilly said.

"Hi, Lauren, nice to meet you. Hilly has spoken a lot about you."

"Hello, Mr. Trueman." Lauren smiled self-consciously.

"This is Tom," Hilly continued.

"Hi Tom, nice to meet you too. How's the nose?"

"Oh, it's much better now, thank you," Tom said bashfully.

"And this is Tom's older brother Mitch," Hilly finished.

"Hi Mitch, I hear you are on the basketball team – I'd love to shoot a few hoops with you later."

"My dad is a huge fan of 'The Kingsland Fishers'," explained Cam. He was even 'Finn the Dolphin' once!"

"No way!" exclaimed Mitch, his eyes lighting up. "You were their mascot?! How did you manage that?!"

"I won it!" Jed confessed. "I got lucky at a charity fund-raiser! The winning ticket was stuck beneath my seat!"

"No way!" repeated Mitch, delighted. "I'm jealous!"

"I had to train every night for two weeks before they'd let me anywhere near that costume! And boy was it tight!" chuckled Jed, his voice deep and rich, like laughing chocolate. "I only agreed to do it to impress their mum!" he roared, catching Hilly's eye in the mirror. "I thought I'd found my calling, until they made me finish with the 'Dolphin Dance'!"

"No way!" exclaimed Mitch again. "With the back flips and the splits?!"

"Yep! Everything! I was so bad I looked more like a flounder than a dolphin!" Jed roared again, his shoulders rocking with mirth at the memory.

His laugh was so infectious. Lauren could see where Hilly got it from!

"It worked though; their mum agreed to marry me… Just so long as I promised never to do that dance again!" The whole car erupted with laughter as he snapped his fingers in glee!

Wiping his eyes, he pulled into the kerb. "Okay, kids, I'm just gonna pop in and pick up some milk." He disappeared into the shop still chuckling to himself.

"Your dad is hilarious!" said Tom, grinning.

"A hero!" agreed Mitch.

"Yeah, he's great," said Hilly with a smile.

"He sure is, and can you believe he's a pastor?!" asked Lee, good humouredly.

"Lee!" groaned Hilly, "You've said the 'P' word!"

"Oh, sorry guys, I forgot." Lee grimaced.

"W-what?" stammered Tom.

"Your dad's a pastor?!" asked Mitch, incredulous.

"Yep!" confirmed Cam proudly. "And our mum!"

"Well, that explains a lot!" declared Lauren. "No wonder you know so much about 'that book'! And your prayers are wicked good!"

"Definitely NOT wicked!" Hilly corrected fervently, "Heaven forbid!"

"Now I understand why they allowed your dad to visit Jess," said Mitch.

"Why didn't you tell us?" asked Lauren.

"I was going to tell you tonight at dinner. After you'd met them. That way you could see for yourself how great my parents are, and hopefully not freak out. You'd be surprised at how many friends I've lost over the years because of what they think my mum and dad will be like because they're pastors."

"Yeah," Cam agreed, "People start behaving differently too. Like they're having dinner with the headmaster or something and have to watch their p's and q's!"

"Yeah, almost as bad as when some folk learn that you are a Christian!" Lee quipped sarcastically.

"So, both my parents are pastors! So now ya know." Hilly grinned. "Moving on!"

"Okay…!" Lauren nodded, rolling her eyes. "So, what does that make you? A 'pastor-ette' or 'pastor-ised'?!" she teased Hilly mischievously, pointing to Jed as he returned with copious amounts of milk.

"Okay, campers, we're in business. Let's get home. I believe there is one of your mother's enormous treacle sponges waiting for me – oops, sorry us!" he corrected playfully, to restrained laughter. He noticed, put the car in gear and slowly pulled out onto the main road. After ten minutes of polite silence and snatches of whispered conversation, he said, "Okay, who died?! When I went into that shop, I left six livin', breathing, laughing souls in my car!" he quipped, "I come out and find they've all been replaced by the cast of 'Les Mis'!" he teased.

Lauren muffled a giggle, reminding Hilly of the first time they'd ever met.

"Soo… It was the 'P' word, wasn't it? Someone mentioned the 'P' word, didn't they?! Who said the 'P' word?!" he carried on, his tone amused and exaggerated. "I guess now you all feel like you've got to be on your best behaviour. So let me tell you something, if everybody I met was on their best behaviour – I'd be out of a job!" he joked. The atmosphere in the car lifted again as everyone began to relax. "So, chill out! Besides if there is anything the good Lord wants me to know about you, he'll tell me himself!" Then he roared at the startled look on their faces!

"Dad's just teasing you, guys!" laughed Cam.

"He truly is!" Hilly giggled. "Although he's not lying about the Lord, He will tell Dad stuff."

"You're not helping, Hilly!" snorted Lee in merriment.

"But it's true!" she retorted, giggling.

They'd barely pulled into the drive, before the car was surrounded by happy smiling faces.

"Cousin Josh!" called Hilly, clambering out of the car, dragging Lauren with her.

"Hi Hilly!" said a taller, almost identical version of Cam.

"Wow! This is your cousin?" asked Lauren. "He looks like your brother!"

"Yep, we're like peas in a pod!" laughed Joshua. "Our dads are twins," he explained, hugging Hilly. "Good to see ya cuz!"

Hilly introduced everyone to everyone.

"And this is my mum," said Hilly with a big smile. "She is the 'Hobbit' side of the family I was telling you about!"

"Cheeky!" Miri laughed, catching her in a one-armed hug, wrapping Lauren in the other. "It's so nice to meet you, Lauren."

"You too, Mrs. Trueman." Lauren smiled, thinking just how much her mum would love this family.

Ten minutes later, eleven happy faces sat around the enormous dining table in eager anticipation of the forthcoming meal. It smelled delicious.

"Joshua, would you like to say grace please?" asked Jed.

Heads bowed, so he began...

"Dear Father, thank You for bringing us all together safely. We praise you for all the blessings You have bestowed upon us today and every day. Those that we are aware of, those that we're not, those that we take for granted and those still yet to come. 'I give

thanks to the Lord for His unfailing love and His wonderful deeds, for He satisfies the thirsty and fills the hungry with good things'. So, 'for what we are about to receive may He make us truly thankful'. Amen."

A fervent "Amen!" resounded around the table as they began to tuck into the feast Miri had prepared.

"I see Josh can pray wicked good too!" commented Lauren wryly.

"Oh, he does! Although definitely NOT wicked!" laughed Hilly. "He's studying at Bible college."

"I didn't know there was a college for Bible study," said Mitch, surprised.

"Yeah, Mattersey Hall, it's in Nottinghamshire," said Cam. "Eventually he wants to be a pastor."

"Like his dad and mum, his uncle and aunt and his nanna and grandad!" said Hilly, grinning.

"That's a lot of pastors!" mumbled Tom around a mouthful.

"Third generation!" interjected Jed proudly. "This spicy fried chicken is a triumph, Miri," he declared, licking his fingers loudly. "More if you please!"

"It's the recipe Deut gave me." She glowed.

"I owe you one, Deut! I think this is going to become a permanent fixture on the 'Trueman' menu!" Jed beamed, winking at Miri.

Deut gave him the thumbs up as he tucked into Miri's fried cauliflower couscous, another one of his absolute favourites.

Tom had never seen so many different choices of food on one table. He did not quite know what to try next, although he did think the Mexican prawns looked rather mouth-watering…!

"I can't believe this is cauliflower!" declared Lauren, "I can't stand cauliflower, but this is DELICIOUS with a capital Dee!" she said spooning a second helping onto her plate.

Miri smiled, she adored cooking. She had always had a knack for creating meals where no matter the dish, no matter how diverse, each one would be a complement to the next.

And her extra special gift, the hidden ingredient of her success, was not so much her talent for cooking, but her talent for making everyone feel truly welcome. In fact, secretly she always ensured that every person at the table had at least *one* of their favourite dishes upon it; and new guests were observed very closely. No one ever realized why they loved Miri's cooking so much, but everyone knew they loved being invited to one of 'Miri's meals'!

Letting her gaze travel around this happy, feasting, chattering circle, her heart overflowed with gratitude. "Thank you, precious Father," she whispered, smiling, "You have blessed me again."

Jed caught her eye and blew her a kiss. He knew exactly what she was thinking, and he loved her deeply for it.

"So, how long have you been at Mattersey Hall?" Mitch asked Joshua.

"This is my second term," Joshua answered. "The course runs for three years."

"And you'll be a pastor by the end of it?" asked Mitch, impressed.

"No, but I'll have a BA in Biblical Studies and Theology. And in my second year I can apply to go on an 'Accredited Ministry Training' course, which would run alongside my degree. And if that goes well, then I will be a fully-fledged 'minister' a year after I've completed my degree."

"A minister?" asked Lauren. "What's the difference?"

"Well, 'minister' is the qualification and 'pastor' is the job you are qualified to do. But you can only become a pastor when there is a church for you to pastor – or rather, be 'the head shepherd of'."

"He will have the status of 'Reverend'" interjected Jed proudly. "The seventh in a long line!"

"So, four years study in total," Mitch observed.

"Yeah." Joshua nodded.

"That's a long time," stated Tom."

"Yeah, but it's worth it." Joshua smiled.

"Mmm, sounds interesting," said Mitch, thoughtfully.

"I've seen that look before!" Jed grinned at Mitch.

"How old do you have to be to study at Mattersey?" asked Lauren.

"Eighteen," answered Joshua.

But before he could say any more, the dining room door burst open and in bounded a large pale vanilla-coloured ball of furry energy, sweeping the room, taking anything knee high out with his 'ninja' tail!

"ZEBEDEE!" cried several excited voices in unison.

"Hello Boy!" laughed Joshua, pounding his side and dodging very wet doggy kisses. "Did you miss me?!"

In answer Zebedee stood up on his hind legs and tucked into Joshua's shoulder. The room was instantly filled with lots of "Awwws" and "Aaahhs"!

Everyone's attention was so focused on the happy reunion, that no one noticed the towering presence standing in the doorway holding the lead, until it spoke.

"Evening everyone, upstaged by the dog again, I see!" the man chuckled.

"I'd have thought you'd be used to that by now!" laughed Jed, embracing his brother and slapping his back.

Lauren stared open mouthed, dividing her attention between Jed and his absolutely identical double.

"Uncle Joel!" exclaimed Missy, slipping from the table and flinging herself at his knees!

"Hello munchkin!" He beamed, swinging her up into his arms.

"Hi Joel." Miri smiled. "Come sit yourself down, there's still plenty to eat!"

"I don't need to be asked twice!" He grinned, setting Missy down and rubbing his hands together.

"No Esther?" Miri asked.

"Nope, she's at a three-day sleepover! God bless and keep that mother!" He grinned cheekily. "The house has never been so quiet!"

"And how long is Ruth away?" asked Jed.

"Just a couple of days," replied Joel. "She loves going to that retreat and always comes back restored."

"I've been to 'Rose Haven' a couple times," said Miri, "It's a beautiful, peaceful place."

"Well, she deserves a break. She's been up to her eyeballs in meetings and training and admin since we agreed to enlist on the 'Safer Communities Programme'. You wouldn't believe the amount of rules there are, the protocols we have to follow and the safeguarding guidelines... It'll be a miracle if anyone actually manages to get in through the church doors!" he chuckled.

Lauren was still staring at Jed and Joel in fascination. She truly could not tell them apart. They not only looked exactly the same, but they sounded exactly the same, they even laughed the same way.

Miri lent over and whispered, "It's quite amazing isn't it. I couldn't tell them apart for ages!"

"They are the spit of each other," Lauren agreed.

"If you ever get stuck just ask them to smile," Miri laughed, "Joel has a gap between his front teeth!"

"So, how's my favourite son today?!" asked Joel, wrapping his arm around Joshua's shoulders.

"I'm your only son, dad!" Joshua laughed. "Nothing's changed since your call last night!" He grinned cheekily. "Oh, except I just heard today that I got an A star on that essay about 'Disobedience and the influence of social media on teenage Christians'." He air quoted.

"Well done son, I knew you'd have nothing to worry about." Joel beamed.

"Yeah, thanks for pointing me in the right direction. Those scriptures really gave me a different perspective to write from."

"Everything you ever need to know can be found in 'The Good Book'!" agreed Jed.

"Amen to that!" several voices chimed.

"Well, it looks like I won't be needing to vacuum in the morning!" laughed Miri, watching Zebedee hoovering up all the crumbs from under the table. "Don't you ever feed this dog?!" she teased.

"He's a Labrador, Auntie Miri!" Joshua grinned. "They're always hungry! Aren't you Zebs!"

At the mention of his name, Zebs rolled over onto his back for a belly rub, lying right across Miri's feet in the process.

"Well, that's it now, I can't move, so I won't be able to do any of the washing up!" she joked, stroking his tum adoringly. "Will I Zebs? Will I?!"

"Don't worry, Miri, we'll clear up," said Deut, patting his full belly.

"Aren't we having pudding first?!" asked Duncan anxiously.

"Of course we are Dunc – I wouldn't want to deprive that sweet tooth of yours!" Miri smiled warmly at her youngest son, painfully aware that he had been noticeably quiet again all evening. What could be having such an effect on him? "So, treacle sponge and custard or ice cream and jelly?" she asked him.

"We'll get it," offered Cam and Joshua, disappearing into the kitchen and re-entering with heavily laden trays. "Now everybody, 'Come sit yourself down, there's still plenty to eat'!" said Joshua in perfect imitation of Miri. He had her voice, her body posture and even the way she used her hands to gesticulate. "Now don't be shy, tuck in, it all has to be eaten!" he continued.

Everyone burst out laughing – even Miri. "Do I really stand like that?!" she asked through fits of giggles.

"Only when you're in your slippers!" roared Jed, slapping his leg in glee.

"Well, Josh, if Bible college doesn't work out, I think you might have a career on the stage!" he chuckled.

Just then the house phone rang. Jed answered. "Good evening, the Trueman residence… Speaking… Oh, good evening officer… Yes, yes that's right… You have…? He did…? Yes, yes of course, I can be there in fifteen minutes… No, not a problem…what about his daughter, Ruby…? Still missing…? Oh dear… Yes, I'll be right with you… Thank you for contacting me."

He replaced the receiver gently, all levity gone. The whole room was silent, waiting to hear the news.

"That was the police, a Detective Stanford. Jess' dad is in custody. He's at the station and he's asking to see me. Unfortunately they still haven't found Ruby.

"You go, I'll drop the children home later," said Miri.

"And we'll clear away," said Deut.

"And I'll make sure everyone's in bed on time," assured Joel, hugging Missy closer.

Nodding, Jed grabbed his coat and keys and headed out the door. "God go with you, sweetheart," said Miri.

* * *

CHAPTER SEVEN

Judges

Pulling into the car park, Jed took a moment to finish his prayer.

"God grant me the wisdom to listen without judgement, the compassion to understand his pain, and the love to help him in any way I can. Let him see You clearly in all my actions and deeds this evening, Lord. Father put Your words in my mouth and Your message in his heart. Amen."

Detective Stanford met Jed at the door. He was young, earnest and impeccably turned out – smart was an understatement. Although currently a large black eye ruined the illusion of complete perfection, which somehow made Jed feel he was more approachable.

"Thank you for coming," he said, shaking Jed's hand. "He's currently in the cells. But I have a few routine questions I need to ask you first." He led Jed into his office. "Please take a seat, Reverend Trueman."

"Thank you."

"My partner, Detective Hughes, will join us when he returns from the hospital."

Jed nodded.

"I must say I was surprised when Mr. Wilkins refused a solicitor and insisted upon seeing you instead. I take it he is one of your congregation?"

"He used to be. Up until eighteen months ago he was part of the leadership team – Head of Men's Ministry; then sadly his wife Cathy, became ill and passed away. Since then, understandably, he has struggled, struggled to come to terms with her loss, struggled with life, with everything. He has also 'backslidden'."

"Backslidden?" asked Stanford.

"Turned away from God, stopped walking with the Lord," Jed explained.

"Okay. So, what is your connection to him now, then?" Detective Stanford asked, focusing on his notes.

Jed paused, choosing his words carefully. "Detective Stanford, are you familiar with the parable of the lost sheep?"

"Yes, sir, I have heard it. Um, a shepherd has a flock of sheep, a hundred I think – one goes missing and he leaves them all to go looking for that one?"

"Correct. He leaves the ninety-nine to look for the one. Well, Peter Wilkins is that one lost sheep, and he and his family all need rescuing."

Stanford paused. "And you see yourself as the person to do that, their 'shepherd' as it were?"

"In a manner of speaking, yes, although ultimately it is the Lord who brings home the lost sheep. Interestingly though 'pastor' is the Latin for 'shepherd'." Jed smiled, hoping to put the young officer at ease, it did not seem to work, so he continued, "They were once part of our church family and we don't turn our backs on family, especially in their time of need, even if they have turned their backs on us."

Stanford nodded politely. "Hm hm. So did Mr. Wilkins contact you for help?"

"No, unfortunately he refused all assistance. But this is a relatively small community and word of his predicament got back to me. We have been keeping an eye on him from a distance, offering support where and when we could; especially to the children."

"How so?" asked Stanford.

"Well, any way we could – friends and members of the congregation would pop round to see how they were doing, until Peter put a stop to that. We'd leave food packages, school supplies, bags of clothes, that sort of practical help. And at every opportunity we'd let them know we were there for them, they could still come to us for anything. And we've prayed for them continually."

"Right, right, even though he was 'backslidden'?"

"Even more of a reason, Detective."

"What did Mr. Wilkins make of that?"

"Sadly, most of the time, Mr. Wilkins was… too far gone to notice anything."

"I see." Stanford scribbled on his pad. He himself had terminated an interview with Mr. Wilkins earlier that day because he was still under the influence of alcohol. Definitely 'too far gone' as the pastor put it. He had been completely incoherent. Stanford had not been able to make sense of anything he had been saying.

"He gave me a card with your name on it. Kept repeating, 'Call him.' It's a little unorthodox, but

I did. I do want to help him, even if it does mean ultimately locking him up."

There was an abrupt knock on the door, it opened immediately and in strode Detective Graham Hughes. Hughes by name, huge by nature. Six feet six inches tall and nearly as wide, and with a personality to match. He was loud and proud and played his persona for all it was worth, yet underneath that bluff was an astute, shrewd, and dedicated detective with a mind that could mangle a Mensa member – no matter how clever they were. He had closed more cases than any other detective in the Met. However, following a life changing near miss on duty, he had opted for a quieter life in Kingsland. A huge result for Kingsland, his wife Peggy, and their dog Bruce – but an ambiguous one for him.

He was used to a faster pace. He had been in the military before becoming a police officer. He had worked his way up through the police ranks very quickly, joining the Armed Response Unit, then moving across to CID (Crime Investigation Department); he had been undercover on several occasions. Ultimately he had been offered a position in the MCIT – the Major Crime Investigation Team. He was a legend within the force. With only five years left before compulsory retirement, he was counting down the days…with dread. The force was his life. Peggy was his love. Bruce was his sanity.

"You must be Pastor Trueman," he said, extending his hand.

Jed got to his feet and shook it. "That I am, sir," he said politely. "And you must be Detective Hughes."

"That I most definitely am, sir!" He grinned. "Sorry to interrupt, but I need a quick word with Stanford." He indicated for Stanford to follow him.

"I won't be long," Stanford apologized to Jed, leaving the room.

"The boy is still unconscious – so no luck there," said Hughes, closing the door to his office. "I've just left PC Burton on watch over night – Dan will be fine, he's a good lad. PC Amos will take over from him at 8.00am. She'll keep any nosers at bay. We still have no idea where the girl is."

He sighed, frustrated. "House to house has revealed nothing. The helicopter has scoured the whole area within a ten-mile radius; the dog teams have come up blank – highly unusual; Scenes of Crime are still there, processing.

PC Crowther is on 'scene guard' at the house – Matt's better suited to keeping a log than Dan. It's at times like this we could do with more people on the ground," he grumbled, rubbing the back of his neck.

Stanford nodded. "What time are MCIT due to arrive?"

"They were due to arrive here an hour ago, but have been diverted back up to North Devon."

"Why?!" exclaimed Stanford, in surprise.

"Another dead body, bearing the same markings as the other victims in 'The Cranford

Case'. So, *all* hands on deck, I'm afraid. It's not official, yet. I only know cos my mate Jim gave me the heads up."

"'The Cranford Case'? How many does that make now?"

"Six," said Hughes, sadly. "All young women under twenty."

"Are they any closer to catching the perp?" he asked, using their slang for 'perpetrator' – the person who had committed the crime.

"Jim couldn't say much. But they are now wondering if it's connected to an extremist terrorist faction, with a very low opinion of women. Not sure how they've arrived at that, but I've volunteered to put in some overtime, when I can."

"So, what's our position now?" asked Stanford.

"We are to keep going until they arrive."

Stanford nodded. "Understood. Any response from the TV or radio appeal?" he asked.

"Nothing of note, a couple of could have beens, might have seens…

The 'community cascade' has been in play since 10.00 this morning – all the local shops and public transport are aware – and nothing has come from that either. It's like the poor kid just vanished," he grated. "Have you got anything from the father?"

"No, he was too inebriated for me to get anything earlier – except to call his pastor. I know it's against regulations, but I thought if it helps find his daughter, I'd give it a try."

Hughes grinned his approval. "Son, this is Kingsland Constabulary, nothing is ever strictly regulation. You've only got to look at the frilly net curtains in the men's loos to see that!"

Stanford returned his grin. "Right, shall I get back to the pastor, then?"

"Yeah. Is Wilkins sober enough to talk now?"

"Not for our purposes, but enough to take 'spiritual counsel' from his pastor, I think," Stanford said pointedly.

"Right, go for it. Like you say, not strictly regulation, but worth a shot. I've got your back. I'll talk to the custody sergeant – get him to bring him up from the cells. And Sam, record it!"

"Yes, sir."

"When you've finished that, go home, get some rest. I'm off myself, now," he said yawning.

Yes sir, thanks, sir." Stanford said, heading back to his office.

"Sorry to keep you, Reverend Trueman. Thank you for waiting."

"Not a problem, Detective."

"Now, where were we?" asked Stanford, checking his notes. "Ah, yes, you were telling me about how you and your church were trying to help the Wilkins family.

"Yes, we tried many avenues of intercession: bereavement counselling, social services, child welfare; but Peter just refused any help and denied there was a problem. Unfortunately, but understandably, the children denied it too. That was not the case of course, and it was blindingly obvious to those of us who knew them. But without his consent, or any evidence to the contrary…" Jed trailed off, shrugging his shoulders sadly.

"But I have a file here that says there were frequent complaints from the neighbours. Surely that was proof enough," bristled Stanford.

"Yes, yes you're right. But Peter managed to convince the authorities it was all malicious lies concocted to make him look bad. Again, supported by his children."

"Yes, well, perhaps if that line of enquiry had been pursued further, his son wouldn't be in the condition he's in now," Stanford said with asperity. "The children were obviously vulnerable and should have been registered as such.

Jed could see that Stanford had been affected by Jess' condition. "You've seen him then?"

"Yes. Poor lad. Wilkins managed to take one swing at me when we were arresting him, and I saw stars for at least twenty minutes," he said, gingerly touching his eye. "God knows what that poor boy's been through."

"Yes, God does know. We have all been very, very concerned about him. The passing of his mother has changed him completely. He was always a polite, respectful boy, who lived for his dog and football. Now he's been expelled from one school for bullying, and he's already got a reputation at his new one," sighed Jed.

"Mmm, sadly that doesn't surprise me," Stanford acknowledged. "So, why do you think

Mr. Wilkins wants to see you now? Why now? After all the attempts you've made in the past?"

"To be honest with you, Detective Stanford, I don't know. But in my experience, when we are at the end of ourselves, we tend to turn to a higher power – and maybe Peter sees me as an intercessor to that power. Or maybe he's just in need of a friend. Either way, God's will be done."

Stanford nodded. "Do you have *any* idea what happened to his son, or the whereabouts of his daughter?"

Jed shook his head sadly. "I'm afraid not Detective, but if I can help in any way, just ask."

"I'd best take you to see him then. I won't come in with you, but I have to tell you that I will be watching from the next room, and I'd like to record your conversation."

"Fair enough," Jed agreed.

Again, not strictly regulation, thought Stanford.

Closing the door quietly, Jed entered a small, cramped, box-like room. The air was heavy with the stench of sweat and stale beer. Peter Wilkins was slumped on the floor in a corner of the room. Jed was shocked to see how the paper suit he wore hung off him. The once big man was now a shadow of himself. Jed could see that he had not shaved in weeks, or slept much, going by the black circles under his eyes. He was a pitiful sight. Jed pulled up a chair and sat.

"So, you deigned to come and see me after all," slurred the dishevelled mound that was Peter Wilkins. "Took you long enough!"

Jed took a deep breath readying himself for the onslaught. Wearing his 'Armour of God', he mentally drew the sword – God's word. And like all good swords, his had a name, a name that struck fear into the very hearts of all God's enemies – 'Vainglorious'. It vanquished all pride and vanity: the very sins that had cast Lucifer from Heaven.

Of course, in reality his armour and sword could not be seen by the naked eye, but in the spiritual realm they were flaming brands, wreaking havoc wherever they fought. Jed's father had taught him and his brother, from a very early age, that the spiritual realm was very real. So he had encouraged them to visualize their armour and sword to help them understand its importance. Jed knew that the 'Sword of the Spirit' was only a symbol of God's powerful word, but it had never stopped him from visualising it as an actual sword, or bringing it into each and every battle. 'Vainglorious' was always victorious and today was no different.

"Call yourself a man of God?!" Peter goaded, "Where have you been all this time?!" His voice rose with his anger. "You promised me, us, that you would always be there for us!" he cried. "Well?! Where were you?!"

"I have watched over you, my brother. You have never been alone," said Jed calmly. "And the Lord has never left your side, never forsaken you."

"Liar! I am always alone! I have been alone since Cathy died." His voice caught in an angry sob. He swore at Jed, foul, disgusting words, designed to offend.

Jed knew that Peter was still grieving, in pain and desperate. But he also knew that if left unchecked, these were the very opportunities that the Enemy would use to gain entry into his life. A gateway into his very soul. Peter had more than one battle on his hands.

Jed had felt the oppression as soon as he had entered the room. He knew Peter had company. The demonic presence was overwhelmingly apparent, the foul language a manifestation of their influence. Jed knew this was a deliberate attack aimed to make him leave; to abandon Peter to them.

"You are a useless pastor!" Peter ranted. "You should give up! What good are you to anyone?! You and your useless God! God?! What God?! There is no God!" He spat. "I don't believe there ever was a God!"

Peter was on his feet now, glaring at Jed across the small tabletop. Jed remained sitting. Throughout the whole of Peter's rant, he had been quietly praying. Now he took command. "In the name of the Lord Jesus Christ of Nazareth, Son of God, you will be silent," declared Jed calmly in a voice not much louder than normal.

Peter stopped mid-sentence, stunned. "Wha…?" Then tried to begin again.

"I said silence!" repeated Jed. "In Jesus' name." Peter swayed on his feet.

"Sit down Peter," Jed said kindly. Peter sat.

Officer Stanford watched in incredulity. He feared for the pastor's safety and had been about to enter the room to put a stop to the interview.

"Now listen to me, Peter," Jed said calmly. "I *have* come here to help you. You and your family. But in order to do that I am going to have to pray for you."

Peter stared at him through haunted, bloodshot eyes. "No!" he snapped. "Prayers don't work anyway!"

"Yes, they do, Peter. Don't listen to the lies of the Enemy," Jed encouraged.

"I don't need prayers! I don't deserve prayers!" he cried.

"Yes, you do, Peter. Everyone deserves prayers. Don't listen to the lies of the Enemy," Jed repeated. Then lifting his hand, palm facing Peter, Jed began to pray.

"Father, I lift your precious son Peter up to you. And in Your mighty name I command all ungodly spirits to reveal themselves quietly and without harm or fuss to Peter or anyone else present."

God had already revealed to him the major culprits. So he began, entering into the 'Battle Proper'.

"In the mighty name of the Lord Jesus Christ of Nazareth, Son of God, I rebuke, bind, and cast out, cast off, cast away, revoke, repent, renounce and reject, forbid from operating within and through Peter Wilkins. I cancel any assignment, agenda, plan, plot, or ploy of the Enemy. And in so doing call forth..."

Stanford was not sure what he was witnessing or if it was even allowed under his 'duty of care'. But Wilkins had asked to see the pastor after all. And pastors and prayers went hand in hand, didn't they?

"...You Spirit of Death, you, your minions, servants and underlings," continued Jed. **"You are to leave Peter now, without causing him or anyone else any further harm; you are never to return, never to be replaced, you are forbidden to return. I apply the blood of the cross upon you and your life Peter, sealing shut any and all ungodly doors that have been opened."**

The demons within and around Peter raged against their spiritual bonds, trying to resist the commands given to them: to be silent and to do no harm, to reveal themselves, to leave Peter in the name of Jesus. How they longed to shriek profanities and hurl insults, scream and curse, cause chaos and fear, hopelessness and defeat. But, powerless against the name of Jesus, they could do no more than submit and flee from the very Lord they feared, and await His eternal judgement.

Peter continued to struggle with the tempest taking place within, mouthing words, broken sentences; switching rapidly between anger and prayers, grief and sorrow, defiance and dejection.

Jed forged on, calling forth each spirit in turn; each one banished. Spirit of Grief, Spirit of Addiction, Spirit of Anger, Violence, Abuse, Neglect, Deception, Denial, Hatred, Hopelessness... the list was endless.

Jed was up on his feet now, wielding God's spiritual sword, word upon word pouring forth, 'Vainglorious' discharging the enemy with precision and authority. Keeping his eyes fully upon God, he gave the enemy just enough attention to do God's will. Sensing defeat, the enemy began an assault upon Jed himself; trying to distract him with threatening thoughts about his family, with whispers of self-doubt, with images of Detective Stanford laughing at him from behind the glass.

Jed immediately began to speak in tongues, praying to the Lord to send forth angels to fight by his side, in the name of all that is good, and noble and right.

Stanford watched, transfixed by the scene unfolding before his very eyes. He had never experienced anything like it. And he hoped he never would again. Although he could not actually see any 'spirits' in the interview room, every hair on the back of his neck was standing on end, he was covered in goosebumps from head to toe, his stomach had flip-flopped like the floor had fallen from under him, and his heart rate was through the roof.

"What on earth…?" he breathed.

He felt what could only be described as pure evil, pure fear and hatred emanating from within the interview room. They were definitely not alone in there. And it scared the living daylights out of him. He did not know what to do, whether he should call for backup or something. But what would he say? 'Ah, guys we have evil demons in interview room two, come in riot gear and bring your shields' – if they even had riot gear in Kingsland! He could only imagine the fallout from that one! He would probably be charged for being drunk on duty and locked up in the next cell to Wilkins!

However, as he continued to watch he could see that with the departure of each demon called forth, the atmosphere changed, and Peter Wilkins became calmer and more coherent. He would not have believed it if he was not actually seeing it with his own eyes; he suddenly wished Hughes were here watching it with him. The moment Jed began to speak in tongues, Stanford hit the 'Translate' button on the recording device, but became confused when it flashed up "Language not recognized – unable to translate". "Well, that was a bloomin' waste of police funding," he huffed at the machine.

Back inside the interview room, Peter began to sob, each sob wracking his feeble body. Jed stood over him, hands resting gently on his shoulders, now praying in English again.

"Dear Father God, thank You for your undeniable loyalty and grace. Precious Jesus thank You for the power of Your name and for Your mercy. Sweet Holy Spirit thank You for Your comfort and guidance. Please come fill Peter with Your presence. Fill the empty spaces vacated by the Enemy. Fill what was once darkness with Your light. Fill him to overflowing with Your love, Your peace, and Your abiding companionship, now and forever more. Amen."

"Amen," croaked Peter.

Jed sat quietly opposite him, mentally sheathing 'Vainglorious'. "How are you feeling?" he asked.

"Tired." He stared fixedly down at his shaking hands, not giving Jed any eye contact.

"Can I get you anything?" Jed asked.

"Thirsty. I'm thirsty," he said, his voice like gravel.

Jed stepped outside the room and met Stanford. "Could I trouble you for a cup of tea, Detective Stanford?"

"Tea?!" he exclaimed, "I could use a whiskey, after that!"

"I think tea will be sufficient for us. Besides, we've had enough 'spirits' in here for one night, don't you think?" Jed said wryly.

108

"Oh, very droll!" Stanford snorted, visibly shaken. "I won't be long." He headed to the kitchen.

Minutes later, Stanford set the tray on the table and took a seat opposite Peter. He quickly surmised that he was now sober enough to interview. "Sugar?" he asked him.

"No…thanks." He sat hunched over his cup, still not looking at anyone.

In the absence of his partner, Jed would be a credible and reliable witness – if not technically 'legal'. He knew he was already going to be in big trouble with Newman – the Detective Sergeant, but the aim of this interview was not to incriminate Wilkins, but to try and find the whereabouts of his daughter, so in for a penny… Pressing the record button in the interview room, Stanford logged the date, time and who was present. There was a brief moment of silence, then he began his questioning.

"Could you please state your name for the records," he instructed Peter.

"Peter John Wilkins."

"Do you have any idea why you are here today Mr. Wilkins?"

"Dunno, I was, I was drunk…?"

"That is part of the reason, yes. But do you have any recollection of the events concerning your son Jess?"

"Jess?" asked Peter, surprised. "Why, what's he done now?"

"*He* hasn't done anything, Mr. Wilkins. It's more a question of what *you* did," Stanford grated out, placing photographs of Jess' battered face on the table in front of him.

Peter lent forward, staring uncomprehendingly at the images before him, suddenly spilling his tea in shock when he realized he was looking at the face of his own son.

"Wha, what happened to him?" he choked.

"We were hoping you could tell us," Stanford said in clipped tones.

"Is he, is he alright?" he asked, becoming more agitated by the second.

"No, Mr. Wilkins, he is not 'alright'," Stanford snapped.

"But where is he? I need to see him."

"He is in intensive care at Kingsland General," Jed said.

"Oh, no. I've got to go to him," he said, standing up.

"Sit down, Mr. Wilkins," Stanford said firmly. "You can't go anywhere right now."

"But I must, he's my boy. I have to see him! He needs me!" he cried, swaying where he stood.

"Peter, he's not alone," placated Jed. "He is never alone – I made sure of that. The whole church has been taking it in turns to sit with him. To pray for him. I promise you, he is in safe hands. Now sit down, my friend, before you make things worse for yourself."

Peter hesitated, then sat dejectedly, burying his head in his hands.

"Now, Mr. Wilkins, what do you remember about Wednesday the seventeenth of July?" Stanford pressed.

"Nothing…I can't remember…anything. But I wouldn't do that to my son! You've got to believe me! Jed tell him!"

"Unfortunately, my friend, I cannot," sighed Jed sadly.

"Oh no, no no no, may God forgive me…I can't remember…I can't remember," he wailed, running agitated fingers through his tangled hair. "Oh, help me, Lord…help me…" He began to sob again. "Oh, what have I done? What have I done?"

Jed and Stanford exchanged looks. Stanford indicated a picture of Ruby.

Jed nodded. "Peter, listen to me, my friend. Although Jess is in hospital, we at least know where he is. We have a surety that he is safe," he said evenly.

Peter nodded.

"But sadly, we don't have the same surety for Ruby." He broke it to him as gently as he could.

It took a moment for it to sink in.

"Ruby? What about Ruby? What's happened to Ruby?!" His panic was escalating once more. "Where is she? Is she in hospital? Is she hurt too?" He was on his feet again.

"Peter, Ruby is missing. She has been since this morning," Jed said, cutting through Peter's rising alarm.

"No, no, no…" he moaned, "Not Ruby, not my baby girl."

"Sit down, Mr. Wilkins," commanded Stanford.

"I can't!" he wailed, stumbling back and forth behind the table. "Missing? Are you sure? Are you sure she's not hiding in the house somewhere?"

"No, Mr. Wilkins. We have torn your house apart looking for her," Stanford asserted.

"What time is it?" Peter asked.

"It's 9.15pm," answered Jed.

"It's 9.15…9.15…all day… She's been missing all day," he moaned.

Neither Jed nor Stanford could get any more sense out of Peter after that, so he was led back to the police cells for the night.

"What happens to him now?" asked Jed sadly, watching as Peter's receding back disappeared down a long dark corridor.

"He will stay here tonight. Then his case will be presented to the magistrates' court judge in the morning."

"That soon?" Jed exclaimed.

"We share one Judge with six other boroughs – and she's back in our court tomorrow, so it's now, or in three month's time…it's not how it's usually done, but…"

"What charges are you bringing?" Jed asked.

"That, I've yet to confirm." Stanford exhaled. "At the moment assault and battery…attempted murder are at the top of the list. Then, of course, there's the matter of his missing daughter."

"Attempted murder?! Woah – I wasn't expecting that!"

"Well, his son is in a critical condition and for all we know, his daughter could be too, or worse…" Stanford left that hanging.

"Oh, merciful Father!" Jed exclaimed. "Any news at all?"

"Nothing. Absolutely nothing." Stanford sighed; exhaustion etched on his face. "It's like she's completely vanished into thin air."

Jed shook his head sadly. "God be with her."

"Indeed," Stanford agreed.

"I'd like to come back in the morning and spend some time with Peter before he sees the judge," Jed requested.

"Of course, Pastor." Then he hesitated. "Will you be…praying for him again?" he asked cautiously.

"Of course, Detective, there's nothing on God's good earth that can't be fixed with the help of petition and persistent prayer." Jed smiled teasingly.

Stanford swallowed nervously. "Will you have 'company' this time?"

Jed grinned. He liked this earnest young man. "I'm always in the company of the Father, the Son and the Holy Spirit." He grinned with a twinkle in his eye. "But no, we won't be mixing with the sort you saw this evening."

"Well, that's just the thing, Pastor, I didn't 'see' anything. But I'd swear on my badge, you weren't alone in there – it scared the living daylights out of me," he confessed.

"You have nothing to fear when you put your trust in the one I do – for '*He who is in you, is greater than he who is in the world*', young man. Don't you ever forget that," Jed said sombrely.

Detective Stanford nodded, but was not entirely sure he understood. "I've no idea what I'm going to write in my report," he stated matter of factly.

"Just write the truth and you can't go wrong," Jed advised.

"Right!" snorted Stanford humorously. "'Mr. Wilkins inebriated, agitated and incoherent. Pastor called as requested, prayed for Mr. Wilkins. Room filled with 'creepy feeling' – I needed a change of underwear. Pastor spoke in a language that couldn't be translated, Mr. Wilkins immediately sobered, became more coherent and calm, requested a cup of tea!'" he finished with air quotes. "That's me and my career – over!"

Jed was chuckling. "Happens to me every day, Detective!"

Stanford stared at him, open-mouthed. "All I can say is you must have an awful lot of pants, Pastor!"

Jed roared, clicking his fingers in glee, shoulders bouncing with laughter, "I do, very big ones!"

"Incidentally, what was that language you were speaking?" asked Stanford, "Our translator didn't recognize it – couldn't translate it."

"It's a language only God understands," Jed said soberly.

Stanford blinked at Jed, then without missing a beat, he said, "In that case we're gonna need an upgrade!"

Jed roared again. "Good night, Detective Stanford."

"Call me Samuel," he said, shaking Jed's hand.

"Then you call me Jed." He smiled. "See you in the morning."

"Good night, sir." Samuel smiled back at him.

***

The following morning Jed was encouraged to see Peter clean shaven and in fresh clothes. He sat staring into the black coffee cradled in his lap.

"How are you feeling today?" Jed asked him.

He shrugged despondently. "Any news about my Ruby?" he asked, his voice flat and hopeless.

"I'm afraid not, Peter," Jed said gently.

Peter's head dropped onto his chest, and he began to sob silently.

Jed took the cup from his trembling hands and squeezed his shoulder. "They are doing everything they can to find her, Peter," he said sympathetically. "The whole Kingsland community is out looking for her too. The youth from church are walking the streets with their parents as we speak, knocking on doors, checking garages, play parks, anywhere she might go. And the elders have been praying 24/7 since she went missing.

"I know it's easy for me to say, but have courage, my friend – don't despair, for He is with her and you. Take your strength from Him. '*For He is strong in your weakness*'."

Peter lifted his head, grief carved in every line of his face. "I can't, I can't, I'm too ashamed…" he sobbed.

"I can understand why you would feel that way. But that's the very reason you need to go to Him," Jed urged. "*Cast all your cares upon the Lord. Be strong and courageous. Be not afraid or discouraged, because the Lord your God is with you to help you fight your battles.*"

"I'm so ashamed…" Peter repeated, burying his face in his hands. "The Lord could never forgive me for what I've done…"

"The Lord always forgives, Peter," Jed said gently. "Remember the parable of 'The Prodigal Son'? That young man asked for his inheritance early, squandered it, was left penniless and begging, yet his father welcomed him home with open arms and feasting – you know God will do the same for you.

Peter nodded, but then shook his head. "But I can't forgive myself," he moaned.

"Peter, would it help to talk about what happened? The Lord is gracious and merciful, and He will not turn away His face from you if you return to Him. And neither will I."

Peter's sobs subsided and he looked at Jed with tortured eyes. "Jed, believe me, if I could remember what happened, I'd tell you… But I can't remember…I can't remember a thing…! Not a thing…! What kind of father doesn't remember how his son got hurt, or where his own daughter is?!"

Jed could see he could not move past his self-recrimination. He was tormented by it. But they

116

needed him to think. Any small detail could lead them to Ruby. "Peter, I know you feel bad. I know you feel that you've let your children down. But you can be strong for them now. You can help them now. It's never too late."

"I just keep seeing their faces and hearing their voices…" he whispered.

"I was so angry… Why did Cathy have to die…? Why did she have to leave us…? I was just so angry…all the time…I had a drink to help me sleep at night…then I couldn't stop…I didn't want to wake up…and every time I did, Jess would be there looking at me, his eyes the same as Cathy's…I hated him…! I'd lash out… How dare he look at me like she used to…! When she was gone…" He sniffed loudly, wiping his streaming eyes and nose on the back of his shaking hands.

"And Ruby, my baby… She would try and cuddle me…with the same unselfish love that Cathy had…! I couldn't bring myself to be near her…I'm so ashamed…disgusted with myself… when they needed me the most…I pushed them away." He was sobbing again.

Jed felt a mixture of pity and sadness. Things had been far worse than anyone had realised. They had all suffered, clinging to their lies for survival.

There was a knock at the door, and it opened to reveal Detective Stanford. By the look on his face, he had been watching from the other room. "It's time to go, Mr. Wilkins."

"Any news on Ruby?" Peter asked in desperation.

"I'm afraid not," he said sadly.

"What about Jess?"

"He's still heavily sedated Mr. Wilkins," Stanford told him gently.

"Jed, promise me you'll look for Ruby and take care of Jess – look after them both," Peter pleaded over his shoulder as he was handcuffed and led away.

"I will, my friend," he promised.

***

The courtroom was austere and empty, except for the judge, court clerk, Stanford, Peter, and his court-appointed defence solicitor Joseph Amos.

It was unheard of for the accused to actually be present at this point in the process. But due to the nature of the case and its locality, Judge Deborah Israel had insisted. She listened with honed intensity to all the charges being brought against Peter, and the mitigating circumstances. Detective Samuel Stanford had been in her courtroom several times and she always made him nervous. She was known for being extremely firm but equally fair; and she had a way of looking at you that made you feel she was peeling you open from the inside out and peering into your very soul.

Looking over the top of her glasses she asked, "Are you sober Mr. Wilkins?" Her voice commanded authority yet was still full of compassion.

"Yes, your honour."

"So, you are fully aware of the gravity of the situation you are in, and the charges being brought against you?"

"Yes, your honour." He nodded.

"Under the circumstances, it gives me no pleasure to rule that you should remain in custody when I'm sure you would rather be out searching for your daughter and caring for your son. However, in my opinion, for the sake of your daughter and that of your son, and for your own safety, you will be confined at Brantwood Remand Prison. God-willing your daughter will be found safe and your son will make a full recovery."

Peter lowered his eyes in shame. He knew he deserved this, but had clung to the hope that somehow, he would be allowed to assist with his children.

Observing his reaction, she asked "Do you have anything you would like to say, Mr. Wilkins?"

Peter hesitated. "I know your decision is final, but I had hoped to be able to do something for my children, to make amends for the complete mess I've made…" His voice trailed off.

"You can, by attending statutory bereavement counselling and Alcoholics Anonymous, both of which I have sanctioned. Think yourself lucky, Mr. Wilkins, that Detective Stanford has not added 'assaulting a police officer' to the charges, for which there would be no other recourse than to send you to Brookmoor," she finished, thwacking her gavel with finality. Firm but fair as always, thought Stanford.

* * *

CHAPTER EIGHT

Ruth the Sleuth

A light tap at the back door followed by, "Hello, hello, hello!" announced the arrival of Ruth and her daughter Esther.

"Come on in!" called Miri, always happy to see her niece and sister-in-law. "Hello my lovelies." She smiled, hugging them both. "How was your retreat, Ruth?"

"It was glorious!" she sighed serenely, "A few days of peace, prayer and personal reflection – perfect!"

As short, curvy, and brunette as Miri was, Ruth was tall, slim, and blonde. Sneeze and she would snap! Her daughter was as tall and as blonde, but enjoyed a more olive skin tone. Miri adored them both.

"And I've come home armed with loads of new reference materials I thought we could both use," Ruth said, plonking down three bulky bags.

"Ooh wonderful!" exclaimed Miri excitedly, they were always on the lookout for new ideas to engage their churches. Joel and Ruth were the pastors of Knighton Pentecostal Church, just three miles away from Kingsland.

"There's an especially good book for use with the youth called 'Your Cake & Eat It!'" said Ruth, keeping a straight face.

"I can only guess what that one's about!" Miri said, her eyes dancing. "And how was your three-day sleepover, Esther?" she asked, hugging her for a second time. "That mother deserves a medal!"

"It was great, Auntie Miri! There were only six of us and we all had to wear pink PJ's and bring our favourite teddy!" She laughed. "It was silly really, like we were trying to be little girls again!"

"Because of course at fourteen years of age you are all sooo grown up!" Miri teased pinching her cheek.

"Of course!" Esther giggled. "Where's Hilly? I haven't seen her in aaages."

"That would be all of three days!" Ruth interjected humorously.

"Yeah, aaages!" Esther laughed.

"She's in the den with some new friends." Miri smiled.

"Oooh, is it Lauren, Tom and Mitch? Hilly texted me all about them!" she gabbled excitedly. "Latersss!" she said hurrying off.

"That girl still comes and goes like a hurricane!" laughed Miri affectionately.

Ruth chuckled. "Yes, she's just like her father in that way! Talking of which, where is my husband? He said he'd be here. And Joshua – I haven't clapped eyes on him since he got back from college!"

"Ah yes, they are both fine; Joel is with Deut collecting his next supply of Bibles, Jed was going to help him, but he was called to the police station; Joshua is taking Zebs for a walk with Missy and Lee in tow! Time to put the kettle on, I think. It's been very eventful," Miri said heavily.

"It has?" asked Ruth, suddenly serious.

Half an hour later, Ruth was up to speed. "Oh, my goodness, those poor, poor children. I remember when Jess was born."

"Yes. We all feel like we should be doing something, so when Jed gets back, we're going to take another walk, down along the seafront. Apparently Ruby loved to play there."

"Count me in."

Ruth had been a child psychologist before becoming a pastor, and had been called upon to assist the constabulary on several occasions.

"It's a wonder the police haven't already been in touch with you," Miri said.

"Yes." Ruth sat lost in thought for a moment. "You know I've recently been heading up the 'Safer Communities Programme' for our church?"

Miri nodded.

"Well, I've met a lot of new people who deal with things like this every day – missing children, runaways, displacement cases. I'm wondering if any of them would be able to help, or at least give me some advice."

"Great idea. It's definitely worth a try," encouraged Miri.

"Can I use your phone?" Ruth asked.

"Of course, use the one in Jed's office."

Just then, Hilly entered the kitchen. "Mum, we're all getting a bit peckish in the den, is it okay to get some snacks, please?"

"Of course, sweetheart. What do you fancy? I've got crisps, fruit, homemade shortbread, nuts, cheese and crackers, chocolate…"

"Can we have it all!?" she asked cheekily, "And some juice?"

Laughing, Miri helped her load up two trays of goodies and carry them into the den.

"Snack time!" Hilly announced.

"Ah! Perfect timing, mum! Can you help us explain what 'speaking in tongues' actually means?" asked Cam, grabbing a bag of crisps. "It's just, we've grown up with it, but Tom, Lauren and Mitch think it's kind of weird."

"Well to be honest it can seem that way, especially if you've never heard it before," Miri said, smiling. "It can sound like a lot of incoherent babbling. And no two 'tongues' are alike. The first time I heard my grandfather speaking it, I thought he was doing a very bad impression of Donald Duck!" They all laughed. Sitting down, she continued, "But, it's a beautiful gift given to us by God, so we can speak with Him directly. It's nothing to be frightened of. It's God's own language. A powerful language that we can use, and the enemy can't understand."

"Soo…it's…like having a direct line to God?" asked Lauren hesitantly.

"Well, it's more like speaking *with* God in His own language; you already have a direct line to speak *to* God, when you pray to Him. It contains more power and authority than any other language – and it is universal. It can sound unique, or God can actually use a recognized

124

dialect from another language that the person speaking it has never been taught."

"So how does 'speaking in tongues' actually happen?" asked Mitch.

"Well, different people experience it in different ways. But you don't have to force it or *do* anything. It will start to flow naturally once you have received the gift. Some people can speak in tongues immediately. Some take years, and some choose not to use it. And whilst some are very self-conscious, others feel completely natural. There are occasions in church when a person will speak out a message straight from God. And when that happens, God will have always given someone else within the congregation the ability to interpret the message."

"I didn't understand a word of what Hilly was saying when we were at the hospital," said Tom. "It all sounded like 'gobbledygook' to me! Sorry Hilly," he finished, slightly abashed.

"No worries, Tom." She grinned.

"If it's any consolation, Tom, a person speaking in tongues doesn't always understand what they are actually saying. It's the intention, focus and commitment driving the words that are important. But God *always* understands them." Miri smiled.

"So, when does God give you the gift of 'speaking in tongues'?" asked Mitch.

"It is *given* to *you*, once *you* have *given* your *life* to Christ. Christians encourage baptism, as the way to publicly acknowledge their love of Christ and to invite the Holy Spirit in, as Jesus

125

explains in Matthew 10:32-33. However, there are examples in the Bible of the Holy Spirit dwelling within people before they have been baptised, as found in Acts 10:44-46."

"So this actually happened in the Bible?" asked Lauren curiously. Once again surprised that something like this was contained within a book she had dismissed as boring, irrelevant.

"Oh yes. It first happened to Jesus' disciples. It's written about in a book in the Bible called Acts – chapter two, I believe. You see, Jesus knew that He would be leaving His disciples and returning to Heaven, so He asked His Father – God, to send them a friend, a comforter, so they would never feel alone or separate from God again. And God sent them His Spirit, His 'Holy Spirit'.

"How did he do that?" asked Tom.

"Well, at the time, all of Jesus' disciples and other followers were gathered together in an upper room, when suddenly the whole house was filled with the sound of a violent wind blowing from heaven. They saw what looked like tongues of fire separate from the wind and come to rest upon the head of each of them. And from that moment all of them were filled with the Holy Spirit and began to speak in other tongues."

"Why were they gathered together in that room?" asked Lauren.

"They had gathered together in Jerusalem to participate in the Jewish festival of Passover, which celebrated their liberation from slavery in Egypt, but they had stayed on for another festival, Pentecost, which was a thanksgiving celebration for the harvested crops. Pentecost means 'fiftieth', and was held on the fiftieth day after Passover. So, there were lots of people visiting from other nations far and wide.

"When they heard the sound of the 'violent wind' blowing from heaven, they came to see what was happening, and could hear their own languages being spoken by the disciples who were Galilean. They were amazed. And some accused the disciples of being drunk. But Peter – one of the disciples – explained that this miracle had been prophesied long ago. And through his declaration and explanation three thousand people were baptised that day."

"Wow! That's a lot of baths!" quipped Lauren.

"It certainly is!" Miri grinned.

"Why do we need the Holy Spirit to live within us?" asked Tom.

"God sends Him to us, to be with us, as our comforter, our supporter and our friend. He connects our spirit to God.

"Sort of like a conscience?" asked Mitch.

"More like God's presence within yourself."

"Wow," said Tom.

"But what happens when you get baptised?" asked Mitch.

"Yeah, what does it mean?" asked Lauren.

"Well, during the baptismal ceremony, you are completely submerged in water, which symbolises the death of your old life and the birth of your new life in Christ – hence the term, 'born again'."

"Does it hurt?" asked Tom.

"No, not at all, Tom," Miri assured him. "It is a wonderful, gentle and life changing experience."

"How does it change your life?" asked Lauren, "Cos I quite like mine as it is," she added wryly.

Miri chuckled. "It changes because you leave behind your old self and enter into your new life. Washed clean. Adopted into the family of God, into His Kingdom, with all the joy and wonder that He brings."

"Part of me thinks it sounds too good to be true," Lauren stated matter of factly.

Smiling at her honesty, Miri continued, "Yes, Lauren, it does, doesn't it? Nevertheless, it is true," she said, her face shining. "God loves you, sweetheart. And gave His only son to save you. Even if you were the only person left in the whole world, Lauren, Jesus would still have died for you, because He loves you above and beyond anything you can begin to imagine."

Lauren blushed a deep crimson red, blinked back tears and felt elated all at the same time.

"It feels strange when you say that," said Mitch quietly, "But good."

"What do you have to do to get baptised?" asked Tom earnestly.

"Before you can be baptised, you need to repent of any sins – so say sorry to God for anything you have done wrong. Accept that Jesus Christ is the son of God, our Saviour, who died for our sins and was resurrected," answered Miri.

"Oh, they've already done that mum! The other day at school!" said Hilly munching on an apple.

"Oh!" exclaimed Miri, "Praise God!"

"They were wondering if they could come to church with us this Sunday."

"Of course they can! Everyone is welcome in our church!" said Miri, delighted. "We'd love you to come!"

Suddenly Ruth called, "Miri?!"

"I'm in the den, Ruth! I'll be right with you! Well, my lovelies, I hope that's been helpful. If you have any more questions, please ask me." She stood up to leave.

"Thanks mum, that was great!" Cam smiled, then with eyes glinting mischievously he said, "Any chance you could bring us some more of those cheese and onion crisps?!"

"Cameron James Trueman!" Miri began, picking up a cushion...

"Uh oh!" giggled Hilly. "She said your full name, Cam, you are so in trouble now!!"

"Run, Cam!" shrieked Dunc in delight, "She's armed and dangerous!"

Jumping to his feet, Cam scrambled for the door, laughing as he fled.

"Bullseye!" squealed Dunc with glee, as Miri lobbed the cushion, clobbering Cam squarely across his retreating backside.

"I am your mother, not your personal assistant!" Miri finished, dusting her hands with amused satisfaction, and comically exited, saying, "Elvis has now left the building!"

Their delighted laughter followed her back into the kitchen, bringing a smile to her heart. "Praise You, Father, for giving me such a blessed opportunity to have this wonderful conversation. These children are so precious."

Ruth returned, bustling with energy. "Miri! They were all a fount of knowledge and only too willing to help."

"Great!" said Miri. "So, what did they tell you?"

"Some things I'd rather not have heard – but I'm choosing to focus on the positive," she said. "I've made a list. Now, I know children of Ruby's age, particularly girls, don't tend to run away to just anywhere, they tend to run to someone or to someplace they feel safe."

"Well, to my knowledge, Ruby doesn't have any family, other than her father and brother, and we know she's not with either of them."

"Right, let's scrub that off the list. What about family friends?"

"As far as I know Peter shut out all friends from both inside and outside the church."

"Right, I'll put a query next to that one. What about friends of the children?"

"Ummm, unfortunately Jess has become a very unpopular boy – so I don't think he has any friends left," Miri said sadly, "But I'll ask the kids."

"Oh, the poor love," tutted Ruth, "And Ruby?"

Miri paused. "Actually, I did see her a couple of weeks ago, she was in the Co-op after school with a friend. When I spoke to her she seemed very withdrawn."

"Was that the night you told me Jed paid them another visit?" asked Ruth.

"Yes, but no one answered the door."

"Can you remember her friend's name?" asked Ruth eagerly.

"Ahh, I'm trying to, she did introduce us." Miri gnawed at her lip as she strived to recall the little girl's name.

"What did she look like? Can you describe her?" Ruth pushed.

"Ummm… Candy floss! Yes! I remember thinking she looked just like candy floss!"

"Okay… How did she look like candy floss?" pressed Ruth, sensing a breakthrough.

"She had curly, flyaway, strawberry blonde hair in two bunches with big pink bows," described Miri. "Oh, her name is on the tip of my tongue," she groaned, "Oh please, Lord, jog my memory," Miri prayed.

Ruth held her breath, silently repeating Miri's prayer.

"Lucy! Oh, thank You, Lord! Yes, it was Lucy! I remember thinking how much it suited her," Miri said with relief. "Oh, praise God."

"Right. We should contact her school and ask if anyone has questioned 'Lucy'," Ruth asserted. "Which school is she at?"

"Kingsland Academy, same as ours," Miri confirmed.

"I wonder if Ruby is close to any of her teachers there?" Ruth added that to her list. "What about places? Do you know of any places she might go to?"

"I only know about the seafront because Hilly has seen her playing there."

"Well, at least we have something new to go on," Ruth said confidently.

The back door suddenly burst open and in charged Zebs, super-excited to see Ruth! "Hello, my gorgeous boy!" greeted Ruth cheerfully, "Did you miss me?"

Up on his hind legs he went, tucking into Ruth's shoulder.

"I don't think I'll ever get bored of seeing him do that!" laughed Miri.

"Hi Mum!"

"Hi, Auntie Ruth!"

"Hello, Mrs. Trueman!"

"Ahhh my other gorgeous ones!" she laughed, grabbing them all in a swift rugby hug!

"They're back!" called Esther from the doorway. "Guys we're in the den, making plans, and we need you," stated Esther imperiously.

Joshua rolled his eyes. "What she means is, *she's* come up with a plan that *we're* going to have to execute!" her brother teased. "It will probably involve my car!" he said jovially.

"Yep! And Zebs!" she said, heading back to the den.

"Zebs?!" They all followed, their interest piqued.

"That girl could lead her brother to the gates of Hades and he'd follow!" Ruth said, shaking her head in amusement.

The front door opened, Joel and Deut entered, deep in conversation, loaded down with boxes of newly printed Bibles.

"Ah, my itinerant husband and his wandering friend!" Ruth grinned.

"Wife!" Joel commanded playfully, placing his box on the floor, "Come here and bring me my hug!" he said opening his arms wide. "Several actually!" He laughed, enveloping Ruth.

"I've missed you, too!" she laughed.

Deut was grinning. "Seems to me that both the Trueman men are going soft in their old age!" he joshed over his shoulder, as he went outside to retrieve another box.

"Could still whup your butt!" Joel laughed, over the top of his wife's head.

Deut's grin widened. "Like to see you try!" he challenged, stacking another box.

"Maybe later!" Joel laughed. "I'm kinda busy right now!"

"Chicken!" Deut baited, laughing.

"Now we'll be having no 'cockerel fights' in my kitchen at this time!" Miri admonished. "I'm trying to fix us all a bite to eat before we go to the seafront. Now, if you scoundrels aren't here to help – shoo!" she laughed, aiming her tea towel at Deut's backside.

"Yes, ma'am!" Deut laughed, going out for another box.

It was good to see him laughing. Understandably he had taken the death of his young Chinese guide extremely hard. It was shocking. Although several humanitarian organisations had now been alerted to the incident, and Deut's eyewitness statement was testimony to it, the diplomatic process still took time. Deut was coming to terms with the fact that those responsible may never be brought to earthly justice, but he had taken some solace in knowing that one day they would stand before God. His grief had turned into grim determination; his forgiveness into fevered preparation. He believed the more Bibles he delivered, the more opportunities for more folk to be delivered, to be set free, to receive their salvation.

The persecution of Christians was undoubtedly escalating. The Enemy knew his time was nearly up and intended to wreak as much pain and chaos as he could. And Deut was equally as determined to bring God's peace – to bring His Gospel to the world. He planned to leave again in a couple of months' time. He was staying just long enough to see his next book published, then he would be off again. Miri marvelled at the courage of their dear friend. She remembered what Cam had recently said: "Not all heroes wear capes, mum, some wear sleeves – book sleeves."

"Right, that's the last box," Deut declared, dusting off his hands. "I'm finished!"

Knowing he liked to be kept busy, Miri joshed, "Oh I'm sure I can find you something to do…! In fact, you can help peel the potatoes!" She grinned, handing him a knife, and herding him towards her kitchen sink.

"Joel! You can help too!" she said, peeling him away from Ruth and leading him over to the sink by his belt buckle! "Peel!" she ordered, "Your wife and I have a couple of phone calls to make."

Miri led Ruth into Jed's office again and closed the door, leaving them to chuckle at her small but mighty, power-house politics!

Ten minutes later, Jed arrived home to find his brother and Deut still peeling potatoes. "Looks like I got off lightly!" he said, grinning.

"There's still plenty more where these came from!" Joel said, still chuckling to himself. "I think Miri's planning to feed the five thousand!"

"Only on potatoes, though! There's not a fish or loaf in sight!" cracked Deut.

"Where is she? It's not like her to leave you two unsupervised in her kitchen!" ribbed Jed.

"She's in your office with Ruth," said Deut mysteriously.

"Well, that's what I like to see, the menfolk hard at work!" teased Ruth, bustling back into the room.

"Nice to have you back, Ruth! Did you have a good time?"

"Yes, wonderful, Jed. Thank you for asking, dear," she said, giving him a fleeting hug.

"Hello, sweetheart. How did it go with Peter?" Miri asked, standing on tiptoes, and pecking his cheek.

Jed proceeded to fill them in.

"And still no news of Ruby?" Miri asked. Jed shook his head.

"It's been over twenty-four hours now..." Deut reminded them.

"Ohhh, such a dreadful situation," sighed Ruth, sadly. "Miri and I have just been speaking to the headmistress of Ruby's school, and she has agreed to let us talk to Lucy, one of Ruby's friends. She might know something that could help us find her."

Jed nodded. "Good idea. I think we should let Detectives Hughes and Stanford know what you're planning, just to be on the safe side."

"Oh, Samuel's working the case, is he? He's very good," Ruth remarked.

"The headmistress said we could pop down any time after 1.00," said Miri, picking up her car keys, "So, we might as well strike while the iron's hot." She headed for the door.

"Okay, I'll call Stanford, then head down to the seafront with the kids, as planned," Jed said.

"Great, can you let Detective Stanford know *I'll* be with Miri – he knows me – we've worked together before," said Ruth.

"We'll let you know what happens," said Miri, heading for the door.

"Keep an eye on your daughter, Joel – she's hatching some plan involving Joshua, his car and Zebs!" said Ruth with a smile.

"Lord help us!" exclaimed Joel, heading for the den.

"Hey, what about all these potatoes?!" queried Deut.

"Thank you, guys, I shall make perfect use of them tonight, for dinner," Miri smiled, blowing them a kiss, "You're all going to join us I hope?"

"What about the whole 'bite to eat' scenario?!" he asked, disappointed.

"There's plenty of fresh bread in the larder and smoked salmon in the fridge." She waved, closing the door behind her.

Deut, Jed and Joel exchanged glances then cracked up!

"I told you she was planning to feed the five thousand!" roared Joel.

***

When they arrived at the school, they were met by Mrs. Luke, the headmistress. She was a quiet, unassuming lady, hiding a keen intellect behind her tortoiseshell glasses; a gentle soul who was fiercely protective of her pupils and staff. She carried herself with a dignity seldom seen in today's world. She reminded people of 'Miss Marple'.

"Good afternoon." She smiled congenially. "You must be 'the Mrs. Truemans'."

"Yes," they said in unison, shaking her hand in turn.

"I recognize you now, you're Cameron, Hilary, Duncan and Melissa's mum," she said to Miri, her smile broadening. "You'll have to forgive me – I never forget a child, but I do struggle with the parents!" she confessed.

"Oh, don't worry, I'm like that with dogs!" laughed Ruth. "I know every name of every dog in the park, and I talk to their owners every day – but I can't remember the name of any one of them!"

"Then I'm in good company!" Mrs. Luke laughed, leading them into her office. "We will be joining Lucy shortly; we're just waiting for her parents to arrive. I'm sure you understand we had to obtain their permission before we could proceed."

"Oh yes, absolutely, we would have insisted," said Miri.

"I've also just received a call from a Detective Stanford, who is happy for you to question Lucy, but wishes to be present."

"Yes, my husband rang him," said Miri, "And Ruth has worked with Detective Stanford before."

There was a knock at the door. They were joined by Lucy's parents, Mr. and Mrs. Bevall, both white faced and anxious. Mrs. Luke made them welcome and asked her secretary to prepare a tray of tea.

Moments later Detective Stanford arrived.

"Now we are all present," said Mrs. Luke, "As I explained earlier, we have already questioned all of our pupils regarding Ruby's whereabouts. Unfortunately, we came up blank. And Miss Lemon, Ruby's teacher, was completely unaware of any close friendship between Ruby and Lucy, in or out of school."

"As were we," stated Lucy's dad, sadly.

"And how Lucy ended up in the Co-op...?" added her mum, perplexed.

"Yes, that is a concern," continued Mrs. Luke, gravely. "Although Ruby is often permitted to leave with Jess, we are completely at a loss as to how Lucy managed to slip out with Ruby, and return unnoticed. However, her actions would appear to be motivated by kindness. She told Miss Lemon today that she had wanted to buy Ruby a lollypop because she was feeling sad. Whilst Miss Lemon praised her for this, she also explained the importance of remaining safely in school. She has also confirmed a note she had given me for our records, saying that Ruby had indeed been more withdrawn and tearful over this last week, and she describes her as a sweet, sociable child who gets on well with everyone, but doesn't seem to have any particular close friend. So Lucy's kindness was well-placed.

"Lucy hasn't ever spoken of Ruby," Mr. Bevall sighed, "But as soon as we heard that one of her classmates had disappeared, we both questioned her about it," he said anxiously. "But she didn't seem to know anything, and she never mentioned going to the Co-op with her."

"But she did get very upset," added her mum.

"Which is why I have taken the advice of Mrs. Ruth Trueman here – a child psychologist, who has worked very closely with the police on a number of occasions, I believe," said Mrs. Luke.

Ruth smiled reassuringly.

"She proposes a less direct approach," said Mrs. Luke. "As requested, I have asked Lucy's teacher, Miss Lemon, to prepare a number of fun activities to keep her calm and diverted whilst she is being questioned."

"When children are engaged in an activity they enjoy, they will often open up more," Ruth explained.

Mrs. Luke led them into a small classroom with a retractable divide.

"I suggest that Lucy's teacher, one parent and one other, be present during the interview. It will be far too overwhelming if we are all in there," Ruth advised, "The rest can listen from the other side of the divide."

"Agreed," said Mr. Bevall. He and his wife exchanged glances.

"I'll go in," Mrs. Bevall decided.

"Will you be the one to question her, Ruth?" asked Miri. "You're very good at that sort of thing – unless you have any objections, Detective Stanford?"

"No, no, Ruth knows what she's doing," he said. Mrs. Bevall nodded her agreement.

Ruth followed Lucy's mum into the room, and was met by a tiny wisp of a girl, who really did resemble candy floss, just as Miri had described. She was a sweet little doll-like child, with big blue eyes, that widened at the sight of her mum.

"Mummy!" she exclaimed, slipping from her chair, and running to her.

"Hello, sweetheart," said her mum, picking her up. "I've come to see what kinds of things you get to do at school," she said with forced cheerfulness. "Isn't that exciting?"

Lucy smiled from ear to ear.

"I've brought a new friend with me," her mum added, "She also wants to see what kinds of things you get to do at school."

"Hello Lucy, I'm Ruth," she said, waving at her.

"Hello." She smiled.

"We were just making a bracelet," Miss Lemon explained. "Lucy has to count every bead she uses and name each colour – they're not easy colours to remember, either."

"That looks fun!" Ruth enthused, picking up a colourful plastic bead. "May I have a go?"

"Yes!" Lucy beamed happily, handing her and her mummy a piece of elastic.

'Lord be with me every moment,' Ruth silently prayed. 'Help me to put Lucy at her ease and to ask the right questions. Amen.'

"I think…I'm going to make a bracelet for my friend," said Ruth. "Hmmm, I think I'll start with a pink one." She reached for a bright, vividly coloured bead.

"That's magenta," said Lucy.

"Wow! I didn't know that!" Ruth smiled, genuinely impressed.

"And this one?" she asked.

"That one is violet," Lucy said proudly.

"And this one?"

That's cerise!" she beamed.

"Cerise! What a beautiful colour! I think my friend Ruby is going to love it."

"Ruby? I've got a friend called Ruby!" Lucy exclaimed, surprised.

"You have?!" said Ruth, smiling.

"Yes, 'cept she's not here at the moment…" Lucy trailed off.

"Oh? She's not at school today?" Ruth asked casually.

"No." Lucy shook her head.

"I wonder why?" Ruth said conversationally.

"I don't know," Lucy answered puzzled.

"Perhaps she's poorly," said Ruth.

"Maybe…" Lucy said doubtfully.

"You don't think she's poorly?" Ruth asked.

"Well, she might be…" Again, she sounded doubtful.

"Or perhaps she's just gone somewhere else for the day?" Ruth suggested brightly.

"Well…Jeremy Hines says that Ruby is 'missing'," she said hesitantly.

"He did?" Miss Lemon sounded surprised.

"Yes, Miss Lemon." She nodded, her eyes shining with the truth of her statement.

"What else did Jeremy say, Lucy?" she asked gently.

"That nobody can find Ruby," she said sadly, threading another bead.

"I'm sure Ruby will be found everso soon, sweetheart," Lucy's mum reassured her.

"I'm sure your mum is right," Ruth agreed. Suddenly, prompted by the Holy Spirit, Ruth decided to change tack. "*My* friend Ruby went missing once," she said conspiratorially.

"She did?" Lucy's eyes grew large.

"Yes." Ruth nodded, dropping her voice, "But she didn't want to be found."

"She didn't?!" gasped Lucy.

"No." Ruth leaned forward like she was sharing a secret. Lucy, her mum, and Miss Lemon all lent forward too.

Little did they know, but everyone behind the dividing screen had also leant forward, craning to hear what was said.

"She was hiding," Ruth continued.

142

"She was?!" exclaimed Lucy, her little mouth dropping open.

Ruth nodded.

"Why was she hiding?" asked Lucy.

Ruth knew she had to be incredibly careful now. She did not want to scare Lucy.

"Well, she was a little frightened."

"Why was she frightened?" Lucy asked, her eyes as wide as saucers.

"She was frightened of someone," continued Ruth. "So she ran away and hid somewhere they'd never find her. Somewhere safe. Somewhere only she knew about."

"Like Wendy's house?" Lucy asked curiously.

"Wendy's house?" her mum jumped in quickly, "Who's Wendy, sweetheart?" she asked, adding another bead to her bracelet.

"I don't know." Lucy shrugged innocently.

"But Wendy has a house?" asked Ruth nonchalantly.

"Uh huh…" Lucy nodded.

"Have *you* been to Wendy's house?"

"No." She shook her head. "But Ruby has," she added, threading another bead.

"She has?" exclaimed Ruth. "Wow! I've never heard of Wendy's house. Have you, Mummy?" Ruth asked Mrs. Bevall.

"No. I wonder where it is?" she asked casually.

Lucy shrugged again.

Ruth tried a different way of asking: "I wonder what it looks like?"

"It's green," said Lucy, "Ruby told me."

"That sounds lovely," Ruth said, mirroring Lucy's smile.

"Oh, but it's not for grown-ups!" Lucy said earnestly.

"Oh? Why not?" Ruth feigned disappointment.

"Cos, you wouldn't fit, silly!" Lucy giggled.

"I wouldn't fit?" repeated Ruth, smiling.

"No!" giggled Lucy again.

"So, it's a very small house?" Ruth asked carefully.

"I think so," nodded Lucy.

Ruth began to wonder if 'Wendy's House' might actually be from the story of 'Peter Pan'. In which case it would be small and built within a wood. "It sounds lovely, I'd love to see it. I wish *I* knew where to find it," Ruth sighed dramatically.

"Second star to the right and straight on till morning!

> Down the lane
> Over the gate
> Under the tree
> Behind the lake.
> Ta Da!" Lucy suddenly sing-songed.

"That's a lovely song," Ruth encouraged, her suspicions confirmed. The first part of that rhyme was definitely directions to 'Neverland', a place in the story of 'Peter Pan'. "Could you sing it for me again, please?"

"Second star to the right and straight on till morning!

> Down the lane
> Over the gate

144

Under the tree
Behind the lake
Ta da!" she repeated, bobbing her head in time.

The second part of the rhyme must be directions to Ruby's 'Wendy House', somewhere she feels safe, thought Ruth. "Thank you, Lucy, that was lovely." She smiled. "Where did you learn that?"

"Ruby sings it." She glowed, pleased with herself. "Jess taught her."

"Her brother, Jess?" asked Miss Lemon.

Lucy nodded, suddenly shy.

"Well, it's a lovely song, thank you. And look, I've finished my bracelet." Ruth said, showing it to her. "I think I'm going to go and give it to my friend Ruby, right now."

"It's very pretty." The little girl beamed.

"Thank you." Ruth smiled. "And thank you for showing me what you get to do at school. You are a very clever girl. Bye for now," she said waving.

Once back in Mrs. Luke's office, Detective Stanford was on his phone, passing on the details to Hughes and the various search and rescue teams.

He thanked Mrs. Luke and rushed out of the school. From the outset he had been concerned that Ruby was not only missing, but might also be injured like her brother, so finding her, and quickly, was paramount.

"Ruth, do you think you could come with me?" he called over his shoulder, "I'm not waiting around for MCIT to arrive – It could be too late."

"Yes, of course, Samuel," she said. "Miri, can you let Joel know where I am?"

"Yes, don't worry. You go, see you back at mine. God go with you." Miri sent up a silent prayer, 'Oh Lord, let us please find this precious child, safe and sound. Amen.'

Slamming the car door, Stanford fastened his seat belt and cautiously pulled out of the school gates, saying, "I think I know where Ruby is."

"Oh, praise God," exhaled Ruth, just managing to fasten her own belt before Stanford sped up and raced onto the main road. He set the blue light flashing, but kept the siren silent.

"We've been looking in completely the wrong direction. Since moving to Kingsland, I've jogged daily. I've been all over this area and there's only one place I know that has a lake and that's Kingscombe Wood."

"I know it," Ruth said, "I've taken the dog there for walks. That lake is huge, it takes us over two hours to walk it. Where do you plan to start?"

Stanford paused, collecting his thoughts. "If we were walking from the direction of the Wilkins' house to Kingscombe Wood, we'd have to come in via the lane at the top, which goes down a steep hill, to an old gate at the bottom…" he said, thinking aloud. "We'll start there."

"Well, that matches the clues in Lucy's' song," agreed Ruth. She repeated the rhyme, "Down the lane, over the gate…"

Stanford nodded, his face full of concentration. "Under the tree…well, that could be any tree," he muttered.

"Did you pick up that 'Wendy's house' was probably taken from 'Peter Pan'?" Ruth asked.

"Yeah, and the star reference. I'm trying to remember if there was a particular tree that was in the story…but it's been years since I've read it."

"Me too, I'll google it," Ruth said, tapping into her mobile – a few moments later, "'Hangman's Tree'!" she exclaimed. "Of course! It's where Peter and the Lost Boys lived!"

"Brilliant, well done!" Stanford encouraged. "So, it's going to have to be a tree that stands out from the rest – somehow," he reasoned.

"Agreed… And going by the rhyme, they have to be able to go 'under' it," Ruth added.

They pulled into a quiet side road and up onto the kerb. They jumped out, swiftly heading toward a gap in the overgrown hedge, Stanford leading the way. Then they began a steep descent down a narrow, nettle-filled lane. Ruth fleetingly wished she had not worn heels and a skirt that morning, but down they went.

"I don't know if a little girl of five could walk this far…" Stanford mused. "And even if she could, why didn't the search dogs follow her scent from the house?"

"Maybe she didn't come from the house," Ruth said.

"Possibly," Stanford agreed.

They had now reached the gate at the bottom of the lane. Stanford helped Ruth clamber over the gate.

"Sorry Ruth, I didn't even stop to think if you would be okay in this terrain," he apologized.

"Oh, don't worry about me, nothing a bit of spit and polish won't fix. Besides, I think you're the one with problems," she said, indicating his ripped and mud splattered trousers.

"Right, let's look for our 'Hangman's Tree'," he said with grim determination.

They pushed their way through the thick undergrowth, the brambles tearing at their clothes and flesh. Battling to keep their balance and their bearings, perspiring and out of breath, they stumbled into a small clearing surrounded by a ring of chestnut trees and one old, gnarled oak – some of its roots exposed, but still green and leafy. It sat crookedly, as if it had been pushed over, looking for all the world like an ancient man struggling to get to his feet. And hanging from the topmost branch was an old hemp rope tied in the shape of a noose.

"I think we're on the right track," panted Ruth, pointing at the tree.

Stanford nodded. They rushed forward, all fatigue forgotten. Circling the trunk, they discovered a hidden trail beneath the roots and fallen branches.

"Under the tree!" Stanford exclaimed, disappearing beneath the foliage. Crawling on his stomach, he managed to squeeze through, followed closely by Ruth. The sight that met them both took their breath away.

"Wow!" murmured Stanford, straightening up.

"Neverland…" whispered Ruth.

They had come through into another small clearing that encircled a beautiful shimmering pond. The trees lovingly embraced it like a slumbering baby. Wildflowers were scattered throughout the small glade and birdsong floated in the air. Faint tinkling drifted from the hundreds of pieces of colourful glass hanging upon every branch. A small homemade swing hung beneath one leafy tree. Sitting beside that, a sweet rickety looking see-saw, made of an old, pale blue, weathered plank of wood. And hidden under the boughs of yet another tree, nestled in amongst very tall grass, crouched what had to be, 'Wendy's house'. A quaint, leafy mix of wigwam and lean-to, complete with door and window, cleverly constructed from driftwood, branches and bamboo, woven together with ivy and sheaves of long meadow grass. It even had a chimney pot made of old chipped terracotta. It appeared as though it had just grown up out of the very woods themselves, along with the other trees and the flowers.

"It's beautiful…" Ruth whispered.

Stanford was speechless, trying to take it all in. He looked around and realized that they were indeed 'behind' the lake – he could see it in the distance, to the east. He had jogged around that lake more times than he cared to remember, and he had never spotted this pond or glade, it was naturally obscured from view. It made him feel faintly nostalgic. Like he had stumbled upon a secret garden.

"I feel like I'm…intruding…" Ruth confessed.

Stanford nodded, feeling the same. Pulling himself together, he said "I can't see her, can you?" his voice barely above a whisper.

Ruth shook her head. "But this is definitely her 'safe place' – we need to proceed carefully – so as not to frighten her. Otherwise, she could grow up believing that nowhere is safe for her."

"Understood. Let's go and see if she's in the house."

Ruth nodded in agreement.

Stanford then crept as swiftly as he could towards the house, hoping that she was in there and safe. Everything within him, screamed at him to run, to hurry up, to find her. Keeping as quiet as possible, he looked in through the window, holding his breath. He was extremely relieved to see her curled up asleep on a makeshift bed of sacks, clutching a little pink dog, her little chest rising and falling peacefully. He could see from her dirty, tear-stained face that she had been crying and his heart twisted at the thought of her here all alone.

He turned and gave Ruth the thumbs up. "She's sleeping and doesn't appear to have any physical injuries, as far as I can see," he whispered.

"Thank God," sighed Ruth, "If she's asleep, let's not startle her. "Ruuby," she called gently.

"Ruuuby, where are you? We've come to take you home, sweetheart," she continued, getting a little louder.

They could hear rustling from within the 'Wendy house', and the door opened slowly. She stepped out, her little face pinched and tired, but as soon as she saw them, her face broke into a smile and she ran forward into Ruth's arms.

"Gloria said you'd find me," she said smiling through misty eyes.

"Did she?" Ruth smiled, picking her up and wondering if Gloria might be her dolly or perhaps an imaginary friend. Ruth was about to introduce herself when Ruby interrupted her.

"I know who you are, Gloria told me – your name is Ruth, and your name is Samuel," she said calmly, "And you have both come to take me home."

Ruth and Stanford exchanged startled glances.

Stanford's immediate thought was to suspect someone involved in the investigation, but how would they have known…?

"You're a policeman," Ruby said to him. "Gloria said you would need this for your poorly hand." She showed him a plaster covered in pink butterflies. "I picked you my favourite one." She smiled shyly.

Stanford watched in stunned silence as she reached over and covered a deep cut on the back of his right hand. One he had not even been aware of.

"Thank you," he said quietly, not knowing what else to say.

"Gloria sounds like a very nice person," said Ruth gently.

"Oh, she is, she's an angel. Gloria isn't her real name. But it's what I call her. I drew a picture of her, would you like to see it?" she said.

"Oh, yes please. So, what's her real name, then?" Ruth asked curiously.

"I don't know – she didn't say," she said matter of factly, "But I think she looks like a Gloria. So, I gave her a name, like I do my dollies."

Samuel had hoped it would have given him a clue to the identity of the person he still had not decided was friend or foe.

Ruby had wriggled out of Ruth's arms and gone back into her Wendy house, beckoning them to follow.

"I need to call in to let them know we've found her," Samuel said to Ruth.

Ruth nodded and followed Ruby into the house. It was snug, yet surprisingly bigger than she had expected. It had two small sack beds with tattered pillows and blankets. Several jam jar lanterns hung with twine from the ceiling. There was even a string of battery-operated Christmas lights.

Ruby pulled out a box with 'treasures' written on the side. Ruth could see pencils, crayons, shells, a pot of gold glitter and a paper pad. Opening the pad, she proudly showed Ruth her picture.

Ruth's first reaction was one of wonder. The whole page seemed to glow. Ruby had drawn an actual angel, with long red hair, standing in the centre of the page, wings wide open, arms outstretched, surrounded by the brightest yellowest sunburst, wearing jeans and a t-shirt, bearing the logo 'God Rocks!' Ruby's attention to detail was remarkable for a five year old, not to mention her spelling.

"Wow, Ruby, this is wonderful," Ruth enthused, "You are very good at drawing."

"Thank you." Ruby beamed.

Just then, Stanford popped his head through the door. "We have to leave now," he said, "Any luck?"

In answer, Ruth showed him the drawing. His raised eyebrows said it all, but aware of Ruby's scrutiny, he smiled. "That is a lovely picture, Ruby. So, Gloria is an angel?" he asked carefully.

"Yes." The little girl smiled. "God sent her," she said simply.

Stanford looked at Ruth, who just smiled back at him. She knew he was way out of his depth. "Can you tell us some more about Gloria?" she asked Ruby.

"Ummm, well…she was very pretty and smelt lovely…like roses… And she sang to me…she said that God had sent her from heaven to take care of me until you came to find me."

"That's lovely," Ruth encouraged.

"She told me Jess was in hospital." Her voice caught and her little chin wobbled. "But he was going to get better," she said, fresh tears spilling down her cheeks.

"It's okay sweetie," said Ruth, gently brushing them away. "He's safe now. You're safe now."

Stanford was using his phone to record what she was saying. He knew this was a conversation they should be having back at the station. In fact, this was really MCIT's case and normally he would not be involved in it at all. But, he reasoned, this was his patch, and this was crucial information and Ruth was a credible witness.

"You're safe now," Ruth repeated soothingly.

"That's what Gloria said, when she brought me Jemima," Ruby wept, cuddling her pink dog. "I left her behind."

"She's such a pretty pink," Ruth soothed.

Ruby nodded, hugging Jemima tighter. "Daddy gave her to me. Gloria said that my daddy is very, very sad. That he misses mummy a lot. But he still loves me and Jess, even though he's sad." She wiped her tears on her sleeve, her little shoulders heaving with emotion.

Ruth embraced her, gently rocking. "Gloria's right. Your daddy loves you and Jess very much."

"I love my daddy, too," she said sniffing loudly. "That bad man, he hit my daddy," she wept.

"What bad man, Ruby?" asked Stanford carefully.

"Daddy's friend. He's a nasty man. He hit daddy and I c-couldn't w-wake him up," she sobbed.

"Do you know the name of the nasty man, sweetheart?" pushed Stanford gently.

She nodded. "K-Kenny," she hiccupped.

"Thank you, darling," he said softly.

"Gl-Gloria, said I have to tell y-you about Jess," she cried.

"Okay, sweetheart, tell me about Jess," Stanford said kindly.

"When Kenny hit Daddy, Jess tried to stop him, and Kenny started to hit him…" she sobbed, reliving the whole thing. "He w-wouldn't st-stop and I shouted at him to stop but he wouldn't stop, and daddy wouldn't wake up. Then J-Jess told me to run! Run Ruby, run to Neverland!" she cried.

Ruth held her, rocking and soothing – allowing her to cry herself out, praying to God to heal Ruby's little broken heart.

Stanford sat quietly waiting. His heart twisted within his chest. He had an uncomfortable idea who 'Kenny' was, and this made him more determined than ever to see justice done. "I think it's time for us to leave now," he said, kindly.

Ruth sat hugging her closely. "I have something for you," she said, delving into her pocket and pulling out the pink bracelet she had made with Lucy.

Her little eyes widened in surprise. "For me?" she asked.

Ruth smiled. "For you," she said, fastening it on her wrist. "Your friend Lucy helped me to make it and she helped us to find you."

Ruby's eyes glowed. "Thank you," she said, watching it twinkle in the light.

They crawled back under the tree, Ruby showing them a less strenuous path back through the undergrowth to the gate and the steep lane.

There was no need for plasters on this route, Stanford thought wryly, looking down at his suit.

Once in the car, they headed for the police station.

There they were met by social services and a doctor. Ruby was taken into the interview room, and throughout the questioning and the examination she would not let go of Ruth's hand.

The Holy Spirit had been speaking to Ruth throughout the whole process and she knew she had to speak to Joel urgently. Under the premise of getting Ruby a drink, Ruth popped out of the interview room, planning to call him, and was not at all surprised to find him sitting in the reception.

"Ruth!" he called, "Is everything alright? Are you alright?" he asked, taking in her dishevelled appearance.

"I'm fine and Ruby's safe," she said, hugging her husband close.

"We've been praying for you all," he said, resting his chin on her head. "Thanks be to God, you are safe."

She gave him an extra squeeze before stepping back. "Joel, I need to ask you something," she said seriously.

He smiled and said, "The beds are already made. Esther has found one of her old nighties for Ruby, and Joshua is clearing out one side of his wardrobe for Jess."

"The Holy Spirit?!" She grinned, already knowing the answer.

"The Holy Spirit!" he chuckled. He's been on my case for the last few hours! Then He started on Joshua and Esther!"

"I was about to call you to ask." She smiled. "Are our licenses up to date? It must be two years since we last fostered."

"Yep, they are, I checked." He grinned, kissing her forehead. "Mmm, You smell like a forest," he remarked, completely unaware of where she had been.

"You wouldn't believe me if I told you." She smiled. "Are you okay to wait here, while I go and make the necessary arrangements?"

"Of course."

After getting Ruby a hot chocolate, Ruth asked to speak with the duty social worker, Dawn Halliwell, outside the interview room. Luckily, Ruth and Dawn had worked together before, and Dawn was only too happy to allow Ruth and Joel to foster Ruby and Jess.

"You obviously have a rapport with her. And they were only going to a temporary placement initially, anyway." She smiled. "I'm delighted. They both need stability and a decent shot at happiness, so you and Joel are perfect. I'll go and sort out the forms and authorisation." She strode off with her phone to her ear. "Jeff…? Great news!"

Ruth was delighted and could not wait to tell Ruby. She slipped back into the room, where she was sitting with PC Jane Amos, both admiring Ruby's bracelet, and sipping their hot chocolates. "Hey, sweetheart, how would you like to come and stay with me and my family for a while?" she asked tentatively.

Ruby's eyes sparkled. "Gloria said I'd live with you, until daddy's all better!" she bubbled happily. "Jess too?" she asked, suddenly serious.

"Jess too! When he's well enough," Ruth assured her.

She slipped down off her chair and climbed onto Ruth's lap. "Thank you," she whispered, wrapping her little arms around Ruth's neck, and tucking in. Ruth and PC Amos exchanged 'Aww, bless her!' looks.

Dawn Halliwell re-entered the room, smiling. "You are free to leave whenever you want!" she beamed.

Stanford followed her in. "I hear you're going to have guests!" He smiled at Ruth.

"We are indeed!" Ruth said happily.

"Can we go and see Jess now?" Ruby asked excitedly.

There was a moment's awkward silence, then Ruth said gently. "Jess is still...recovering, sweetheart. He's still...sleeping."

"Yes, but Gloria said he'd be awake by 'tonight', and it is 'tonight', isn't it?" she asked hesitantly, looking out at the evening sky.

Just then Stanford's mobile rang. Ruth was vaguely amused at the 'Star Trek' ringtone. She did not have him pegged as a sci-fi fan.

"Excuse me, I've got to answer this," he said, leaving the room.

Ruth finished signing the paperwork brought in by Dawn. Ruby stood pensively staring out at the darkening sky.

Stanford re-entered the room, looking bemused. "That was my partner, Hughes, he's at the hospital, Jess has *just* regained consciousness," he said, astounded. "I'm heading over there now."

"Can I come?" Ruby asked excitedly.

Stanford hesitated, thinking of Jess' injuries. She was traumatized enough, without seeing her brother in that state. He crouched down to Ruby's level. "Ruby, you have been a very brave and courageous little girl. In fact, you are *the* bravest and *most* courageous little girl I have ever met. So, I'm going to be honest with you. Jess *is* awake but he's still very poorly. I think he needs a bit longer before you can visit him."

Her little brow puckered, her bottom lip trembled, and her eyes became misty, but all she said was, "Okay." Then returned to Ruth and stood holding her hand patiently.

"Thank you, Ruby." Stanford straightened up. "Amos, you're to come with me. Ruth, I'll be in touch," he said, then left.

"Well, how about we go meet the rest of my family, Ruby?" Ruth asked brightly.

She immediately perked up. "Joel, Joshua and Esther?" she asked.

"Yeeees…" said Ruth in surprise. "How do you know their names?" she asked, already knowing the answer.

"Gloria," Ruby said nonchalantly. "She made me say them again and again, 'til I could remember them!"

"What else did Gloria tell you, sweetheart?" asked Ruth tentatively, as they walked to the reception.

Joel stood up smiling at her. But before he could say anything, Ruby beat him to it.

"Hello, I'm Ruby and I'm coming to live with you," she said, offering Joel her hand.

Amused, Joel shook her tiny little hand in his enormous one. "Hello Ruby." He smiled. "I'm Joel."

"I know," she said matter of factly, keeping hold of his hand. "Can we go home now?"

* * *

CHAPTER NINE

1st Samuel James Stanford

Samuel Stanford was exhausted. He had just arrived home after visiting Jess in hospital. Following the statement Jess had given, truth be told, he knew he was in way over his head with this case.

In the space of thirty-six hours, he had experienced things that he never in a million years would have believed possible. It presented him with more questions than answers. His mind was so full, 'fit-to-bust' full, that it made his nostrils ache!

"I need a shower," he muttered to himself, "Clear my head."

So saying, he hopped in, letting the stress and strain of the day drain away.

Sitting in his lounge, half an hour later, with a large mug of tea and a bacon butty, he reflected upon the day. He was thankful beyond belief that they had found Ruby, that Jess was now conscious and would make a full recovery, and that their father, Peter Wilkins, was not, after all, personally responsible for his son's injuries, or his daughter's disappearance; although he was indirectly, due to neglect and dereliction of parental duties. However, his grief and remorse were palpable, so with counselling and the support of his social worker, the damage to himself and his family could be rectified. All in all, a good result in a case where it could have all gone horribly wrong. A ripped and muddy suit was a small price to pay.

He knew he needed to write his report, but how he was going to word it truthfully without sounding like a 'nut job', he did not know. He never thought transferring to quiet, rural, seaside Kingsland would present him with his most inexplicable case to date.

The irony was not lost on him. He had not chosen to transfer to Kingsland, but had been informed by his superintendent that his 'presence had been requested'.

Two weeks later he had found himself ensconced in a rustic, but homely, police cottage in Devon.

When he arrived and had discovered *who* had actually 'requested his presence', it had softened the blow. Graham Hughes was someone who anyone would have given their back and front teeth to work with, no matter where the location.

Hughes had transferred to Kingsland at his wife's insistence. Apparently they had holidayed here at least once a year since they were first married and had planned to retire here. However, when Hughes had suffered a near fatality during his last MCIT job, they had both agreed enough was enough. She worked in the admin side of the force and had kept an eye open for any 'quieter' vacancies. When Kingsland came up, she practically frog-marched him into the interview! His one stipulation had been that he could choose his own partner. Kingsland would have been prepared to re-staff the entire force in order to secure *his* engagement!

Stanford had grown to love Kingsland. It was a place of natural beauty, rolling hills and fields tumbling into rolling waves and beaches. The locals were friendly and had somehow hung on to their community spirit and old traditions, embracing all the good aspects of modern life, yet actively keeping all the negative at arm's length – rather like handling a beautiful, but poisonous, snake on a hook. He had to admit they were all very suspicious of anything too new. But he liked that about them!

It had been this very spirit of community and tradition that had saved the local constabulary. The proposal that each household would pay extra on their Council Tax bill, in order to keep their small police station open and comfortably manned, had won by a massive majority. The nearest station open was sixty miles away and understaffed to a dangerous level; a problem all too common in today's economy. As Hughes had pointed out on several occasions, The three R's universally stood for Reading, wRiting and aRithmetic, but in the force it stood for lack of Recruitment, lack of Resources and likely Redundancy! He had a point.

Except in Kingsland. The police force were well supported, well provided for, and well equipped. The station itself was small in comparison to some, but had been extended, updated, and boasted certain features that you would not find in an average station.

For starters, there was a sumptuous 'viewing room', complete with a two-way glass window into not one, but two interview rooms! On top of that, they had installed the latest in technical equipment: recording devices that could translate a language as it was being spoken (well, all languages known to man! he thought wryly); cameras that could give you a detailed image of even the smallest crater on the moon; and personal surveillance apparatus that would make the Met – the well-equipped Metropolitan Police Force in London – drool, including a van, for 'covert operations'. Of which, to date, there had been one! He had a sneaking suspicion that the architect, the builder, and the technician, were all closet fans of American cop shows!

It must have cost hundreds of thousands to achieve – how such a small community could afford it had been a mystery to him – until he discovered that the mayor was the grandfather of one of the bobbies! No one could blame him for wanting to ensure his grandson had everything he needed to do a good job. Kinship had its perks!

Still, he was not complaining. He had a good life, and he loved his job. It was not how he'd originally planned it – the Met had been his dream. He had made a very good impression in the three years he had been there, earning himself a reputation for being a go-getter, reliable and hard working. That was how he had first encountered Hughes, their cases had overlapped. Little did he know where that brief alliance would eventually lead. He had lived here for two years now and had not looked back.

Stanford had always wanted to be a policeman. When he was a boy, at every opportunity he would dress in his 'constable's uniform' usually made from black bin liners and an old bucket for a helmet. Until, on his sixth birthday, he had received a 'cops and robbers' set. He had practiced reciting 'The Caution', every day, until he knew it off by heart, and arrested his first piece of toast when he was just seven and a half, unfortunately observed by his older brother, Luke, who had never let him forget it!

He found it amusing, but not surprising, that Luke had become a defence solicitor – he had always liked to play the baddies when they were growing up. He was only a couple of years older than Samuel, but he still remained very protective of him, keeping a close eye on him throughout his police training in Hendon; encouraging him, advising him, cheering him on with each promotion and career move. Luke had told Samuel he would always have his back, because Samuel was one of the 'good guys' and he, Luke, should know: he was well acquainted with the type of people Samuel would be up against – he had defended enough of them. Luke had confessed that he was relieved when Samuel moved out of the Met, but Samuel's attitude was 'if your number's up, your number's up'. It would not matter where you were.

When his best mate, Jack, a fellow Met detective, had visited him in Kingsland, he had likened it to 'Sandford' – a fictional rural town in one of his favourite films – 'Hot Fuzz' – all about a local constabulary. Stanford had to confess there were similarities, especially after attending the summer fête, where coincidently 'splat the rat' and a tottery tombola were also on offer, as in the film!

Jack had found it hilarious that 'Stanford' had transferred to 'Sandford', but, like Samuel, he had grown to love Kingsland and was always popping down to see him.

So, all in all, today had been a good day. Yawning, he flopped into bed without bothering to clean his teeth. "I'm such a rebel!" he yawned into his pillow.

The following morning found him at his desk, trying to make sense of his notes. From start to finish each page sounded weirder than the last. What with Peter Wilkins' demons and Ruby's angel, he didn't know where to begin. Some of Jess' statement had also taken some swallowing.

That Jess *believed* he was telling the truth, Stanford was in no doubt. That it was *actually* true, he really could not say. But either way, it had to be documented word for word.

When he had arrived at the hospital last night, Hughes was talking to the doctor in the corridor, and had indicated for him to go on into Jess' room, with PC Amos, who would now be on 'security duty'.

Jess was sitting propped up by several pillows. His face was a little less swollen, he could open his eyes now, but the cuts and bruising had really developed. He was a mass of blue and purple, red and yellow. Stanford was glad that he had not let Ruby see him like this.

"Hello Jess, I'm Detective Stanford, but you can call me Samuel if you like," he said gently, "And this is PC Amos – Jane."

She smiled.

Jess nodded, then winced in pain.

"How are you feeling?"

"Okay," he mumbled, making the split on his lip bleed.

Stanford offered him a tissue. "Jess, I need to ask you some questions about what happened to you," he said sensitively. "Are you up to answering?"

"Yes." He nodded.

With PC Amos in the room, he was legally allowed to question Jess, but still felt it was a big ask given his condition. However, the sooner they knew all the facts the better.

"Tell me what you can remember about Wednesday morning."

Jess closed his eyes briefly. "My dad's friend Kenny came," he began, his voice dry and husky, "He brought a box of beer for my dad."

"Do you know Kenny's last name?" asked Stanford.

"No…but…" He seemed to be trying to remember something, Stanford waited.

"He works at the harbour," Jess added, suddenly remembering.

"Thank you, Jess, well done, lad. That's a great help," Stanford encouraged.

Jess' whole countenance seemed to lift with Stanford's praise. Stanford felt pity, realizing that he'd been starved of love and attention. Looking at him now it was hard to believe that he had a reputation for being a bully. "Can you remember what happened when Kenny brought the box of beer, Jess?" he asked.

Jess nodded. "Kenny said my dad needed to pay him for it and the box he'd had before. My dad said he'd only pay him for this box because the last box was 'dodgy'…"

"Okay, this is all very helpful. What happened next?" Stanford probed.

"Kenny and my dad argued, started shouting at each other. Ruby got upset, so I took her upstairs. Then my dad shouted for me to come down and help him find the money he kept in the kitchen jar." A tear slid down his bruised and battered cheeks.

"It's okay, Jess, you're safe," Stanford comforted, "It's all over now, lad."

Jess nodded again, embarrassed. "I didn't want to go down because…*I'd* taken the money from the jar the day before, for mine and Ruby's school dinners…" he explained, wiping his nose on the tissue. "Dad never normally noticed…so I didn't think it would matter…but it did…"

"I think that was a very brave and sensible thing to do, Jess," reassured Stanford, "You were taking care of yourself and your little sister."

Jess stared at him, desperate to believe what he said; desperate to believe something good about himself. He blamed himself for what had happened to his dad.

"But, if I hadn't taken the money...my dad could have paid Kenny," he said.

"So, your dad didn't have the money to pay Kenny?"

"No...Kenny got really angry with my dad, and they started fighting...so I ran downstairs...I told Ruby to stay where she was...but she didn't, she came down..."

"What happened when you went downstairs?" prompted Stanford.

"Kenny and my dad were fighting...he was hitting my dad so hard...dad fell down... And he didn't stop hitting him even when he was on the floor...so I tried to stop him... Ruby was screaming at him to stop hitting me...but he wouldn't...I called to dad to help me, but he didn't move...I was worried he'd hurt Ruby too, so I told her to run away to 'Neverland'..." The horror of the event could still be clearly seen in his eyes.

"You are a very brave young man, Jess," consoled Stanford, "You tried to protect your dad and your little sister even when you were under attack."

Jess just hung his head in defeat. He felt he had let them down.

"There are very few men I'd trust to cover my back, young man, but you'd be one of them," came Hughes' gruff comment. "I could use a good man like you on my team," he said, smiling at Jess. He had entered the room quietly and been listening intently.

Jess took a shuddering breath and exhaled as if the weight of the world had been lifted from his shoulders.

"So, what happened next?" asked Stanford.

"I saw Ruby run upstairs…so I pushed Kenny away and ran to the front door and pretended to shout to her…I shouted that she mustn't DOUBT that she knows the way to 'Neverland'…Kenny ran down the road looking for her…and…I don't…I can't…remember what happened after that."

"That is top intelligence, that is, son," praised Hughes.

Jess managed a wan smile.

"So, Ruby ran upstairs?" questioned Stanford.

Jess nodded.

"You told her to run to 'Neverland'…" Stanford checked.

Jess nodded again.

"So why did she run upstairs? Is 'Neverland' upstairs?" Stanford asked, carefully.

"No, but that's where the escape hatch is," Jess explained.

"Escape hatch?"

"We've got an attic that joins on to next door, so we crawl through a loose panel, and after that it comes out onto a fire escape at the end. I tied a rope that we swing from into the tree with a star on, *right* opposite. That's the 'Second star to the *right*'."

"Well thought out, son," encouraged Hughes.

He might be loud and brash, but Hughes had perceived exactly what Jess needed to get him through this trauma. He could also see that at heart he was a good lad despite his faults. He just needed steering back on the right path.

Sitting forward in the bed, Jess confided, "'*Straight* on 'til morning' is climbing from tree to tree, *straight* along the back until you reach the shops at the end. Then we run down *their* fire escape onto the pavement.

That would explain why the search dogs had not picked up Ruby's scent from the house, thought Stanford. No one would have thought to take a dog up into an attic, and the shops were at least five hundred yards away from the house – which was why she had just seemed to 'vanish'.

"Who planned this escape route?" asked Hughes.

"Me," Jess said uncomfortably, fearing he'd done wrong.

"Well thought out!" Hughes praised. "Sure had our dogs fooled!"

"I used to get Duke, our dog, to search for Ruby, but he couldn't ever find her either!" he said animatedly.

"Smart!" Hughes grinned.

"So, where did Ruby go next?" asked Stanford tentatively, already knowing the answer.

"She went to 'Neverland'," he said simply, as if that explained everything.

"So where and how does Ruby get to 'Neverland'?" Stanford probed.

"Second star to the right and straight on 'til morning.

Down the lane,
Over the gate,

Under the tree,
Behind the lake,
Ta da!" he sang.

"I told Ruby that she would never forget the way, if she learnt that song." He smiled, proudly. "She should never DOUBT that she knows the way."

Samuel had noticed that he'd mentioned the word 'doubt' twice now.

"So, once you're on the pavement, where do you go from there?" Stanford asked.

"You walk to the end and go into '*Downsbury*' Road," Jess emphasized.

Then '*Down*' the lane at the top. Then '*Over*' the gate at the bottom. Then '*Under*' Hangman's Tree, the one with the rope. Then you're '*Behind*' the lake – *T*a da! It spells D.O.U.B.T. – DOUBT," he said.

"Show me," said Hughes, thrusting his pen and notepad at him.

Jess weakly wrote it all down, his hands shaking uncontrollably, then handed it back to Hughes expectantly.

"Well, I'll be a monkey's uncle!" chuckled Hughes, proudly, "This is clever stuff, son!"

Jess beamed, wincing as his lip split open again.

"It's a long way for you and your sister to go," said Stanford.

"We practiced – we can do it in twelve minutes! Although Ruby gets stitch," he shared.

"Impressive!" said Hughes with a smile.

Jess, can I ask why you and your sister built 'Neverland'?" Stanford asked, delicately.

172

A shadow seemed to pass over his face. He dropped his eye contact and seemed to close in on himself. Stanford thought regretfully that he might have just pushed him that bit too far.

Hughes stepped in to soothe the way. "I'm sure a young man with Jess' talents, had a *very* good reason." He winked to Stanford.

Thankfully, Jess nodded. "My mum…she said 'Neverland' was a magical place, where Peter and the Lost Boys were safe. She used to read it to us," he said, dashing away another tear, hiding his face, abashed.

"Never be embarrassed about shedding a tear for your mum, son. It's the price you pay for loving her," Hughes rumbled, squeezing his shoulder very gently.

He nodded. "She used to say that our dad was Peter Pan when he was young. And that she had changed her name from Wendy to Cathy to hide her identity – but Peter Pan liked to crow and show off, so Dad had kept his name for all to see." No sooner had a small grin appeared like a burst of sunshine, than it had faded behind a cloud of sadness again, as he said, "Ruby thinks Dad has changed into Captain Hook though."

"What do you think, son?" asked Hughes, shrewdly.

Jess shrugged. "Sometimes he is…but mostly he's like Mister Smee!" He grinned cheekily.

Hughes laughed. "So, he's not the crocodile, then?"

"No! That was Duke, our dog. When Dad turned into Hook, Duke used to growl at him and chase him away," he said proudly.

"Where is Duke?" asked Stanford, realising that there was no report of a dog at the house.

"Dad gave him to Kenny…" Jess said, hiding another tear.

"Well, when we find Kenny, maybe we'll find Duke," said Hughes positively.

Jess stared at him, eyes hopeful.

"No promises, mind," Hughes said, "But we'll do our best."

Just then Sister Martin popped her head around the door. "Excuse me, gentlemen," she said politely. "Five more minutes, then Jess will need to rest." She smiled at Jess. "I'll be back in to check on you in five, okay? Shall I bring you a hot chocolate?" she coaxed, eager to get him to drink.

"Yes please." He nodded eagerly.

"Great! I wonder if you'll have another visit from your angel?" She beamed, bustling out again.

"Angel?!" repeated Hughes and Stanford together. 'Oh no,' thought Stanford, 'This is about to get weird again.'

Jess blushed.

Hughes and Stanford exchanged glances. "This 'angel' gets around," muttered Hughes under his breath. Stanford didn't know what to say.

"Go ahead son, tell us about your angel," Hughes prompted, pen poised.

"Well…" He hesitated. "I dreamed that I was asleep in bed and a bunch of angels were singing to me. It sounded wonderful…" he said, searching for the right words. "I didn't want

174

them to stop." His voice was full of awe. "Then one angel told me I wasn't to worry because Ruby was safe in 'Neverland'; that a kind lady called Ruth was going to find her, with the help of a policeman called Samuel."

Something stirred within Stanford, he felt like his chest was about to explode. Hughes had gone white and was, for once, speechless.

Clearing his throat, Hughes said, "Carry on, son."

"She said that Ruby and I would stay with the kind lady, Ruth, and her family, until Dad was better – Ruby's with her now and I can go once I'm out of hospital. She told me that Ruby had called her Gloria."

Jess suddenly looked wistful. Stanford thought he was about to cry again. "She said that God had sent her to me and Ruby. That God loves us both…" His eyes misted over. Blinking, he said serenely, "Then she told me that I would wake up very soon," he finished.

Hughes had actually been present when Jess had woken up. He had popped in for an update, on his way home. Checking his notes, Hughes clocked the time as 8.15pm. He had called Stanford straight away, and Stanford had arrived at the hospital at 8.30pm. They had not discussed anything at the hospital. This was unbelievable. There was no way that Jess could know about Ruby, or Ruth, or Samuel for that matter.

"This case is gonna get us both locked away," muttered Hughes bewilderedly under his breath.

"Can you remember what Gloria looked like?" asked Stanford.

Jess nodded. "She was…shining. She had… kind eyes…and she smelt like roses…" He paused. "She was wearing a t-shirt that said 'God Rocks' – which is funny, don't you think? For an angel."

Stanford nodded. "Is there anything else you can remember?" he asked, trying to keep the interview 'normal'.

"I don't think so." Jess hesitated. "She was pretty…with red hair and really big wings." He smiled.

Sister Martin re-entered the room. "Here we are." She smiled, handing Jess a cup of hot chocolate. "Just what the doctor ordered!"

Jess took a careful sip, a huge smile spreading across his face.

"Now that's what I like to see," Sister Martin said, gently ruffling his hair. "I'm afraid it's time for you gentleman to go," she said pointedly. "There's a hot chocolate waiting for you outside, Constable Amos." She grinned. "I take it you'll be here for the night too?"

"Yes. Thank you!" Amos beamed appreciatively. "We'll have to compare notes!" She winked at Jess. Jess grinned back.

"Cheeky!" laughed Sister Martin. "You can be making your own hot chocolate in the future!"

"Jess, thank you for telling us what happened – you've been a great help. We'll be in again to see how you're getting on," said Stanford in a friendly manner, getting to his feet. "If you think of anything else, you can tell Constable Amos, and she will pass it on to me, okay?"

Jess nodded.

176

Hughes stood, towering over Jess. "Young man, I meant what I said earlier. If you ever consider a career in the police force, you contact me, okay?" he said, handing him his card. "It might be a few years before you're old enough to join, but you contact me first."

Jess' eyes were sparkling, and his smile could not have grown any wider.

Despite the cuts and bruises he already looked very much better.

Once out of earshot, Stanford and Hughes exchanged thoughts.

"I am too tired to even try to make sense of all this 'angel' stuff," stated Hughes, grumpily. "I'm going home to my wife and my dog. Take my advice and do the same – and as you don't have a wife or dog, I suggest you get yourself one!" He smirked. "And get a copy of Amos' notes – she might not have said much, but she is very observant, and her notes are always accurate to a fault."

"Yes sir. Giving Jess your card was a nice gesture," Stanford said, changing the subject. Hughes was always trying to marry him off or foist a dog on him.

"The lad needs something good to focus on – besides, how many other eleven year-olds could pull off a strategy like this 'Neverland'? He's bright – got something about him – in a few years, who knows. I take it you'll continue tracking down this 'Kenny' piece of dung, tomorrow?"

"Yeah, I've got a nasty idea that it's Kenny Samuel."

"Yeah, he had crossed my mind too. Haven't seen him around in a while though."

"I'll chase up the 'harbour' lead."

"Take PC Crowther, with you. Kenny doesn't just like beating up kids. I'm going to retrace Jess' 'escape route' – want to confirm that it can be done, for my own satisfaction. It all sounds far-fetched – especially this 'Gloria' character."

"You gonna be swinging on ropes and climbing trees, sir?!" Stanford asked incredulously.

"Don't be daft! That's why I'm taking PC Burton!" He grinned wickedly. Right, I'm off! See you in the morning."

"Yeah, night sir."

* * *

CHAPTER TEN

2nd Samuel:
Kenneth Stewart Samuel
– to be exact!

He stank. Kenny hadn't showered in over a week. He had been on the run from so-called 'colleagues' and the police. Wilkins had seriously landed him up the proverbial creek without a paddle. He had only agreed to supply him with the booze in the first place to get rid of a dodgy batch. He didn't think Wilkins would be sober enough to realize it was 'off'. That he *had* sussed it and then refused to settle his tab had made things very 'awkward' – a hundred quid 'awkward'. Not a lot in the big scheme of things, but enough to get Kenny into serious trouble.

He already owed the Phillips brothers seven and a half grand from a previous 'awkward' transaction with a dodgy Swedish gin supplier that had gone horribly wrong, leaving him in a weeping puddle of broken bones from a beating he would never forget. The brothers had figured whoever could leave Kenny in that state was way out of their usual petty league; so they had given him the benefit of the doubt and allowed him to continue to work for them; at least until he'd paid back every penny he had 'lost' them. Never mind that Kenny had nearly 'lost' his life in the process. That was eight months ago now, and he still limped.

So, by refusing to pay him, Wilkins had practically signed Kenny's death certificate, not to mention his own. They wouldn't let him off for a second time – even if it were for just a measly hundred quid.

And as for the Wilkins boy, he should have stayed out of it. Stupid idiot. Who did he think he was, taking *him* on? Didn't he know *who* he was dealing with? Kenny took great pride in teaching people *who* they were dealing with. Unfortunately, he only usually taught those weaker or smaller than himself.

It made him feel validated, powerful, when actually he was nothing more than a snivelling coward. Sadly, however, he believed in his own hype, even though the last time it had nearly cost him his life.

He did not know what had become of the boy's sister, he had done a quick search for her but had given up and made good his own escape; though not before snatching anything of value from Wilkins' house. His pockets jangling with collectable buttons, silver coins and medals, he stepped over the unconscious boy, smirking, with not a flicker of remorse. Dumping the family photographs, he pilfered the silver frames – they would buy him enough petrol to fill his car and get him to where he was now heading – a change of plan, but it would keep him alive. He jumped into his car whistling 'Eye of the Tiger', before pulling away from the kerb, wheels screeching. He thrilled at the thought of 'being seen'. He *wanted* full credit for this. He *wanted* the Phillips brothers to know he had meant business and was not conning them; *and* he wanted to send out a clear message to any other 'business associates', who might find paying him 'awkward'. They didn't call him 'Kenny the Sledge' for nothing, he thought, admiring his own reflection in the rear-view mirror.

His inflated ego was almost as large as the delusional bubble he lived in. Nevertheless, he was still a dangerous man.

Within twenty minutes he had disposed of his stolen wares to his fence – a 'colleague' who never asked questions about where the stuff came from – and was on his way to a tiny village in the middle of nowhere. He had unwittingly stumbled across it once when he'd been lost. It was so remote he figured anyone driving through this village was probably also lost. But he knew its isolated location made for a good place to lay low, and a vacant property would be an ideal hideout. And judging from the state of the 'For Sale' sign outside, this place had been empty for a very long time.

Breaking the glass in the back door, he reached through and turned the key, stiff from lack of use. A damp, musty smell immediately assaulted his nostrils. Screwing up his face in distaste, he quickly entered the kitchen, making a beeline for the internal garage door, opened the garage and swiftly secreted his car inside. Luckily for him there was no neighbour within a two-mile radius. Smug with his own sense of success he explored the property. It was a 1950's bungalow, run down and in dire need of modernisation. The loud orange and green wallpaper was hanging off in places and the russet carpets were threadbare. 'Pity', he thought – he quite liked it – apart from the stink of the mildew.

There was still running water and electricity – an oversight on the part of the estate agent, but a bonus for him. 'Kenny, your luck is changing' he gloated, flicking the switch on the immersion heater. He found an old lump of carpet soap under the kitchen sink, called 'Vanish'. He chuckled at the irony.

All the curtains in the property were drawn shut, which suited him fine. Dumping a large black duffel bag on the floor, he proceeded to empty its contents. He never went anywhere without this bag. It was his 'getaway' bag, his lifeline, always stashed in the boot of his car. It carried everything from sticking plasters to sticky toffee pudding – out of date but still edible. You name it, it was in that bag somewhere. He loved that bag. He'd even named it – 'Colossus' – a word he had learned from his last stint in prison – meaning something vast, enormous. He was proud of this name, it fed his belief in his own superiority.

He dragged a mouldy old mattress in from the garage, throwing his sleeping bag over it. The two-bar electric fire in the lounge would help to dry it out. He'd slept in worse places, he mused.

Now for some chow. His guts were rumbling. It would take a while for the immersion to heat up. So, plenty of time to fix a meal. Tinned sausage and beans – it wasn't steak and chips, but, it would fill a hole.

Later, wiping the steam from the bathroom mirror, he contemplated his next move. He knew he would have to put things straight with the Phillips brothers, but he would hunker down here for a week or two, first. Give things time to cool off.

To save his neck, he would post them a package, with not just one hundred quid, but five hundred quid in it, courtesy of Wilkins' medals. He'd also include a note:

"Wilkins reneged on our deal (reneged – another word he had learnt in prison). This should put us square. Be in touch."

K.

He knew they would still be suspicious. But at least they would call the dogs off. He hoped. He wondered if the police had paid them a visit yet. They would eventually. Which he knew would seriously rattle their cage – he took vengeful satisfaction in rattling the Phillips brothers.

He allowed himself to relax a little. It had taken him days to get to this place; navigating along the back roads and mud lanes, parking in fields, under bridges, in abandoned quarries; avoiding any route that had a camera. It should have only taken a day, instead it had taken four. He was exhausted but elated. There was nothing he enjoyed more than playing cat and mouse with the police, unless of course, there was

someone who needed 'teaching a lesson' –
Kenny style.

* * *

CHAPTER ELEVEN

1st Kings

"Meeting in the den, now!" commanded Esther, imperiously. Everyone followed her in amiably, used to her habitual bossiness.

She sat, consulting a long list in front of her.

"As you all know, our family has grown again," she said, taking charge. "Joshua, Mum, Dad and I want to make Ruby and Jess feel really welcome. So, we are going to throw a party for them!" She beamed.

"Ooo, what a lovely idea!" exclaimed Hilly.

"When?" asked Tom.

"As soon as Jess is well enough to come home from hospital. Which, if all goes to plan, will be this Wednesday," explained Joshua.

"So, Mum figured that we should give him a day or two to settle in and then surprise them both with a party on Saturday. Are you all free to come?" asked Esther excitedly.

They all confirmed they were.

"Great! So, this is the plan that I've come up with."

"I hope it's better than your last plan!" teased Cam.

"Hey!" Esther admonished her cousin, "It worked, didn't it?!"

"Sort of..." said Dunc, grinning at the memory.

"I don't think Zebs would agree though!" chuckled Lee.

"He made a great 'tracker dog'," Esther huffed, defensively.

"Yeah, but Joshua nearly lost his license, following him *in the car*!" laughed Mitch.

"I thought that policeman was very understanding, once we'd explained what we were doing!" giggled Hilly, finding it hard to contain her merriment.

"Thank goodness Dad arrived in time to support our explanation," agreed Joshua, also grinning widely. "Mind you, he wasn't too happy with me afterwards. He said I should have used more common sense."

"Well, I *still* think it was a great plan," Esther stated stubbornly.

"And Zebs did do an amazing job," agreed Lauren, hiding her smiles.

"Thank you!" puffed Esther, "He made an amazing tracker dog."

"Yes, Zebs definitely did an amazing job, he *tracked* a shoe, a tin can, three balls and a bucket and spade! But not a sniff of Ruby!" snorted Hilly, unable to contain herself anymore.

The entire group fell about laughing, including Esther.

Right on cue, Zebs dashed into the room, swiping everything off the table with his 'ninja tail'.

"Here he is! The hero of the moment!" laughed Joshua, patting his side. "Who's a good boy? Who's a good boy?!"

They all made a huge fuss of him, sending him loopy with attention until, finally exhausted from all the love, he flopped contentedly across Joshua's feet, and enjoyed a blissful belly rub.

"Right! Back to the planning!" commanded Esther, checking her list. "Mum and Dad also want to buy them a few gifts to make them feel at home. Any ideas?"

"They don't have anything of their own with them. It's all back at their house and we aren't allowed to go there, as it's still a crime scene," explained Joshua.

"And they're sharing our bedrooms – Ruby is in with me, and Jess will be in with Joshua," continued Esther.

There was a moment's thoughtful silence.

"So, they don't have anything of their own? Nothing? No clothes or shoes?" queried Mitch.

"Nope, Ruby's wearing an old nightdress of mine at the moment," replied Esther.

"Well, what about buying them their own jim-jams? That would make a nice gift," suggested Hilly.

"Yes! Brilliant!" said Esther.

"What about their own duvet cover?" offered Tom. "I always feel more at home when I sleep in my own duvet – my nan even keeps a Spiderman one for me at her house.

"Yes! Great idea!" said Joshua.

"That would give them a sense of ownership and belonging," said Mitch, nodding.

"That's deep," said Lauren.

"Psychology 101." Mitch grinned cheekily.

"It would certainly help to make them feel more at home," agreed Hilly.

"I think Ruby would simply adore a 'Lion King' duvet. She told me she loves Simba and is always singing 'Circle Of Life'!" said Esther.

"Or one with angels on!" chipped in Joshua.

"Angels?" asked Hilly.

"Yeah, she talks *a lot* about angels, especially one she named Gloria." said Esther and proceeded to tell them everything Ruby had told her. They listened, agog.

"Wow! How wonderful!" breathed Hilly in awe.

"Incredible," agreed Mitch.

"I'm jealous!" declared Lauren.

"Me too!" said Tom.

"Yep. That's something I will definitely be discussing in my theology class next term," declared Joshua.

"So, so far, we've got jim-jams and duvet sets…" said Esther, bringing them back to her list, "Anything else?"

Well, Dad's carving them a coat hook with their initials on – like the ones he made for us," said Joshua.

"And Mum's ordered them toothbrushes with their names on," Esther said, adding those to her list.

"I've got one of those. They're really cool, they light up!" said Dunc. "That will cheer them up!"

"It certainly will, Dunc!" said Cam, ruffling his hair affectionately. He had always been close to Dunc and could see he was not himself, Cam knew his brother too well, but Dunc wasn't ready to share yet…

188

"What about slippers?" asked Lauren.

"Yep! I'll add that to the list," said Esther happily.

"How about we each give them 'a promise'," Lee suggested thoughtfully.

"A promise?" asked Lauren.

"Yeah, you know, to make them feel part of our 'gang', our 'family'. We could make a 'promise' to them and write it in a card."

"Like?" asked Lauren, curiously.

"Ummm, like, Jess can have a go on my bike, whenever he wants," said Lee.

The mere mention of Lee's bike made Lauren blush uncontrollably.

"That's a really great idea!" approved Hilly. Everyone agreed.

"Yeah, I could lend Jess my football!" Enthused Dunc, his eyes alight. Then, inexplicably, the light was extinguished… "Or, or perhaps my fishing rod would be better," he mumbled sadly.

Cam knew something was really bothering his brother. He had never seen him look so unhappy. He exchanged a worried look with Hilly.

"I'm sure he would love to borrow your fishing rod, Dunc!" encouraged Hilly. Dunc just nodded.

"I think Mum and Dad will love all these ideas! Anything else?" asked Esther.

"Is the party going to be at yours?" asked Cam.

"Actually, Mum and Dad thought it might be a nice idea to have it at 'Beachy Manor', if the weather stays nice," said Joshua.

"Oh lovely! Are Nanna Penny and Grandpa Walt going to be there?" asked Hilly.

"Yes! They're back from their conference on Friday," said Joshua.

'Beachy Manor' was the affectionate name given to their grandparents' seaside beach hut, tucked away in sleepy Kingsland Cove. Sitting sedately on the sand, she dozed in the sun, like an antiquated duchess – her white flaky paint rippling in the breeze, reminiscent of white lacy petticoats, her crooked umbrella, now a filigree of fluttering weathered holes, as delicate as any Victorian parasol. But still beautiful. Still a lady. And still a place of tranquillity and adventure! She had been in the family since Jed and Joel were children themselves. Only six feet by six feet outside, but her inner dimensions appeared to rival those of 'Doctor Who's Tardis'. The picture postcard 'residence', with her stripey blue and turquoise door, billowing polka-dot curtains, colourful bunting and twinkling fairy lights, was home to a small gas stove, shiny blue whistling kettle, delicate cups and saucers, thick warm towels, and plenty of Nanna's cream teas! It was perfect. Many exploits and memories were made and enjoyed at 'Beachy Manor'.

The children spent the rest of the day excitedly planning the forthcoming party with glee. Esther periodically dispatched people off on various missions, to find, to buy, to borrow, to pack, stack and prepare for next Saturday. The house was abuzz!

190

***

The following morning found Tom, Mitch and Lauren sitting in the front row of Kingsland Pentecostal Church, sandwiched between Hilly, Dunc, Cam, and Lee.

It was a beautiful old church that had been around since the early 1800's. At night its illuminated cross made a comforting sight shining out all across Kingsland from high atop its tall proud steeple, from which the bells still rang out every Sunday morning. Built from local red sandstone, it exuded a warmth that invited you in.

Two beautifully arched stained-glass windows, depicting doves symbolising the Holy Spirit, stood like sentinels, one either side of the enormous deep-blue double arched doors. These welcomed you through into a light airy foyer which housed a tastefully furnished café to the left, scattered with small chairs like miniature pews, round wooden tables, and deep comfortable sofas. To the right beckoned a bright bustling information reception, and beyond it, the creche, various multipurpose rooms, offices, and a cavernous church hall, in which French windows opened out onto a large garden – a wide green lawn framed by a meandering border of colourful flowers, plants, and shady trees. The views across the cliff tops and out to sea were breathtaking. Benches were secreted throughout the garden, providing pockets of quiet tranquillity. It was idyllic.

Back in the foyer, suspended from the centre of the high ornate ceiling hung a monumental glass and brass chandelier radiating a hue so golden it felt like the sun was actually rising within – even on days when it was raining without.

A little further forward, entering through four smaller arched doors brought you into the place where the congregation sat, a mixture of traditional pews and single wooden chairs with blue cushions, neatly but informally arranged either side of a blue carpeted central aisle, which led you right to the front, where a slightly raised platform hosted the worship band and the lectern, where folk rested their Bibles during a sermon. On the wall behind were God's 'Ten Commandments' to His people, beautifully scripted in blue and gold, with the addition of Jesus' commandment to **'Love your neighbour'.**

I am the Lord your God. You shall have no other gods before me.

Do not bow down and worship idols

Do not use the Lord's name in vain

Observe the Sabbath day – keeping it Holy

Honour your father and mother

You shall not murder

You shall not commit adultery

You shall not steal

You shall not give false testimony

You shall not covet

Following the path of the aisle, suspended from the ceiling, were three smaller versions of the chandelier hanging in the foyer, also glowing like miniature suns.

The walls were completely whitewashed and left bare, making a perfect backdrop for the stunning stained-glass windows that ran down either side of the church, bathing the room in glorious colour. Each window exquisitely narrated the story of Christ from His birth to His death and His resurrection.

A peace hung in the air along with a joy that could almost be tasted, garnered from generations of prayer and worship. God's presence was palpable. People felt better just entering this room.

The church had originally been St. Stephens – part of the Anglican diocese – until sadly, like a lot of churches in contemporary England, its congregation had diminished, the building had fallen into disrepair and eventually been sold off.

Fortuitously, it had been exactly what the AOG – the Assemblies of God denomination – had been seeking to enable them to plant a Pentecostal church in Kingsland. That had been over thirty-five years ago, and now, thanks to the Lord's blessings, it had grown into a living, thriving house of God once again. And Jed, only the third Reverend to be selected to pastor here, loved it, counting his blessings every day. This morning was no different. Standing out in front of his eagerly awaiting congregation, peppered with new faces, he was bursting with God's message, his happiness complete.

Beaming, he welcomed everyone to church and into the presence of God. The worship team of singers and musicians began the first song, 'I Declare!'. It was a call, a promise, and a declaration to God, and to one another. Tom, Lauren and Mitch soon picked it up.

Looking around, Lauren was struck by the honest, heartfelt way in which everyone was singing with such joy and abandon, as the worship team led them in praising God. Arms raised heavenward, eyes shining, clapping, swaying, and dancing. She was swept up in a wave of unabashed adoration. Her pure voice felt effortless in its strength and beauty: her first experience of Godly unity.

The worship team flowed seamlessly into 'When You Cried', a song that urged them all to reach ever higher, draw ever closer to the glory and presence of God, acknowledging His sacrifice. Tom was completely lost in his emotions, each swelling note matched by the swelling within his heart. He had thought a lot about the conversations he had shared over the past two weeks and knew that he could not go back to life the way it was before. It had changed. He had changed.

The congregation followed as the team poured themselves into a rousing rendition of 'Hallelujah! Hallelujah!' leading them all *'through His gates with thanksgiving and into His courts with praise'*. Celebrating God. Loving Him. Thanking Him. Rejoicing, relying, trusting Him in all His glory.

It was an experience Mitch would never forget. He had never encountered anything like it in his entire life. In that moment he was given an absolute assurance of what his future was to be. He was shown a vision – a supernatural glimpse of what God had planned for him. He knew he would never be the same again – he had received his calling – his personal God-given purpose in life. He knew from that instant on he would choose to serve God and His church. He sank to his knees, marvelling at the wonder of God.

Lauren was singing at the top of her lungs, tears streaming down her face. Why was singing having such a profound effect on her? she wondered. Self-consciously, she glanced around and was startled to see Mitch on his knees. Lee and Cam were either side of him, laying their hands on him, praying over him.

Hilly smiled and nodded her encouragement. "It's okay," she whispered, handing her a tissue, "It's the Holy Spirit."

Tom, self-contained and completely oblivious to all around him, sang with every fibre of his being, eyes closed, heart open. A quiet determination grew within him. He was getting baptised – nothing was going to stop him now – nothing!

The Lord had His hand upon the lives of these children. Never before had Jed observed God summon, equip, and prepare anyone for service in His Kingdom as swiftly as He had these three children. Their Christian walk had begun at a run. Within two weeks they had become acquainted with it, committed to it, and given a mission for it. Their anointing was profound! "Praise You Father! Praise You!" he cried, awed by the power and majesty of his God. 'When the King calls', you decide, you choose – reject or respond – they had responded! Answered His call! Rallied to His side! Enlisted in His righteous army! Joined His family.

Jed's chosen sermon that morning would have to be preached on another day. The Holy Spirit had just given him new instructions!

The worship repeatedly soared, crescendo after crescendo like an eagle riding upon thermals of praise. Ever higher and higher. Heaven was open. Jed could see it in spirit. Feel it in his soul. More aware than ever that God was here with them – here in Kingsland Pentecostal. Jed could see some folk lying down – 'slain in the spirit', some openly weeping, others laughing and joyous, others serene, heads bowed. The pastoral care and prayer teams quietly worked amongst them, covering some with blankets, offering prayers, support and encouragement where needed. The

Holy Spirit was doing a great work within them all.

Awed by God's love for them, His faithfulness and mercy. Jed extended his arms out over his flock and began to pray deep intercessory prayers.

Miri was at his side praising and doing battle. The Holy Spirit had already given her the alert that there would be huge enemy opposition to the work God was doing today, and she was having none of it. Spiritually she was engaged in a fierce and brutal fight, confidently defeating everything the Enemy threw at her, holding her husband's arm aloft as he tired.

Deut joined her, raising Jed's other arm. Speaking forcefully, he entered into the fray. "God's will be done," he declared.

The power and authority of God pulsed through Jed as he prayed deliverance, liberation, healing, and protection for all of the folk the Lord had given him the privilege to lead. Lives were saved. Lives were transformed and lives were given to God that morning.

Gradually the worship drew to a natural conclusion. The congregation, remaining in the presence of God, prepared to receive Jed's sermon.

Jed wiped his perspiring face upon his hanky and thanked God for all He had just done for them. He took a moment to collect his thoughts before he said, "I had already prepared my sermon for this morning, and I was bursting to share it with you. It was a good one! But I think the Lord had other plans!" he chuckled, wiping his brow.

Appreciative laughter rippled across the congregation.

"As the lyrics say:

'Sing praises to our King of kings
The Lord of all the wondrous things,
Let everything that takes a breath
Praise the Lord! Praise the Lord!

Several "AMENS!" rang out in agreement.

"And that is exactly what the Holy Spirit has prompted me to focus on today. The Lord truly is our King of Kings. He sits at the right hand of His Father God. Interceding on our behalf. Making ready for the day we join Him at the heavenly banquet, celebrating His return, His victory, and our own coronations. You see, He is 'The King' and we are His princes and princesses. He has prepared a crown for each and every one of us. Unique, beautiful, and promised to all of His people – the King's people. For that is who we are. The King's people. *Members of a chosen race, a royal priesthood, a dedicated nation, God's own, special, purchased people.*

"In this world, we know that in a race *all* the runners run, but only *one* gets the prize. *Therefore, run in such a way as to get that prize.* Everyone who competes in the games goes into strict training. We are currently 'Training for Reigning'. We are 'Monarchs in the Making'. They – the worldly – do it to get a crown that will not last, but *we* do it to get a crown that will last forever!

"Now it's not easy in the everyday hustle and bustle of life, of living *in* this world, to remember that. We know what we are up against – *who* we are up against. But the Enemy has already been defeated. He is beneath our feet. And *'He who is in us is greater than he who is in the world.'*

More "AMENS!" swept across the room.

"So, when faced with the trials and tribulations of this world," continued Jed, "We have to remember not only who we are, but WHOSE we are! We are ROYALTY and we are SONS and DAUGHTERS of 'THE KING'!"

Rousing claps and "AMENS!" filled the room.

Jed forged on, "Complete with all the privileges, power and duties of that station. You have the King's favour. *He has plans to prosper you and to do you no harm. He has commanded His angels concerning you to guard you in all your ways. He gives you victory wherever you go. No weapon formed against you will prosper. He prepares a table for you in the presence of your enemies. He offers you the keys to His Kingdom. He has promised never to leave you or forsake you. Nothing you do could make Him love you any more or any less than He already does. Your King died to save you!*"

Agreements and praise echoed around the room.

"*And in His name, He has given us the power and authority to drive out demons, to speak in new languages, to lay hands on the sick so they recover, and he gives us protection from harm.* You have been set apart, you are the Ecclesia – 'the called-out ones', *chosen for such a time as this.* Why try and fit in when you have been called to stand out!? You are not of this world. You are heaven-bound," Jed assured them.

"Now, knowing this, knowing how precious we are to our King, knowing our royal status, and knowing where the true source of our trials and tribulations originate, ask yourselves: How would a prince respond to that person who has just insulted him? How would a princess react to that person who has just been unkind to her? Ask yourselves how would *you* expect to see a prince or princess behave? Given all the power and authority afforded them. And remember, you aren't just any old prince or princess, and not just the son and daughter of any old king, but the son and daughter of THE KING! THE KING OF KINGS!

"So, the next time the Enemy tries to bring you down to his level, the next time he tries to use that insult or that unkindness to take you out, the next time the Enemy tries to remind you of your past, you remind him of his future!" You get back up on your feet, dust off your armour and run the race to the finish line. Because your crown awaits you! And you can say to him – *Get thee behind me Satan! I have fought the good fight, I have finished the race, I have kept the faith.* Because *he* is already a defeated foe and *you are more than a conqueror through Christ who loves you!* For the Lord sees you as *more* than a conqueror, he sees you as *more* than a champion, *more* than a warrior – He sees you as a ruler! Seated with Him in Heaven! Crowned, coronated and complete in Him!

The congregation erupted, expressing their understanding and support for 'The Word' Jed had been given by the Holy Spirit.

He indicated that his message was concluded. The worship team spontaneously began to play 'When the King Calls'. They were enthusiastically followed by the congregation, reignited with God's burning fire.

Jed made an 'Altar Call' – an invitation come to God, to surrender and be transformed. "If there is anyone here today who has not yet given their life to Christ, who has not yet received their salvation and feels that they want to 'get right' with God; equally if you have already given your life to Christ and for whatever reason have turned away, have backslidden; please join with me in the following prayer. Congregation, please help them. Repeat after me... Dear Jesus,

"I repent of every and all of my sins,
I believe that You are the Son of God,
I believe that You died for my sins and rose again,
I give you my life,
For the rest of my life,
Amen."

"If you have just joined with me in this prayer and you meant it, please raise your hand. We don't wish to embarrass you. But we do wish to bless you and give you some information and welcome you into the family of God."

Five hands flew up. Mitch, Lauren and Tom, and a newly married couple. The church celebrated. Heaven celebrated. Jed celebrated, blessing them all in the name of the Father, the Son and the Holy Spirit.

In the aftermath, Mitch sat, slightly stunned, saying nothing, quietly basking in God's presence, with Cam and Lee silently supportive on either side.

Lauren was holding Hilly's hand, receiving a steady supply of fresh tissues. Her eyes were red and swollen, but she had never felt so happy.

"I get why you are always smiling, now," she hiccupped. Hilly hugged her tight, knowing exactly how she was feeling.

Tom was chatting away to Dunc, nineteen to the dozen, beaming from ear to ear. He looked like a different boy. More confident. More upright. More 'Tom-ish'.

Jed, Miri and Deut joyously congratulated them with hugs, kisses, and handshakes, inviting them all round for lunch later that day. They had not only become part of the family of God, but of their family too.

It was a day the children would remember forever.

* * *

CHAPTER TWELVE

2nd Kings

Wednesday eventually arrived. It had taken Jess more than three weeks to recover enough to be allowed 'home'. Ruth and Joel had spent a lot of time with him during his hospital stay, and with daily visits from Ruby, Esther, and Joshua, they had all soon got to know one another very well. To Jess' complete surprise, he realised that he actually liked the Truemans a lot and was excited at the prospect of living with them.

His stay in hospital had given him plenty of time to think about his life. The angel – 'Gloria' as Ruby called her – had also spoken to him about a great many things – his bullying, for one. And facing a bully like 'Kenny' had made him realise just how he had made others feel. He was ashamed and desperately wanted to say he was sorry to everyone he had ever hurt. And knowing how awful he felt about himself, had helped him to understand and forgive his own father's behaviour.

So, when he had been allowed a supervised visit from his dad, their conversation had healed much and had filled Jess with renewed hope. It had done him the power of good. So much so that the doctors had declared him fit for discharge the very next day.

***

Saturday dawned bright and sunny, promising a glorious outing to 'Beachy Manor'. Both Jess and Ruby were surprised and super excited about their seaside 'welcome party' and could hardly contain themselves. Ruby ran around all morning singing 'Circle of Life', whilst Jess packed and repacked every bag, box and container prepared for the day – with the full support and approval of his new best friend, Zebedee! It had been love at first sight for both of them. They were inseparable. Jess was a changed boy. Joel could see the re-emergence of the young man that Jess had been before his troubles had begun, before the loss of his mum. His whole countenance had been restored. Praising God for His mercy and grace, Joel bundled the final batch of burgers into the back of his car, declaring in his best 'Trumpton' voice "Right, folks! Ruth! Josh! Esther! and Roob! Zebedee! Jess! And Joel! That's me! Time for us to leave!" he called.

There was a happy stampede for the car, with everyone ensconced even before Joel had time to get himself in. "Well, that has got to be the quickest roll call on record!" he laughed, starting the engine.

Arriving ten minutes later at 'Beachy Manor', they were greeted by his parents. "Great to have you back, Dad! How was the conference?"

"It's great to *be* back, Son!" He smiled, slapping Joel's back. "The conference was excellent – you would have loved it – there were some superb speakers, and the Holy Spirit's presence… Whoo! Off the scale!"

Joel and Jed were younger versions of their father, who was still tall, broad, and dapper, sporting a goatee, a white Panama hat, white cotton shirt, cream shorts and a wide cheeky grin. Retirement agreed with him.

Penny, his mum, came bustling out of 'Beachy Manor' arms outstretched. "Joel Trueman, come give your mother a hug, I have at least a month's worth to catch up on!" she exclaimed, smiling widely. Tall, slight, and athletic, her white-blonde hair sparkling with sunshine and silver made a striking contrast against her sun-kissed skin and vivid blue eyes, which twinkled with mirth. A picture of health and vitality. Retirement obviously agreed with her, too.

Jess and Ruby hung back shyly, watching in fascination.
"Ruth, darling, you too!" Penny ordered happily, opening her arms wider, laughing as Ruth skipped in for a hug. "Esther, Josh! Don't think you are getting away without one!" she chuckled, stretching her arms wider still, making room for a full-on family scrum.

Jess, amused, could see where Esther got her bossiness!
Then espying Ruby and Jess, Penny turned her full attention on them. "And you must be Ruby and Jess!" She smiled kindly. "I'm Penny and this is Walt, we're Josh and Esther's grandparents, Joel's parents. Welcome to the

family! We have a family rule – we 'never say hi without a hug!' She beamed. "You are welcome to join in if you wish!"

Ruby ran forward and practically threw herself into Penny's arms. "Hi!" giggled Ruby, never backward in coming forward. Jess grinned at his sister, but shyly settled for a handshake, still not quite used to such displays of affection – unless it was for Zebs!

The sound of another car pulling up drew their focus. "It's Missy!" squealed Ruby excitedly, running to the car – they had become firm friends when she had discovered they both loved 'The Lion King'!

Jed, Miri, Hilly, Cam, Dunc, Missy, Lauren, Tom, and Mitch all piled out of the people carrier. "Lee's on his way," explained Cam, "He's riding his bike down. And Uncle Deut's gone to pick up some ice for us."

Soon more folk began to arrive. Miri's parents, Nigel and Dawn Tyler, and her brother Marcus, much to the delight of his nieces and nephews. He was by trade an estate agent specialising in commercial farming, although with his casual dress sense and 'Ken Dodd' hairstyle he more closely resembled a stand-up comedian. However, appearances aside, he used his astute business mind and unique sense of humour to successfully buy and sell agricultural land and property all across Devon. His business was thriving. It was surprising given the name of his agency – 'Ewe Mooove'.

One could be forgiven for not taking him seriously. It made folk laugh and they would contact him just to see if he was actually legitimate! But once you had a conversation with him you realized it was all part of a very clever marketing plan, simple in its ridiculousness! His signs were ludicrous – a chicken standing on the back of a sheep, standing on the back of a cow, reading…

"With 'Ewe Mooove'
Stay calm and smooth
Don't cluck or bleat
Your needs we'll meet!
Call 080 282828
Don't wait! Don't wait! Don't wait!"

And it had to be said, he was extremely good at his job. His customer service, fast legal process, care and attention to every detail, not to mention his honest, trustworthy approach and incredibly competitive rates had earned him respect and a reputation for excellence amongst the farming community. Miri adored her brother. There were very few estate agents like him. And he *was* very funny – the children hung on his every word!

She knew five minutes with him would have Jess and Ruby feeling right at home.

As the numbers steadily grew, so did the party atmosphere. The laughter surrounded them all like warm fluffy towels. Jess and Ruby were truly welcomed into the Trueman family, and overwhelmed with their gifts.

Jess was a little awkward to start with, which was not surprising given his previous behaviour, but the children didn't mention it. They had made a promise to forgive and forget and treated him kindly. Amidst all the present opening and excitement, Tom was completely taken aback when Jess quietly apologized to him for all that he had said and done to him. And Tom was further surprised when he thanked him for praying for him. "Mr. Trueman, Joel, he told me what you did," Jess explained meekly. "Thank you."

Tom just nodded and shook his hand, unable to think of what to say. But Jess looked so sad in that moment that he felt he *ought* to say something to him, so not knowing what else to do, he called out to the Father. 'Lord I don't know what to say, what can I say to him?' he prayed inside. And as clear as a bell he heard in his heart – 'Tom, tell him the truth – all of it!'

Tom's stomach flip-flopped – first he was shocked that he had heard God so clearly – because he knew these were not his thoughts – he would never have wanted to tell Jess anything, let alone the truth. Then he panicked at the ramifications of sharing his truth with anyone, especially someone like Jess. 'Really Lord? Do I have to? He might not believe me. He might laugh at me,' he thought.

'He might, but that mustn't stop you, Tom. Do not be afraid, I am with you. I will never leave you or forsake you,' assured the Lord.

Suddenly aware that Jess was still watching him, Tom swallowed nervously and said, "Actually, I couldn't stand you, you were a nasty bully and you scared me." Jess went scarlet and stared at the ground, abashed. "But God showed me how to see past all that," Tom rushed on, "I couldn't have done it without God – because God... Well..." Tom hesitated, his face burning self-consciously. "God loves you, Jess. And he knew what was going on...and well..." he stammered, "You looked so...awful, in that hospital bed...and...I felt sorry for you. And I could see why you were the way you were... and...I'm sorry about your mum," he finished, clearing his throat anxiously.

Jess stared at him for a moment, then said, "That's what Gloria said. *She* said God loves me."

Tom blinked, he wasn't sure what he had expected Jess to say, but it certainly wasn't that!

"So, I guess...it must be true," Jess continued, really taking it in for the first time.

Tom nodded. "It is," he said simply. "So you're gonna be alright."

Jess smiled.

"Jess, Tom, come and meet Great Aunt Mary and Uncle Roly!" called Hilly.

They turned and were met with the most eccentric vision drifting along the promenade towards them.

Great Aunt Mary was a little round ball of colour. Vivacious curly orange hair, piled high on top of her head, spilled out of holes in what appeared to be a bright red straw hat, the brim strewn with plastic cherries. From a distance it looked like she was wearing a tomato pot on her head! A stripy turquoise and blue ankle-length dress billowed in the wind, revealing pink flowery Doc Marten boots. A large green handbag was slung across her shoulder, and grasped in one hand was a sparkly gold walking stick, which she fervently waved in greeting. "Hallooo!" Clutched in the other hand was probably the strangest sight of all, a tangle of bejewelled, ribbon-like leads, each attached to the collar of a small dog. A cacophony of perpetually swirling sound and movement, wrapping and unwrapping themselves around her ankles and knees, yapping and wagging in their excitement.

Hovering above her was a large yellow parasol held gallantly aloft by Great Uncle Roly. He was tall, skinny, and resplendent in a purple crushed-velvet suit, midnight blue shirt, mauve tie, and matching shoes. Their beaming smiles and rosy cheeks made them both a jolly sight.

It reminded Lauren of an ambulant circus tent – the dogs' leads reminiscent of guy-ropes, and Great Uncle Roly a perfect tent pole. And yet, as she watched Great Aunt Mary spinning around untangling herself for the umpteenth time, a fairground carousel also sprang to mind. Either way, she couldn't wait to meet them.

"Halloooo darlings!" Great Aunt Mary hollered, waving her stick again.

Tom counted eleven dogs! Pekingese, Chihuahuas, Pugs, Shih Tzus, Bichon Frises, miniature Poodles and a bizarre looking dog that could only be described as a small furry sofa.

Great Aunt Mary could be heard admonishing her charges on the wind. "Freddie, do stop pulling, I'm sure if you weren't in such a hurry, you wouldn't get so breathless! You're like quicksilver!" she scolded a golden pug with a heavy black moustache-like muzzle, whose naturally protuberant eyes were made more so by a lack of oxygen as he strained against his lead.

"Well, Freddie by name, Mercury by nature, my dear," placated Great Uncle Roly, used to his wife's grumblings.

"And Jasper, put that down!" she hissed at a russet Chihuahua that was chewing on a discarded bread roll.

"Jasper, do as mummy says," echoed Roly.

More hugs, kisses and gift giving abounded upon their arrival. Then collapsing into a plump cushioned chair, Great Aunt Mary declared, "The party has started!" and promptly handed Miri a large bottle of Great Uncle Roly's homemade cherry sherry. "Pour me a glass, dear, would you please," she whispered, winking at her.

Grinning, Miri took it inside Beachy Manor, surreptitiously showing it to Jed *en route*. "Use a small glass!" he chuckled, "That stuff is potent!"

"How are the bread rolls coming along Ruth?" called Joel, flipping the burgers and sausages on the Barbecue. "Cos these are almost ready."

"They're on their way!" she said, bringing out a large tray. Then catching sight of Joel, she roared with laughter. "What *are* you wearing?!"

"It's a present from Great Aunt Mary!" he grinned, executing a perfect pirouette. Sitting atop his head was a flying seagull, complete with flapping wings. "It's to keep the sun off my ears, apparently!" he chuckled. "You should see what Jed and Dad got!"

She turned to see Jed and Walt posing for a selfie. Jed sporting a huge spouting blue whale and Walt an enormous orange crab, strung with Australian-style corks from each leg!

The children couldn't contain their hilarity. It was a sight never to be forgotten. Great Aunt Mary was a firm believer in making memories and would go to great lengths to achieve them. She had certainly outdone herself this time!

"Grub's up!" called Joel.

Everyone eagerly tucked into the feast, watched closely by twelve pairs of pleading, hope-filled eyes and waggy tails.

"Bishop! Stop begging!" commanded Great Aunt Mary, to a particularly enthusiastic Bichon Frise who was drooling profusely all over her feet.

"That's a cool name," said Lee.

"Yes, I like to give them names that suit them. He's Bishop because his knees are bad," she said, as if that explained everything.

"One assumes that as a Bishop, one would be on one's knees praying a lot," said Great Uncle Roly with a wink.

"Ahh," said Lee, grinning, "I get it!"

"Are they all yours?" asked Jess, delighted to be surrounded by so many.

"Yes, all mine. Well, they are now, anyway." She smiled.

"They've all been rescued," explained Great Uncle Roly. "Mary has a big heart," he said, smiling adoringly at his wife.

"What's this one called?" asked Ruby, stroking a blonde Shih Tzu. "I love the pink ribbon in her hair, it reminds me of my friend Lucy."

"Yes, she's a beauty, isn't she? Her name is Monroe. Named after Marilyn Monroe – another beautiful blonde." Great Aunt Mary smiled indulgently.

"And this one?" asked Mitch, scratching a gorgeous chocolate brown Pug behind the ear.

"Oh, that's Mo – named after a particular favourite gent of mine, Mo Farrah. We took a while to find a name for him, didn't we Roly – until we came to realise that it took a *marathon* length run to wear him out!" she chuckled proudly.

Mitch was laughing into his burger. He couldn't believe she had named a pug after an Olympic gold medallist!

"What about this one?" asked Lauren, pointing to a dark golden Chihuahua, now completely in love with Great Aunt Mary.

"That's Setta – short for Poinsettia, a plant native to Mexico, which is where Chihuahuas are from. And we rescued her on Christmas Eve, so it seemed fitting. She was the only dog left in the shelter. All alone. And we couldn't have that could we," she said sadly. "So, we offered to foster her over Christmas and well, she never went back."

"That was five years ago!" said Great Uncle Roly. "And this fellow named himself!" he chuckled, stroking Jasper, the bread eating Chihuahua. "What are you called, Jas? What's your name, boy?!"

Sitting up very straight, Jasper yapped "Jah… Jah! Jah…Jah!" He did indeed sound remarkably like he was saying Jasper!

"And we have no idea what breed that strange little chap there is, but with his square shape and squat wee legs, we called him PK for Parker Knoll – as he puts us both in mind of a dinky roving sofa!" Great Aunt Mary laughed.

"I thought that too!" exclaimed Tom, grinning.

"Excellent boy!" she praised.

"Tell them about these two!" laughed Dunc, cuddling two Pekingese.

"That's Ant and Dec!" She grinned wickedly.

"Why Ant and Dec!?" asked Mitch, unable to contain his laughter.

"I named them!" laughed Roly mischievously, "Because Ant is a very cheeky boy and Dec is a very naughty boy!" he said pointing to each in turn. "And together they bring us both hours of comical entertainment!"

Everyone laughed – even those who had heard it all before.

"What about the poodle?" asked Lauren expectantly.

"That's Brian – Brian May. Well with hair like that what else *could* we call him!?" She twinkled mischievously.

"Yes, Mary is a huge fan of the Queen!" said Roly affectionately.

"I am indeed! Both of them – Freddie and Elizabeth! Long may Her Majesty reign!" she said, raising her glass and taking a glug.

"Hear, hear!" said Great Uncle Roly, joining in her toast.

"And last, but by no means least, is Lotty," continued Great Aunt Mary, pointing at a golden Pug. "Named after another favourite of mine, Charlotte Church."

"Why?" asked Tom, not seeing any resemblance whatsoever.

"Because she can sing, my boy! And just like Ms. Church, when that girl opens her mouth, you wouldn't believe the heavenly sound that comes out!" chortled Great Aunt Mary.

"Sing for us Lotty!" encouraged Great Uncle Roly, throwing back his head and howling.

Immediately Lotty joined in, "Wrooo wroo wroof! Wroo wroo wroo wroof!" she sang in a sweet high-pitched perfect doggy soprano!

Not to be outdone, Zebs decided it was time for him to join in the fun too

and began 'woo-woo-wooing' in a rich, woofy kind of way!

"Oh! We have a Pavarotti!" exclaimed Great Aunt Mary delightedly.

The children found it all hilarious, especially when Uncle Marcus began barking in tune!

"Marvellous! A three-part harmony!" chortled Great Uncle Roly.

"Yes, the dogs are our life!" continued Great Aunt Mary, thoroughly enjoying herself.

"You're forgetting Tinker!" said Great Uncle Roly.

"Never!" she said fervently. "Where is he, by the way?"

"Still in his basket, fast asleep I believe! Are you awake yet, old chap?" he asked, lifting the lid of what the children had taken to be a picnic basket.

'Purrrraow!' came the soft reply. "Oh! You are! About time, you lazy ole troll!" Great Uncle Roly chuckled. Reaching in he pulled out a large fluffy ginger tom cat with huge green eyes. He was beautiful.

"Here he is, Mummy's precious boy!" exclaimed Great Aunt Mary. His purr grew louder.

Ruby squealed at the sight of him, "Oh please, oh please, oh please, may I hold him?!" she asked breathlessly.

"Of course you can, my dear," said Great Uncle Roly magnanimously, plonking him in her lap, where he promptly fell fast asleep again. Tinker was so big that he swamped Ruby like a giant rug, but her happy little face said it all.

No one else seemed to find it strange that they had brought a cat to the seaside – not even the dogs! Tinker had just purred all the louder when Zebs had given him a friendly lick on the nose –

obviously, this was 'the norm' for them all. 'Batty, the lot of 'em!' Tom thought, sharing a smile with Lauren.

"Well, at least he's behaving himself today," said great Aunt Mary, "The last time we were here, he disgraced himself!"

"How?" asked Lauren eagerly, hoping for another eccentric tale. She wasn't to be disappointed.

"Well, he really was a very naughty, naughty boy," whispered Great Aunt Mary, conspiratorially, her eyes twinkling. "Tinker has a real penchant for cream…"

"And Miri had made one of her scrumptious raspberry trifles…" continued Great Uncle Roly smacking his lips.

"A temptation that poor Tinker couldn't resist and later lived to regret!" sighed Great Aunt Mary. "The cream and sugar proved to be too rich for him you see, and he availed himself of his lavatory in…" she paused for effect.

"MY shoe!" finished Great Uncle Roly. "A positively unpardonable misdemeanour on his part!"

"Unfortunately, Tinker won't do his 'business' outside – it always has to be *in* something… It took him days to recover, poor boy!"

"Poor boy?! My shoe still hasn't recovered!" grumbled Great Uncle Roly.

"Oh, yes, but you were so gracious about it, my darling," cooed Great Aunt Mary, "And Tinker did buy you those lovely red cowboy boots as an apology…"

"Oh, yes, he did, and they are rather splendid!" he agreed. "It was just unfortunate that I didn't discover his little accident until *after* I'd placed my bare foot inside the shoe!"

Muffled giggles, snorts and a few 'Eeeews' echoed around the table!

"And what about you, Mary, my dear? You weren't left unscathed by the incident either!" he remarked solicitously. "She didn't discover the extent of Tinker's troubled tum, until she raised her parasol!" He grimaced, miming the action.

"Yes, it smelt just awful!" agreed Great Aunt Mary, "But do you know, my hair was in lovely condition for weeks after that!"

The table erupted!

"Needless to say, trifle is strictly off Tinker's menu from now on!" laughed Great Aunt Mary, jovially.

"Yes, Tinker by name, Tinker by nature!" chuckled Great Uncle Roly.

The rest of lunch passed without event, and Tinker continued to behave himself appropriately. Shortly afterwards Joshua asked, "Dad can I go and get the boat out now?"

"Of course, but you know the rule, don't go alone," he said, throwing the keys to him.

"Thanks! Lee, Cam, Mitch you wanna come?"

"Where are we going?" asked Mitch.

"To the harbour," answered Lee.

"That's where 'The Glory' is moored," said Cam.

"'The Glory'?"

"Yeah, a boat – owned by both our dads. its full name is 'The Glorious Lord'."

"But we mostly call her 'The Glory' or 'Glory' for short," explained Joshua.

"Cool name!" said Mitch.

"Cool boat!" said Lee. "She's a beaut! A thirty foot blue and white fishing boat."

"Dad and Uncle Joel bought it together the day they became Reverends – to celebrate," said Cam.

"She's a dream to sail!" said Joshua, "She waltzes on the waves." He sighed, happily. "I might ask Dad if we could spend the night on board tonight – she's a four berther."

The afternoon wound sleepily on, the ocean calm and peaceful, dozing beneath a blanket of gentle sunshine. 'Glory' tiptoed around the bay, not wishing to disturb the sea in its slumber. The soft, salty breeze caressed each new face as they came aboard, bringing with it the scent of suntan lotion and toffee apples, ice cream and candy floss. Seagulls called and soared above, and below, sunlight sparkled upon the waves like a thousand flashing cameras at a concert. Everyone thoroughly enjoyed their trip, returning time and again for yet another voyage along the shoreline.

Joshua loved sailing. He was in his element. Here is where *he* felt closest to God. This was *his* secret place. His dad had often remarked that he had learnt to sail quicker than he had learnt to walk!

Meanwhile back at 'Beachy Manor' the conversation had taken a comical turn once again thanks to Great Aunt Mary.

Walt had been talking about the conference from which he and Penny had just returned. One speaker had been teaching about the many different ways in which God will communicate with us.

Walt had been particularly touched by the testimony of a lady who had nursed a baby squirrel back to health. She had explained that throughout the whole process God had used each new development to speak to her about her own life.

"Well," Great Aunt Mary declared, "If God can use a donkey's ass to speak…I'm sure he can use a squirrel!"

Jed choked on his drink. "I think you mean an Ass' mouth, Great Aunt Mary!" he exclaimed, quickly.

"Donkey! Ass! Whatever you call it, it still spoke!" she said emphatically. "Or would you prefer I call it a burro?!"

"No, it's just you said… Oh never mind!" He grinned, giving up as the children's laughter grew more unruly by the second! "How many cherry sherries has she had?" he asked Miri, amused.

"Only the one!" she whispered, covering her mouth with her hand, desperately trying to disguise her own laughter.

"Yeah, but have you checked her handbag for another bottle?!" muttered Joel, his mirth evident.

"It's probably inside the parasol!" chuckled Walt, from beneath his Panama.

"Great Aunt Mary is of course referring to the example of Balaam and the talking donkey in Numbers 22-24," explained Nanna Penny, trying desperately to regain a semblance of order, but too late, Great Aunt Mary's faux pas would be remembered forever! Penny's sister had always had that knack!

Just then Jess arrived back from his turn on 'Glory'. "Josh says would anyone else like a trip on 'Glory' or should he weigh anchor for a bit?

"I think everyone's been – all except Great Aunt Mary," said Joel, looking around. "Would you like a trip on 'Glory', Great Aunt Mary?"

"A what?" she asked.

"A trip, with Joshua, on 'Glory'?" Joel repeated.

"Where's Joshua?" she asked, her hearing sometimes a challenge.

"He's on 'Glory'," Joel repeated.

"Where? Where's he gone?" she asked, confused.

"He's gone to 'Glory'," Jed interjected.

"Who's gone to glory?" she asked.

"JOSHUA!" said Joel and Jed raising their voices.

"Oh! Oh! My goodness! Gone to glory?! Not Joshua! When?! When did he go to glory?!"

"NO!" bellowed Jed and Joel together. "Not *gone to Glory,* as in gone to be with the Lord, but gone to *'The Glory*! Our BOAT!" they clarified, quickly.

"Oh, thank heavens for that!" she huffed, relieved. "Honestly, you should be clearer with your communications!" she admonished them. "How do you expect your flocks to understand you if you can't even make yourselves clear to me! Penny dear, you need to take your sons to task!" she said, wiping her brow with a red spotted hanky. Stifled laughter rippled around the group.

Great Uncle Roly had hidden beneath a newspaper and could be clearly heard snorting with glee. "Never mind, Mary, m'dear, you at least make yourself very clear!" came his muffled comment.

She glared over in his direction, assessing whether she had just been insulted. Uncle Roly shrewdly refrained from further comment.

"Let me make you a cup of tea," suggested Miri kindly.

"Oh, lovely idea! Oooh and one of your excellent cream scones, Penny, if you please!" She smiled, mollified.

"Of course, Mary," said Penny, smiling at her sister, "Or perhaps a piece of my honey cake!?"

"Oooh, rather!" She beamed, her eyes alight with anticipation. "Your honey cake is known as 'The Bee's Knees' after all!"

"I'll go and tell Joshua to weigh anchor then, shall I?" said Jess, grinning.

"Yes. Thank you, Jess," said Joel, glad to see him looking so relaxed and happy.

"Tell Joshua I've saved him a piece of my honey cake," called Penny. "That should bring him in!" She winked.

"Okay!" He smiled, heading off to the harbour at a trot.

"Wait up, Jess, we'll come with you," said Cam. Then like a gaggle of noisy geese they all followed after him, leaving Ruby and Missy building a sandman with Walt.

"That is a different boy than the one we met three weeks ago," remarked Joel.

"Praise God!" agreed Jed. "I think today has gone really well – they both seem to have settled right in – made new friends too."

"Talking of which, Ruth, didn't you say that Detective Stanford was coming today?" asked Joel.

"Yes, Samuel said he'd pop by. I think he was rather touched when Jess asked him to come. Him, Detective Hughes and Jane, that nice Police Constable," said Ruth. "I'm sure they'll be along soon – they wouldn't let Jess down."

***

In truth, Detective Stanford would have much preferred to have been with them and had planned to arrive hours ago. But he had received a 'heads up' from an informant that Kenny Samuel had been seen in the area. Stanford was keen to get his hands on him and had been following up on the intelligence, the first bit of useful information since the incident had occurred. So far, every avenue he had explored had led to a dead end. He had confirmed that Kenny had been employed at the harbour, loading and unloading cargo – mostly fish. But he had gone AWOL around the time of the incident and had not been seen there since. It was as if he had just disappeared off the face of the planet.

Both Jess and Ruby had positively identified Kenny, picking him out of an album full of 'ne'er-do-wells' just like him. As part of the ongoing investigation, Stanford had had to correlate all the evidence against him, including the doctor's report on the injuries Jess had sustained. Stanford was determined to see Kenny locked up, powerless to inflict *that* kind of damage on anyone ever again.

He was now *en route* to a local pub, 'The Smugglers Cove', a favourite haunt of Kenny's and the last place he had reportedly been seen.

PC Amos and PC Burton were currently there keeping it under low-key surveillance, posing as holiday makers in Dan's old VW camper van, as the all-singing all-dancing official surveillance vehicle was in use at another location by Hughes. He knew of Kenny's connections to the Phillips brothers, knew that Kenny owed them a lot of money and knew they would be looking for him too. So, where they went, he went – at a safe distance. They only had to take an extra breath and he would know about it. Not for the first time, Hughes found himself thanking the generosity of Kingsland's residents. Generous to a fault, he smirked, eavesdropping on the Phillips' conversation. Ironically, they had already dropped themselves in it by unknowingly admitting to several petty crimes in the area. He

224

would arrest them for that lot later – right now he was using them to catch Kenny.

***

Kenny, however, was *not* having a good time. His brilliant plan to lay low had come to an abrupt end when he had been seen posting the money to the Phillips brothers. He had hidden away for nearly two weeks undetected, but knew he could not wait any longer to put things straight with them. His very life now hung in the balance. If *they* found him before his package found *them* – he would be a goner.

But he had no understanding of how close-knit such a rural community was. For the folks who lived in that quiet, picturesque village it was a bonus (provided you could dodge the gossip!), but for an outsider it was anything but – as Kenny had now discovered, much to his chagrin.

He had been spotted by Stan, an elderly gentleman, out walking his dog late at night. Stan had been a coast guard in his youth and had never lost his ability to 'scan the horizon' for trouble. His eyes, still sharp at eighty, had marked Kenny's shifty demeanour and knew he was an unsavoury 'squall' out to 'rock the boat' in their otherwise calm village 'harbour'.

'But not on my watch,' thought Stan, immediately on the phone alerting the local 'Neighbourhood Hub'. He informed Gladys at number three, she passed it on to Cyril and Sandra in number six, who contacted Richard at number ten, who took his role as local MP very seriously, and instantly deemed it police-worthy. And to his and their credit, the local bobbies had quickly responded, vigilantly cruising around the village in search of said 'unsavoury squall'. The crime level in that area was zero and they all wanted to keep it that way, thank you very much.

Kenny, like a hunted animal, was always on the alert. He had noticed the police car passing by the house twice in the last ten minutes and decided he wasn't going to wait around for a third time. Hastily stuffing everything into Colossus, he threw it into the boot of the car and beat a hasty retreat in the opposite direction, cursing his bad luck. He had posted all the cash he could spare to the brothers, hoping to appease them *before* his return. Now he knew he was heading back into shark infested waters. For the first time ever, his life depended upon the price and prompt delivery of a first-class stamp, and his absolution upon the efficiency of the Royal Mail.

He desperately needed more funds and knew just the bloke to squeeze – he owed him one anyway. So, with no other option he headed back to Kingsland, once again travelling along the back routes, avoiding the cameras, arriving exhausted and angry several days later. His first port of call: 'The Smugglers Cove'.

***

PC Daniel Burton, keen to make a good impression on Detective Hughes, had volunteered to work an extra duty. But by 10.30am his enthusiasm was beginning to wane. PC Jane Amos, on the other hand, was still in 'highly diligent' mode.

"Whose car is that parked over in the corner?" she asked. "You think we should call it in – check its number plate?"

"I don't recognize it and I can't see the number clearly," Burton answered, squinting through the split screen.

"Hang on," said Amos, delving into the left-hand side of her top and producing a small pair of binoculars. "Here try these."

Focusing the lenses he said, "Have you got a pen handy?"

Delving next into the right-hand side of her top, Amos produced a pen *and* pad. "Ready," she said.

"WF19 ZRB... Local reg., that is," he said.

"I'll call it in," she said, once more delving back inside her top, to the centre this time, drawing out her mobile.

"Crikey, Amos, what else have you got stashed in there?!" he asked, startled.

"Handcuffs, Swiss army knife, couple of Mars bars!" She grinned.

"You're kidding me?!" he gaped.

"Nope! Meet TESSA," she beamed, lifting up her top.

"Woah! Amos! What are you doing?!" he yelped, covering his eyes. "You trying to scar me for life?!"

"Don't be such a plonker, Burton! Open your eyes and just look!" she snorted.

"No way! I've got a girlfriend!" he declared, "And she'd kill me, if I even took so much as a peek!"

"Burton, for goodness sake, what kind of girl do you think I am?!" Amos exclaimed. "Take a look, it's a prototype that mum and I have been working on. T.E.S.S.A. stands for Tactical Equipment Secret Storage Attire. My mum's an amazing seamstress and she made it for me."

Cautiously Burton opened his eyes, and was met with an impressive looking bit of kit. A kind of black pocketed 'utility bustier'. "Woah!" he exclaimed, gawping open mouthed.

"It's cool, isn't it?" We're thinking about making the next one with Kevlar!" She glowed proudly. "I'd have preferred to call it, Tactical Equipment *Covert* Storage Attire, but it meant it would have been called TECSA, which sounded too much like 'Alexa', and I didn't want people walking around talking to my chest, and you know they would!" she accused. "It can be worn under *or* over your clothes. As you can see, I'm wearing mine *over* a t-shirt and *under* my top!" she emphasized as if talking to a child. "I'm gonna try wearing it under my uniform on Monday, see how it feels. If it works, we're putting the design forward to H.Q. It's got a pocket for everything – even a lippy!"

"Don't suppose you have any coffee in there, do you? I could murder a cup," Burton grumbled.

"Nope, but I do have teabags!" She grinned, unzipping one of the smaller pockets.

"What about hot water?" he asked cheekily.

"Now you're pushin' it Scoob!" she laughed, pointing to the flask at her feet. "There's milk and sugar in the bag too!"

"Amos, you're an angel!" Burton declared, grabbing the flask. "I think your TESSA is a really great idea. Will it just be for the women? Or will you design one for us blokes?"

"Ummm, I hadn't really thought about it, to be honest. My mum got fed up with me shoving everything inside my bra, so we came up with an alternative! Besides, I think a bloke lacks certain anatomical requirements necessary for the pocket design to really work!" she teased.

"Point taken!" He blushed. "'Ere! That car's gone!" he said suddenly.

"Oh flip! I'll call it in now!" she said, dialling in a panic. "Sergeant Newman will have our guts for garters if it turns out to be important!"

"I didn't see anyone come anywhere near the car!" he moaned.

"No, you had your bloomin' eyes closed!" she quipped. "Hi, Sarge, can you run a reg. check for us, please?" she asked, giving him the details. "…Well, it was parked in 'The Smugglers Cove' car park… We're not sure exactly when it left to the second, Sarge," she said biting her lip. "We were…focusing on another line of enquiry," she mumbled. "Yes Sarge, I'll put it *all* in my report."

"That could be awkward," muttered Burton.

She mock-smacked his shoulder in reprimand. "Yes, Sarge. Yes sir, thank you sir." Ending the call, she let out a sigh of relief. "Phew!

Apparently it belongs to a little old lady of eighty, who is unlikely to be a person of interest."

"More tea?" asked Burton grinning. "Or perhaps we could have one of TESSA's Mars bars?!"

"Burton! It's not funny!" She grinned, mock-smacking his shoulder again.

"*Au contraire*!" he laughed, earning himself another wallop.

Suddenly her mobile rang. "It's Detective Stanford," she said, answering it. "Amos here." She listened intently. "Has he? When?… Okay… Right, we'll keep our eyes peeled." She nodded as the call ended. "Stanford is on his way, cos Kenny is definitely in town and heading in our direction, driving a clapped out old green Golf, with the reg. WW67 YDS. Hughes is *en route*, because the Phillips brothers have got wind of Kenny and they are also on their way here!"

"Cor, it's all go, innit!" said Burton gleefully, slurping his tea.

***

'All go' was probably not how Kenny would have described it. Walking along the beach from the next cove brought him to the rear of the pub and gave him the advantage of not being seen. He was, at that moment, scrambling up the side of a cliff, trying to drop down into the hidden entrance of 'The Smugglers Cove'. He had used this way many times before, thus avoiding any unwanted attention – much as smugglers of the past had avoided the customs officers. He could enter the pub without anyone knowing. It was one of the reasons why he liked this pub so much. Jarvis, the Landlord, was about to get a nasty surprise. Kenny needed somewhere to stay, and he needed cash, fast. He did not care how he got it or from whom he got it. Little did he know that his plans were about to be scuppered again.

***

Hughes pulled up in the surveillance van, anticipating the arrival of the Phillips brothers.

Stanford arrived minutes later, parking next to Amos and Burton. Already dressed for the beach in casual blue shorts and a t-shirt, he jumped out and approached them, waving, for the benefit of anyone who might be watching. "Hi guys! So glad you could make it!" he enthused loud enough for everyone to hear.

Amos wound down the window and leaned out giving him a hug. "No sign of him yet," she whispered in his ear.

"You go in and order a drink at the bar, let me know if you see him," Stanford murmured under his breath, surreptitiously handing her two earpieces.

"Righto." Burton nodded.

"You go on in, I'll wait for the others to arrive," Stanford said loudly, popping a pair of sunglasses on. "Mine's a pint of Rusty's, mate!" he joshed, leaning against his car.

"Righto, mate! But you're getting the next round!" returned Burton, playing the happy camper to the full.

As they disappeared inside the pub, Stanford discretely scanned the car park. There were two other vehicles parked now.

"I've run the plates on both those. They're all clear," Hughes said in Stanford's left ear, "And the Phillips brothers should be arriving here any minute now."

Right on cue, a bright red Ford Ranger pickup truck coasted in, doing a loop around the car park before parking near the exit. Three men got out: one huge, blond-haired, muscle-bound behemoth of a man, and two smaller, hard-faced, square-featured men, their darting eyes scanning the surroundings with the focus of seasoned hunters.

"That's them," Hughes said, "And 'Godzilla' there is their hired muscle – Giovani Gonzolas – a nasty piece of work. Used to work for the Trent family in London, until he fell out of favour with the boss. Not sure of his connection with these two or why he's turned up here in Devon. I'd have thought the scene down this neck of the woods was too tame for him. He's wanted for at least three grievous assaults and a robbery in Charing Cross."

Stanford pulled out his phone and pretended to talk into it. "What's the plan then?"

"Let them find Kenny, then arrest the lot of them," said Hughes, simply.

"Just you, me, Burton and Amos?!" asked Stanford, a tad concerned at the odds.

"No, Crowther's here with me and Sergeant Newman's on his way."

"Who's running the station, then?" he asked, surprised.

"A civilian volunteer."

"A civilian volunteer? Who?" asked Stanford, confused. As far as he knew they didn't have any civilian volunteers.

"Peggy."

"Peggy?! Your wife, Peggy?!" exclaimed Stanford, startled.

"Yep!" said Hughes proudly, "She's worked in the force for years."

"Yeah, in admin!" Stanford clarified.

"Yes, but she knows what she's doing. She's only going to be answering the phones and taking messages," he replied glibly.

"Uhh, we've got our drinks and are currently wandering around the bar, but there's no sign of Kenny in here," interrupted PC Amos, nervously.

"Good, take a seat and keep your eyes open," commanded Hughes.

"A couple of nasty looking chaps and 'The Hulk' have just walked in," reported PC Burton.

"As you were," said Hughes. "That's the Phillips brothers and their pet goon. Keep an eye on them, but don't get too close."

"What now?" asked Stanford.

"We wait," Hughes replied.

***

Kenny slipped unnoticed up the steps from the cellar and tiptoed along the corridor towards the private rooms in the back of the pub. He had lived this way his entire life, his senses honed, alert, ready for any trouble. The bully in him thrived on a bit of 'aggro' – especially if he was the cause. The coward in him, however, was another story.

Slinking past an open door he caught a glimpse of his quarry. He waited for him to leave the room, then pounced on him in the corridor, slamming him into the wall, then dragging him back down the stairs to the cellar.

Jarvis, stunned and bleeding from a gash on his cheek, cowered in shock and fear. Small and stocky, he was no match for Kenny.

"Hello, Jarvis, my old cocker!" purred Kenny, menacingly, "Thought it was about time you paid me what you owe me."

"K-Kenny, ya only had to ask," he stammered, holding his nose. "I'd have given it ya."

"Where's the fun in that?" Kenny laughed, taking a step closer.

"How much ya want?" Jarvis asked, swiftly emptying out his pockets.

"All of it!" Kenny snarled, snatching the small roll of notes out of his hand.

"I owe you two hundred quid, there's four hundred in that bundle!" Jarvis protested weakly.

"Call it an investment!" Kenny sneered.

"An investment, in what?! Jarvis asked, nervously.

"Your future. Whether you get one or not!" He grinned, clenching his fingers.

"Now, Kenny, there's no need for that!" he pleaded. "I was always goin' to pay ya – ya know that! It's just ya disappeared before I could give ya your cut." He swallowed nervously, taking another step back, his breathing ragged.

"You told me that booze was only out of date – not that it was off! Kenny raged, "Wilkins refused to pay me. And now I'm in a whole lot of trouble because of you!"

"How was I to know that Wilkins would taste that it was off!" he reasoned. "Half the time he didn't even know what time of day it was! I didn't set ya up, Kenny, honest I didn't! You can ask the Phillips boys – I just spoke to 'em – asked if they knew where ya was so I could pay ya!" he claimed desperately. "They said they didn't know where ya was and was looking for ya too!"

"You what?!" asked Kenny, stopping in his tracks.

"Yeah, honest, Kenny. Go and ask 'em yourself. They're up in the bar!" he explained, hoping this would put a stop to another beating.

Violently shoving Jarvis into a stack of empty barrels, he rasped, "You ain't seen me, got it?"

"Wh-wh-what?" Stammered Jarvis, confused.

"GOT IT?!" Kenny bellowed in his face.

"Yeah, yeah, whatever ya say, Kenny, whatever ya say!"

Giving him a final shove, Kenny marched out, slamming the door behind him. Shaking uncontrollably, Jarvis slid to the floor in relief.

Kenny headed up towards the bar, taking a careful look through the curtains screening off the private rooms. Sure enough, there they were, in the bar, *both* the Phillips brothers and they didn't look happy. They had obviously not got the package he had sent them yet. Time to leave. Then he caught sight of Giovani Gonzolas sitting at the same table sipping a pint. What was *he* doing with them? He was the Swede who had stolen seven and a half grand's worth of gin from them, leaving him, Kenny, for dead and forced to pay the thieving git's debt!

Kenny saw red. "Two timing, double crossing, shyster sons of scum!" he cursed under his breath, retracing his steps back down and out through the cellar, jogging back across the beach to his car. He needed somewhere to go, somewhere to hide, somewhere no one would expect him to be. "Think Kenny, think!" he admonished himself… "The old net shed at the harbour – perfect!" he thought. He had been the only one who had regularly accessed it. He could lock down in there for a few days, give himself time to regroup, and give the Phillips brothers time to receive the package he had sent them. Turning the car around, he headed towards the harbour.

***

Kicking the ball back and forth between them, Jess and the others 'footsied' their way along the beach towards the harbour.

Dunc had been true to his word and had promised Jess the loan of his football *and* his fishing rod. Jess had been very moved by all the 'promises' made by the children. He had never known such generosity and kindness. But he had been particularly touched by Dunc's 'promises' because Jess was a keen footballer and used to go fishing a lot with his dad.

Dunc was a really talented player – showcasing his skills with lots of volleys, headers, tricks and kicks that had them all cheering him on. Lee belted the ball down towards the shore, sending it spinning into the surf. They all charged in after it, splashing and squealing with glee. Their laughter drew the attention of a large group of lads sitting on the sea wall.

"HEY! IT'S DUNC THE PUNK!" shouted one of the boys, jumping down off the wall, followed closely by the rest of them.

"ARE YOU GONNA, DUNCADONNA?!
ARE YOU GONNA DUNCABALL?!
ARE YOU GONNA, DUNCADONNA?!
ARE YOU GONNA TRY AND SCORE?!"

They began to chant loudly and repeatedly. Dunc stood rooted to the spot, all merriment washed away. Moments of fear, sadness, and anger flashed across his blanched face. "Go away, Walker!" he said, turning his back on him.

"Why? What're you gonna do, Duncadonna? Pray?" jeered Walker. "You gonna ask that God of yours to help you again?" A spiteful snicker rippled through the group of lads, they cackled like a pack of hyenas.

Hilly and Cam exchanged a brief look, they knew instantly *this* was what had been troubling their brother.

"I suggest you leave him alone," Cam said, firmly. Hilly immediately shoulder to shoulder with her brother began praying under her breath.

"Why? So he can lose us another game?" came Walker's bitter retort.

Tom and Jess shared an uncomfortable moment. Walker's 'bully boy' tactics were reminiscent of Jess' past behaviour and served as an unwanted reminder. Jess dropped his head in shame.

Tom, on the other hand, held his higher; and ever conscious of other people's feelings, whispered, "You're not like that anymore, Jess, and remember, *God* has forgiven you." Then he surprised everyone by stepping in front of Walker, looking him straight in the eye and saying, "*You* will *stop* this, right now!"

Walker just stared at him in disbelief. "And who the hell are you?!"

"Never mind who I am," said Tom, emboldened by a steady courage rising up from the pit of his stomach.

"Oooooh!" jeered Walker's cronies, in mock awe.

"Well, well, well," sneered Walker, taking a threatening step towards Tom. "Looks like 'Dunc the Punk' has at least one friend!" he taunted.

"One more than you have Walker!" Tom said calmly, standing his ground, fully aware of who the *real* enemy was, who he was *really* standing against. Inside, Tom's resolve was further strengthened by a deep calm that came upon him as he prayed to the Lord. "Now, leave in peace, you are not welcome here and you have no right to pick on Dunc," he said with authority.

Walker stopped in his tracks, faltering at Tom's utter surety.

Hilly, fully aware of the hidden battle taking place, asked the Lord to equip, strengthen and seal them all safely inside their 'Armour of God'.

Walker, not wishing to lose face in front of his cronies, blustered, "Out of my way, freak!" and stepped around Tom.

Dunc's loyal family and friends were about to step in, when Dunc held up his hand, abruptly stopping their intervention. Turning, he said, "Do you know something, Walker? I never realized, until today, what an absolute bottom feeder you are!"

Cam and Hilly were both taken aback by Dunc's comment. They'd never heard him speak ill of anyone. He was the quietest, most reserved, most sensitive sibling out of them all.

"Oh, now you're brave, when you're surrounded by your pals!" Walker sneered, stung by his comment, and annoyed to hear laughter coming from his own friends.

"Oh, *I've always* been the brave one, Walker," stated Dunc calmly, "It just took me a while to realise it."

"YOU?! YOU lost us the game!" accused Walker, angrily.

"No, *the Truth*, lost us the game!" stated Dunc.

"The TRUTH?!" snarled Walker, incensed. "YOU were the one that did a 'Maradona'! YOU were the one that did a handball! YOU were the one that did a 'Hand of God'!" DUNCADONNA!"

"Yeah. You're absolutely right, I did. And it was an accident. An accident that no one saw. Not you, not the goalie, not the linesman, not even the ref. So, I could have got away with it. BUT *I knew*. And *God knew*. And I couldn't live with that! I couldn't lie, I wouldn't want to win the game by cheating!"

"A win's a win!" Walker shouted, frustrated.

"What are you *more* annoyed about, Walker? That I accidentally did a handball whilst *scoring* a goal, or that you *missed* a goal taking a penalty shot, and *that* lost us the game?" asked Dunc, forcefully.

"We wouldn't have had to go into penalties, if you had just kept your mouth shut!" shouted Walker. "But no, you had to go and blab!"

"But what kind of win would that have been?!" yelled Dunc, in return, "It's dishonest! It's dishonourable! It's downright unsportsmanlike!"

"You just don't have the guts to do whatever it takes!" bawled Walker.

"That's exactly what I *do* have! I have plenty of what it takes to *do* the *right* thing!

"If it was the *right thing*, then why has Coach benched you?!" spat Walker spitefully. "You haven't played a game in weeks! Your services are no longer required!"

This came as a shock to Dunc's family and friends – he had not told anyone that he had been benched.

"Dunc?" asked Hilly, concerned.

240

"I wasn't allowed to play because of this," he sighed resignedly, lifting his t-shirt to reveal heavy, but faded, signs of bruising all across his rib cage. "Thanks to some 'gentle persuasion' at half time, I've got a cracked rib."

There were collective gasps from all around – even from Walker's cronies.

"Oh Dunc!" exclaimed Hilly in shock.

"Did *he* do that to you?!" asked Cam. "Did *you* do that to him?!" Cam demanded angrily, taking a step towards Walker.

"Cam, stop! He really isn't worth it," said Dunc calmly.

"Loser!" said Walker scornfully.

"*I'm* not the loser, *I* never was. *I* walk in victory wherever I go," Dunc said, proudly lifting his chin.

"Oh, more of your 'God chat'!" Walker spat, derisively.

"Yeah, I *have* been chatting to God, a lot, actually," nodded Dunc smiling, "I've been trying to work out whether being a Christian was worth all the aggro."

Cam and Hilly were both alarmed to hear this.

"I've *even* been praying for you," continued Dunc, "And thanks to you, I've made up my mind. Without God, what is there? Without God, who would I be? Without God," continued Dunc," I'd be just like you…"

"Oh, shove yourself and your God up your…" BAM! Dunc's football smacked Walker right between the eyes, knocking him flat on his back.

The collective "aaooww!" spoke of the force with which the ball hit Walker and the force with which he in turn hit the ground.

"Oops!" said Jess innocently, "Sorry, my foot slipped!"

A couple of Walker's cronies ran to his aid. The rest were openly laughing, a couple even applauded. They had had enough of Walker too. No one likes a liar. No one likes a cheat and certainly no one likes a violent bully.

Retrieving his ball, Dunc, stood over Walker. "Oh and by the way, from Monday, Coach has made *ME* captain of the team, so *'your'* services are no longer required'!"

Turning his back on Walker, he walked away, '***kicking the dust off his sandals***'."

"*That* was a *fantastic* shot, Jess!" exclaimed Lee, grinning widely.

"It was, bloomin' AMAZING!" laughed Lauren, "AMAZING with a capital A!"

"It was a really cool shot," agreed Dunc, "But I'm not sure fighting violence with violence is the answer." He grinned wryly.

"Nonsense!" proclaimed Hilly. "There is such a thing as 'righteous anger'."

"I dunno about 'righteous anger', more like 'righteous angle'! That shot was superb!" snorted Lee, sending them all into fits of laughter.

"Jess you're a legend!" chuckled Cam.

Jess exchanged a shy but happy glance with Tom.

"Have you ever thought about joining the football team?" Tom asked.

"You should!" encouraged Hilly.

"And I am going to be needing a new striker now!" said Dunc.

"Yes, Jess, God didn't give you that fabulous right foot of yours just to put Walker on his back!" laughed Esther, "Even though it was rather terrific!"

Jess was beaming from ear to ear. His belief in himself and the promise of a new beginning was restored.

"Tom you were flippin' incredible too!" bubbled Lauren, "You were so brave!"

"Yep, you were armed and dangerous too!" smiled Hilly, proudly.

Tom's face burned. He understood now. ***With God all things are possible.***

Arriving at the harbour, they re-lived it all over again, falling over themselves to tell Joshua and Mitch what had just occurred.

"It will be all around school on Monday!" Lauren declared.

"I wish I could have seen it," grinned Mitch.

"Dunc, you've done yourself and God proud, you really have," said Joshua, smiling.

Dunc shrugged. "I guess, the whole thing was pretty cool, but I know what Dad would be saying now…"

"What?! What, would your dad be saying?" asked Lauren, "Surely, he wouldn't be cross with you for standing up for yourself?!" Her woodpecker temperament was beginning to rise again.

"No, no! He'd agree that *sometimes* the only way to get a bully to understand is to speak their own language. *But* he would also say '*Do not laugh at the downfall of another person*' – to forgive them. To '*Do unto others that which you would have done unto yourself*'. So, I'm *still* going to pray for Walker."

"And *that's* what makes *you* a legend," said Jess quietly.

"Yes, today will go down in the annals of history as the day Dunc dunked a dunce!" declared Cam to much laughter.

"Nay," said Joshua, impersonating Sir Winston Churchill. "Today Dunc defeated his enemy – a berk. We witnessed the same courage demonstrated by the brave at Dunkirk. Today is Duncberk Day!" he finished to rounds of appreciative applause. "Right! I can definitely hear Nanna Penny's honey cake calling me! To Beachy Manor!" he commanded, leading the way, followed by an entourage of laughing people!

"That was class! Class with a capital CLA!" Lauren roared.

***

Kenny dumped his car down a dirt track behind an abandoned railway siding. Dragging Colossus out of the boot, he headed for the harbour on foot. Using his peripheral vision to keep watch, he kept his head down and hood up, super alert to his surroundings with every step. Five minutes later he forced the door on the old net shed and slipped inside, narrowly avoiding a loud bunch of kids as they straggled past, their happy voices grating on his nerves.

Jess and Dunc were playing 'keepy uppy' and had dropped behind the others a little. Missing the last header, Jess pursued the ball as it bounced against the old net shed and rolled past its weather-worn doors.

As he bent down to pick it up, he noticed the broken lock and splintered wood, the door slightly ajar. Curious, he took a peek. Inside, a man crouched rummaging through an enormous black bag, mumbling to himself. As he looked up, he caught sight of a kid watching him from the door. "You shouldn't be in here, kid. Clear off!" he bluffed – acting like he owned the place.

Jess, whose eyes had not quite adjusted to the dark yet, recognized the voice. He would have recognized *that* voice anywhere. "You!" he exclaimed in anger. Too late, Kenny realized who Jess was. Covering the distance in two swift strides, he grabbed Jess by the throat, dragging him inside. "So, we meet again, me old cocker!" he hissed maliciously.

Dropping the ball, Jess struggled against Kenny's choking grip. 'Not this time,' he swore to himself, kicking Kenny in the shins as hard as he could. In pain, Kenny loosened his hold enough for Jess to break free. Scrabbling for the door he collided with Dunc, who had come to see where he had got to. "RUN!" yelled Jess, "IT'S KENNY!"

Slamming the door closed behind them, they sprinted to catch up with the others, Dunc calling out to them as they ran, "Guys! Guys! Wait up! We've just seen Kenny!"

Breathlessly Jess explained what had happened.

"Right, let's get back to Beachy Manor, all our mobiles are there – we can call the police from there!" said Joshua.

Although Jess was shaken by his encounter with Kenny, he suddenly felt a strange calm descend upon him. "You go back to Beachy Manor and call the police. I'm going back to Kenny," he said assertively, turning to go.

"Jess! NO!" they all cried together.

"I must!" he said, bravely, "I don't want him to get away again."

"Well, we'll come with you then!" said Tom.

"No, I don't want to put anyone in danger," he said.

"YOU are not *putting* anyone in danger – WE are *choosing* to do it!" declared Esther, passionately.

"Exactly!" agreed Hilly, "There's strength in numbers!"

"Okay, this is the plan," said Josh, taking command. "I can see there's no talking you out of it, Jess, so Lee, you are the fastest sprinter here, run back and inform our parents. Tell them he was last seen at the old net shed. GO! The rest of us, follow Jess and STICK TOGETHER!"

By the time they arrived back at the old net shed, there was no sign of Kenny – he had left in a hurry, leaving his enormous bag behind. So

246

they spread themselves out around the harbour in twos.

Jess was the first to spy him, running up over the field, away from the seaside, into the woods. "There he is!" he cried, pointing. He set off at a sprint, not waiting for the others. Joshua was hard pressed to keep up with him.

Kenny crashed off the path, heading deeper into the woods.

The afternoon had crept unnoticed into the beginnings of evening, twilight making it harder to see clearly under the shade of the trees.

This did not stop Jess; he was determined to catch him. He could feel his fear turning into strength, his anger melting away, being replaced with a calm implacability. Kenny was going to pay for what he had done. For what he had done to his dad, his sister and himself. Jess was going to make sure of it.

***

Meanwhile, Lee had arrived back at Beachy Manor and explained the situation.

It was 'battle stations'.

"I'll call the police!" said Penny.

"I'll call Samuel!" said Ruth.

"Dad, call the harbourmaster!" Jed instructed Walt, "And the coastguard!"

"This way!" said Lee, heading off in the direction of the net shed on his bike and hotly pursued by Jed, Joel, Miri, Deut and Great Uncle Roly.

"I'll stay and keep an eye on the little ones!" declared Great Aunt Mary, helpfully. "Come to Aunty Mary," she crooned to Missy and Ruby.

"I'll wait for Samuel and show him where you've gone!" said Ruth.

***

Back at 'The Smugglers Cove', things had just shifted up a gear. As far as Hughes and Stanford were concerned, Kenny had not showed up.

However, judging by the current state of the landlord, there was a possibility he had already been and gone, surmised Stanford, eyeing Jarvis' bloody cheek.

"Uhh, the landlord has just stumbled into the bar. Looks like he's taken a beating," said Stanford under his breath.

"What?!" snapped Hughes in his ear.

"Do I break cover and investigate?" asked Stanford calmly.

"No!" Hughes snapped again, "Send Burton over in the guise of a concerned citizen. What are the Phillipses doing?"

"They haven't noticed yet," said Stanford, watching Burton approach the injured landlord.

"They have now!" whispered Amos, nodding in their direction.

"Burton, abort!" ordered Hughes, "Just get out of their way." Burton changed direction, heading towards the loos.

All three men had risen as one, making a beeline for the bar.

"Hey Jarvis, what's up, mate?" asked Judah, the shorter of the brothers.

Flinching, Jarvis stammered. "N-nothing, man. I'm okay. Just took a tumble down the cellar stairs, that's all."

"Must have been a nasty fall," drawled Jonas, the other brother, eyeing his injuries with interest.

Skirting past him, Giovani Gonzolas disappeared behind the curtains which led to the private rooms.

"Hey! You aren't allowed back there!" Jarvis protested.

"Why?" Jonas asked.

"Brewery rules," bluffed Jarvis, avoiding eye contact.

"Do you need to go to hospital, mate?" asked Judah.

"No! I'll be fine," he protested, nervously touching his cheek.

"Cos if I find out that you are lying to us…" threatened Jonas, "You will definitely need to go to hospital."

"Look, I don't know what you're talking about. I just fell down the cellar stairs!" he asserted. "Now, buy a drink or leave me alone."

Giovani Gonzolas, returned shaking his head. "No sign," he said, his English slightly accented.

"No sign of what?" asked Jarvis, bluffing his way out of a lie. It had always struck him as very odd, that 'Giovani Gonzolas' was blond and Swedish, when his name was so obviously not. He had asked him about it once and had been *made* to mind his own business! But not before

Giovani had boasted about its *meaning:* 'Battle Castle'. Jarvis still winced at the memory.

"You know who we're looking for…!" said Judah. "Fifty quid says you know where he is…" tempted Jonas.

Dabbing his bloody cheek, Jarvis grimaced. "Make it five hundred and I'll throw in a kidney," he laughed in an attempt to divert them.

"Make it a thousand and we'll *take* your liver too," Judah said nastily, baring his teeth.

"Look, I don't know anything!" protested Jarvis, swallowing nervously.

Jonas' mobile rang. "Yeah…? Where…? Yeah, I know it – cheers…I owe you one," he said, ending the call. "Kenny's car's been seen down by that old train siding."

"I think I know where he's gone," stated Judah, "He used to park there when he worked at the harbour."

"Let's go," said Jonas.

"Heard it! On it!" said Hughes. "Meet you down there." His surveillance van had already left the car park before the Phillips brothers had left the pub.

Suddenly Stanford's own phone rang. It was Ruth.

"Okay, slow down, Ruth, Jess is what…?! When…?! Right, I'm on my way! Hughes is already on his way to the harbour. Yep, stay calm, we'll find him, I promise," he said, hanging up. "You two, with me!" commanded Stanford, rushing out the door, already dialling Hughes. Filling him in, he screeched out of 'The

Smugglers Cove' and headed for Kingsland Cove.

***

Jed, Joel, Miri and Deut sprinted along the beach to the old net shed, with Great Uncle Roly bringing up the rear. Dunc and Lauren were there waiting for them.

"Joshua asked us to wait here for you – he said to tell you they've gone up into Brashcombe Woods," said Dunc.

"Right, let's go!" said Jed, "Everyone stay close! Great Uncle Roly, can you stay here and direct the police when they come?"

"Absolutely, old boy!" he puffed.

"Right, which way?" asked Joel.

"This way," said Lauren, taking the lead.

***

"Oh, Samuel, thank goodness you're here!" exclaimed Ruth as he pulled up at Beachy Manor.

"Show me the way to the old net shed," he said without preamble.

"Amos, when we get there, I want you to keep your eyes open for the Phillips brothers and their tame gorilla – we need to get to Kenny before they do. Burton, I want you to question anyone in the vicinity who might have seen Kenny or have any idea where he might be heading – we need to locate him before he locates Jess," he said, jogging ahead.

***

"Jess, wait for us!" called Joshua. "Flip! That boy is fast!" he exclaimed.

Kenny sprinted along the top of the woods, taking a short cut up out of the valley and back to his car. Sliding down over a steep grassy bank he sprinted along the dirt track towards the railway siding, skidding to a halt when he saw the bright red Ford Ranger parked in front of his Golf. Cursing profusely, he turned and headed back the way he had come. Stumbling down through the undergrowth, he was suddenly aware that he was being followed. In fear for his life, he ducked behind a large tree, holding his breath, trying to make himself as small as possible, terrified that the Phillips brothers had tracked him down. Cautiously he scanned the valley, and was full of rage when he realized *who* his pursuant was. "That Wilkins brat has got it coming!" he grated, climbing up the tree.

Kenny waited silently, poised, watching his quarry draw nearer, revelling in the thought of what he planned to do to him, his grin growing wider with each approaching footstep, each panting breath.

He sprang heavily down upon Jess as the boy passed beneath the large oak into a clearing.

"Gotcha!" he shouted, gleefully, knocking him to the ground, winding him. "Now, to finish off what I started." He smirked, yanking him to his feet. "You obviously haven't learnt your lesson. So, I'll just have to teach you all over again, won't I!" he ground out sadistically, raising his fist.

"No, you won't!" declared Jess, shoving Kenny away. "Cos… Cos I've got THIS!" he said, with some surprise, finding himself suddenly brandishing a baseball bat!

"AND US!" exclaimed Joshua, bursting into the clearing with Tom, Mitch, Hilly, Esther and Cam.

"AND US!" shouted Lee, joining them with Jed, Joel, Deut, Miri, Lauren, and Dunc. His bike showered Kenny with dry mud as he screeched to a halt.

"AND THEM!" added Jed, indicating the army of angels, surrounding the children. He could see them all in spirit. Each child, each person, protected by several angels. Swords flaming. Great golden, glowing beings, breathtakingly beautiful and ready for battle. *"For He will command His angels concerning you, to guard you in all your ways!"* Jed murmured in wonderment. He could also see a flaming wall of fiery protection burning fiercely, surrounding them all. Their faces blazed with scorching light against the darkening sky. He looked to his right, exchanging a nod with the enormous angel assigned to protect him. "Praise You Lord!" he exclaimed under his breath. "Thank God you're on my side," he said in awe! The angel winked.

Bringing his focus back to Kenny, Jed could see from the terrified look on his face, that God had also revealed this to him. Although no one else present seemed to be consciously aware of their celestial company, Kenny could obviously see them all!

Jess saw Kenny cower in sudden fear and felt a satisfaction course through him. 'Amazing what having a baseball bat can do,' he thought to himself. Although he had no recollection of where he had got it.

They *all* saw Kenny's sudden fear and put it down to the threat their sheer numbers posed.

Kenny, his mouth agape, stared in horror at the scene before him.

So many people, so many…whatever they were…so much light. A burning wall of fire encircled them all, the heat forcing him to step back. Yet they seemed impervious to it, oblivious to it. Shielding his face, he straightened up, brandishing a knife from his belt. "Back off!" he shouted, "Back off, or I'll…"

"You'll what?!" demanded Jess angrily, raising his bat. "Beat me up again?!"

"Give up, Kenny," called Deut, "IT'S ALL OVER!"

"YOU THINK IT'S ALL OVER?!" he spat maliciously, then threw the knife at Jess, and ran.

Stepping in front of Jess, his angel swept the knife aside with a contemptuous flick of his sword, sending it deep into a tree.

Jess had instinctively ducked, found Dunc's football at his feet and toed it as hard as he could at Kenny, smacking him square on the back of his head. BAM!

"IT IS NOW!" he shouted in defiance, as Kenny collapsed in a heap.

Ruth, Hughes, Stanford, Amos, Burton, Crowther, and Newman all ran into the clearing, witnessing Jess' shot.

"Cuff that piece of scum!" Newman ordered Amos and Burton.

They ran forward, rolling a stunned Kenny onto his stomach, securing his wrists behind him. Burton was privately relieved to see Amos take her cuffs from her back pocket.

"Oh, them's just me spares!" she smirked, catching his look.

"That was *some* shot!" Stanford grinned at Jess. "You okay?"

"Yes, he's okay!" chuckled Hughes, proudly. "I told you he'd make a great copper! He's made his first arrest at eleven!" he joked.

The family crowded around Jess, hugging, congratulating and generally making a huge fuss of him.

"You gave us all quite a scare for a minute there, Jess!" said Miri, smiling and squeezing him tight.

"Choking, not breathing!" he teased when she wouldn't let him go.

"Get used to it, Jess!" laughed Cam. "I'm still trying to straighten out the crick in my back!" he stage-whispered.

"Cheeky blighter! Just you remember, young man, you're still not too big for me to put over my knee!" Miri grinned.

"Are you kidding me mum?" Cam teased. "You only come up to my kneecaps, these days!" Their relief and pride was evident in all the teasing and friendly banter, but Ruth, knowing how it *could* have ended, took a moment to thank the Lord for His mercy and grace.

***

It was a loud, happy, babbling band of tired but triumphant folk that returned to Beachy Manor. Pappa Walt, Nanna Penny, Great Aunt Mary, and Great Uncle Roly were much relieved to see them all back, safe and sound, their fervent prayers answered.

Newman, Crowther and Burton escorted Kenny back to the station, leaving Stanford, Hughes and Amos behind.

"Sorry, we're late, we've been a bit busy!" said Amos, to much laughter.

"Oh, *do* tell, my dear!" begged Great Aunt Mary. And she was, much to her delight, beset with the tale, as everyone fell over themselves to tell their bit. And it took some telling, Jed's contribution in particular.

"Well!" declared Great Aunt Mary, "As I said earlier, God will use anything to speak to us. Today it would appear he used a football! For I'm sure Kenny *heard* God's displeasure loud and clear! I'd say that was, God ONE – Kenny, NIL!" she roared, delighting in their shared laughter."

"I bloomin' LOVE your Great Aunt Mary!" whispered Lauren to Hilly.

"We ALL do!" Hilly giggled.

Later they gathered around an open brazier, quiet and reflective, Ruby and Missy both snoozing beneath Nanna Penny's snuggle rug. Everyone else had gone home hours ago and the beach was now deserted. Not a soul in sight, except for their party. Miri began to raise her voice in praise. Gradually, one by one, everyone joined in.

**'We lift our hearts
And praise You Lord
Hear our joy
Hear our joy!'**

"Father, we thank You for today. Thank You for bringing us all together. Thank You for family and friends – old and new. Thank You for your protection, for keeping us safe. Thank You for Your justice, grace, and mercy, for Your wondrous miracles and boundless love. Amen," prayed Jed.

The stars were out, the sky a deep midnight blue, the air fresh and cool, the moon glowing and full. Sitting beneath such majesty humbled even the most hardened unbeliever. Hughes had seen things in his life that he would never forget, and he had lost hope in humanity. But hearing them sing, listening to their prayers he marvelled at the strength of their faith and wondered…

"Oh, and Lord, I'd like to ask one more thing," added Jed with a smile, "Despite the late night, could you make sure everyone is on time for church tomorrow! Amen!"

***

Kenny paced angrily back and forth in his cell. He could not settle, could not believe that he was locked up again, could not believe that he had allowed a *kid* to get the better of him. He had seen stars when that ball hit. The back of his head still hurt.

But what bothered him more were the images he had seen. He could not get them out of his head. What were those…things? Were they really what he thought they were? Was it possible? *Angels?* Had he really seen *angels*?

And what about that fire? Had there really been a fire all around them? *He* could see it. *He* could feel its heat. But *they* didn't seem to see anything – not even the Angels. How? How come *he* could see them, and *they* could not? Unless the bump on the head was making him hallucinate? 'NO!' He reasoned, 'I saw them *before* I was hit by the ball.' And what about what he had seen as he had turned to run? Shuddering, he tried to block *that* memory out. Those terrible *things* – jet black, evil-looking, vile things with red eyes, reaching out to grab him. Burying his head in his hands, he slumped on the cell bed.

"It's all real, Kenny," said a soft voice.

Kenny's eyes flew open. He yelped and scrambled off the bed, for sitting on the end of the bed was a woman with long red hair, in jeans and a t-shirt.

"Do not be afraid," she said, calmly.

Startled, he said, "How did you get in here?"

"The same way as you," she replied.

"What?" he asked nervously, "Through the door?"

"No," she replied, "Through choices."

"What?" he asked again.

"Kenny, what you saw today was very real," she asserted. "There is a Heaven, and a Hell. There is good and evil. You were shown both."

"What are you talking about? Wh-who showed me?" he stammered.

"God," she answered simply.

"God?!" he spat derisively, "I don't believe in God!"

"Well, He believes in you." She smiled. "And He loves you, Kenny."

"Loves me?! God?! The great and powerful Oz?! That God? Loves me?!" Kenny scoffed.

"Yes," she answered.

"Why?! Why would *He* love *me*?!" Kenny mocked.

"Because, God *is* Love," she replied.

"Oh right! God is love! And who are you?" Kenny asked disbelievingly, "His P.A.?"

"I am but His messenger," she replied softly.

"His messenger?!" He laughed. "So, what's the message?"

"Repent," she replied.

"Repent?" he scoffed, "What does that mean?"

"Turn away from your old ways. Start a new life."

"Oh, okay, well, let's say just for a minute I believe you. How do I do that?!" he sneered.

"Confess your sins. Ask for forgiveness. Receive your Salvation."

"Confess my sins?!" he roared, "Confess my sins?! Is this some kind of joke?!" he raged. "You must think I'm stupid! This is all a ploy to get me to admit stuff! To admit to stuff I haven't done!" he continued to rant. "This is all a set up! There's a camera in here somewhere, isn't there?! You haven't been sent by God! You're working for the coppers!" he accused, angrily. "Well, it won't work!" he shouted to the walls. "It won't work, cos I'm not stupid! I'm not confessing anything!" he screamed, gesticulating rudely at the wall, using his finger in place of his mouth.

The woman stood up. "Kenny," she said softly.

"What?!" he snarled, turning to face her.

"This is your last chance," she warned, gently. "Those things you saw today, those *terrible* things that frightened you, *they* will be with you for eternity, if you do not repent," she said, pointing to the corner of the room.

Kenny screamed, covering his eyes. There they were again.

"They are your demons, Kenny," she explained. "Demons that you allow to operate within you, and through you, and for you, because of your past. They are with you all the time, wherever you go, they follow. Repent and they will no longer hold dominion over you."

Kenny was terrified, quaking where he stood, horrified at what he was seeing. "Make them go away!" he pleaded. "Make them go away!"

"*I* cannot," she said solemnly, "Only *you* can do that, Kenny."

Suddenly angry again, he shouted, "This is all a trick! None of this is real! It's all a con to catch me out!"

He began cursing at the wall again, cursing in the direction he thought a camera was hidden.

"Kenny, stop this. Come back to God. He longs for your return."

"Never!" he screamed defiantly. "Leave me alone! Leave me alone!"

"Goodbye, Kenny," she said, sadly.

He turned to see her rising, held aloft by two beautiful, enormous white, golden wings that filled the room. She glowed, her light growing ever brighter and brighter, until in a flash, she was gone.

Kenny fell to the floor, laughing and weeping maniacally, "'God Rocks!' She's gone, she's gone! She's an angel. They were all angels…!

God Rocks…! And there are demons! Where are the demons…?! Where did the demons go?!"

Sergeant Newman thought Kenny was just 'kicking off' and headed down to his cell to tell him to keep it down…and was met with…this.

***

Early the following morning, after arresting the Phillips brothers and Giovani Gonzolas, Hughes and Stanford stood looking in through the bars of Kenny's cell, baffled by his behaviour. According to Sergeant Newman, Kenny had insisted on confessing to every single crime he had ever committed since turning sixteen. Including the assault on Jess and his father.

"Do you think he's going for the insanity vote?" asked Hughes suspiciously.

"Well, if he is, he's got mine!" quipped Stanford. "That man is not the sane man we arrested yesterday!"

Hughes nodded in agreement. "And I hear he's had a visit from another one of Ruby's 'friends'."

"Apparently," confirmed Stanford. "An angel and a few 'demons' by all accounts. An angel with long red hair, blue jeans and a t-shirt with the logo, 'God Rocks'!"

"She's got a lot to answer for, that woman!" grumbled Hughes.

"Angel, sir," corrected Stanford, wryly, "Angel."

"How the heck did he get wind of *her*?!" asked Hughes, incredulous.

Stanford shrugged. "I have no idea – unless…"

"Unless…?" asked Hughes.

"Unless Ruby's 'Gloria' is 'legit'," Stanford said, seriously.

"After yesterday, I'm willing to believe anything!" Hughes sighed, rubbing his eyes in fatigue. "Still, I'm pleased we've locked a few more 'bad uns' up! Can't believe they were *still* waiting by Kenny's car, this morning. Apparently some woman with long red hair, dressed in jeans and a t-shirt, told them to wait for him there!"

"Gloria?!" Stanford grinned. "Our reports are gonna sound certifiable!"

"Won't be the first time!" Hughes laughed, good humouredly.

"Well, we need to leave now, if we're going to get to the church on time," Stanford said, checking his watch.

"You go on ahead, I've gotta check something out first," Hughes said, heading for the door.

"Tell Gloria I'm sorry…" came Kenny's broken voice. "She'll be there."

"And that's not creepy at all!" muttered Stanford, following in Hughes' wake.

***

The morning had dawned bright and clear, promising to be yet another beautiful day. Kingsland Pentecostal was busy, bustling and preparing for seven baptisms!

Lauren had arrived first, bringing her mum Jenny, dad Frank and brother Ben who, it turned out, already knew Lee from football club. She sent up a silent prayer hoping that Lee would *never* mention the whole 'Tuchus debacle' to Ben, or she would never live to hear the end of it!

Next to arrive were Tom and Mitch with their nan Doris, parents Nancy and Jack and siblings

263

Davis and Libby, all dressed in their best, hair brushed and faces scrubbed squeaky clean.

Last to arrive was the surprising addition of Jess. Last night he had quietly asked Joel if he would baptise him – in the presence of his new friends. Joel had delightedly agreed, leaving his own church in the capable hands of his junior pastor Malachi. So there Jess was, escorted by Joel and Ruth, flanked by Joshua and Esther. And happily bringing up the rear, was his dad, Peter, with Ruby clinging ecstatically to his hand. He looked much improved – so much happier. His social worker, Dawn Halliwell had welcomed the opportunity for Peter to spend time with his children during his recovery and had sanctioned the whole thing.

They were introduced to the other baptismal candidates by the 'meet and greet' team, then Miri led them to their seats, all chattering away, excitement evident on their faces. The baptismal pool was waiting and ready.

Jed joyously welcomed his flock, and the worship team led them all in rousing song, praising God, raising the roof and the spirits of everyone present. Then, following Jed's short but sweet sermon on the baptism of Christ, he invited each candidate to give their testimony telling everyone why they were doing this.

Lauren went first.

"Umm, I don't really have much to tell." She blushed profusely. "All I *can* say is, since I met

264

Hilly, my life has changed, I've changed. She seemed *different* from other kids. Well, I actually thought she was weird!" She grinned. The congregation chuckled. "But when I got to know her, I could see she was nicer, kinder, stronger than other kids, and I liked her. And I came to realise that it was her faith, her belief in God and Jesus and the Holy Spirit, that made her that way. And I wanted to have what she had. Then I realized that I couldn't actually have what Hilly had without having Jesus. And that it was Jesus that I really wanted.

"But at first, I didn't believe that it was her faith that made her that way. I thought it might just be the way she is." Her blush deepened. "Anyway, then I met her family…and…well, you've met her family!" She grinned. The congregation laughed. "So here I am. I want, need Jesus," she finished, her eyes filling with tears.

Smiling, Jed thanked her, inviting Tom up next.

"You see, sweetheart, you never know who's watching you!" whispered Miri to Hilly, hugging her.

If at all possible, Tom blushed even pinker than Lauren had.

"Hi," he muttered nervously, "I'm not very good at this sort of thing."

"You can do it, Tom!" called Dunc.

Nodding, he said, "Like Lauren, I met Hilly and thought she was different from others, better in a way…but it was learning about how God works in our lives, about how much Jesus loves us and how the Holy Spirit helps us, that *really* made me want to be baptised. I saw how Dunc handled a really difficult situation, I saw how happy Hilly was, even when things got tough. But mostly I saw how much my nan loved Jesus, every day of her life. And if he's good enough for my nan – he's good enough for me!" The congregation laughed. His nan blew him a kiss.

Beaming, Jed thanked him, inviting Mitch up next.

Clearing his throat, he began. "Hello. Like Lauren and Tom, the Trueman family have a lot to answer for!" The congregation laughed. "I *am* studying Religious Education at school, but there's nothing like experiencing it for real in the field!" he continued. "And I have to say the experiences of the last few weeks, since getting to know the Truemans, has been much like a biblical version of what can only be described as commando training!" he joked. The congregation roared. "I've been brought to my knees more times than a monk! Had my previous conception of Christianity turned on its head! And I've cried myself dry at some point, every day since. And yet I have never been so happy!" Laughing appreciatively, the congregation applauded. "When I first came to this church, I didn't know what to expect, but in a very short time I've come to realize that with God, we must expect the unexpected. And I thank him for that every day. I want to dedicate my life to Him and today

I'm taking the first step. Thank you," he finished, humbly. The congregation cheered.

"He is so eloquent!" beamed Miri.

"He's preaching it like a pro already!" said Jed, clapping.

"He is a natural!" agreed Joel.

"I'm sending him an application for Mattersey as soon as I get back!" Joshua asserted, proudly.

Thanking Mitch, Jed asked Joel to say a quick word on behalf of Jess at Jess' request.

"Hi all! As most of you know, I'm Jed's twin brother – so don't worry you're not seeing double – unless of course you've been overdoing the communion wine!" he joshed, to appreciative laughter.

"I'm also the pastor at Knighton Pentecostal Church – another KPC – just three miles away. Not to be confused with KFC – one letter does make all the difference, you know – you'd be surprised the amount of folks who've arrived expecting a 'Bargain Bucket' and left with a Beloved Bible and a side order of prayers!" The congregation chuckled.

"But today I've been given the honour of baptising a very special young man, here in *your* KPC. A young man who, despite some extraordinarily traumatic times, has shown an enormous amount of courage, resilience, and determination. As you and I know, ***anything the Enemy intended for bad, God will use for good***." The congregation vocalized its agreement.

"The challenges this young man has undergone would have brought even the strongest adult to their knees – but instead it brought this young man to God. Jess would you like to add anything?"

Jess shyly stepped forward.

He was surprised and chuffed to see everyone present who had been at Beachy Manor the day before. Great Aunt Mary (minus the dogs!) dressed in fuchsia pink, waved enthusiastically. Sitting next to her was Great Uncle Roly, sporting a huge pink carnation tucked into the pocket of a lime green suit, giving him the thumbs up. Nanna Penny, Pappa Walt, Uncle Marcus, the whole shebang! The church was packed, standing room only. And standing right at the back by the doors were Stanford and Amos, smiling encouragingly.

Speaking very quietly, Jess began. "I just wanted to say thank you to everyone who came to visit me in the hospital… And for praying for me…and for my dad and sister. Thank you to everyone who's helped me… Thank you for bringing God to me." Then he quickly returned to his seat – ears self-consciously pink, as the congregation erupted, cheering and clapping. His dad patted him on the shoulder. "Well done, Son." He beamed. "Your mother would be proud."

Gradually the other candidates shared their testimonies. Then Jed and Joel briefly left to change, returning in shorts and t-shirts sporting

268

the scripture, Jeremiah 3:15 *'And I will give you shepherds after my own heart, who will feed you with knowledge and understanding.'*

First to take the plunge was Lauren, dressed in leggings and a t-shirt inscribed with 2 Corinthians 5: 17 *'Therefore, if anyone is in Christ, they are a new creation. The old has passed away; behold, the new has come.'*

She stepped into the baptismal pool, helped by Jed and Joel.

Hilly stood ready with the scripture God had inspired her to give to Lauren. "Lauren, the Lord prompted me to give you Psalm 139: Verses 1-5. He really wants you to know how much He loves you and that after your baptism today, you will never be alone again, for He will never leave you or forsake you; He's got you and will continue to bless you forever more," she said, then read aloud,

"O, Lord, You have examined my heart
And know everything about me.
You know when I sit down or stand up.
You know my thoughts even when I'm far away.
You see me when I travel
And when I rest at home.
You know everything I do.
You know everything I'm going to say
Even before I say it, Lord.
You go before me and follow me.
You place your hand of blessing on my head.

Once Hilly had completed her baptismal scripture, Jed read her 'The Baptismal Vow'.

"Lauren, do you believe that Jesus Christ is the Son of God, that He died upon the cross to save you and is resurrected?" asked Jed.

"I do," stated Lauren solemnly.

"Then I baptise you in the name of the Father, the Son and the Holy Spirit," he said, plunging her under the water with the help of Joel.

She surfaced to the deafening cheers and clapping of her family and the congregation, celebrating her re-birth. As she climbed out, Hilly wrapped her in a towel. "Welcome to the family!" she said, hugging her tight.

Next Tom stepped in. Dunc came forward with his scripture.

"Tom, I've been praying for the right scripture for you, there are so many that would have been good, but my heart beat faster when I came across this one. So, I know this is what the Lord wants you to know," he said. "1 Corinthians 16, verses 13 and 14."

"Be on guard.
Stand firm in the faith.
Be a man of courage.
Be strong.
And do everything with love."

Once Dunc had completed his baptismal scripture, Jed began.

"Tom, do you believe that Jesus Christ is the Son of God, that He died upon the cross to save you and is resurrected?" asked Jed.

"I do," nodded Tom, emphatically.

"Then I baptise you in the name of the Father, the Son and the Holy Spirit," he said, now plunging him under the water with the help of Joel.

Tom surfaced grinning from ear to ear, much to the amusement of his nan and those around him. Cheers and clapping rang out. Dunc handed him a towel saying, "You belong to God now, Tom, you're part of His family and mine!" Tom grabbed him around the shoulders with one sopping wet arm, soaking him too!

Next came Mitch. Joshua strode forward. "Mitch, God gave me this scripture for you the very first time we met. It's a weighty one, but I absolutely know it is meant for you. Ironically, it's from Joshua!" He grinned. "Joshua 1: 6-9."

"Be strong and courageous, for you are the one to lead these people to possess all the land I swore to their ancestors I would give them.

Be strong and very courageous.

Be careful to obey all the instructions Moses gave you.

Do not deviate from them, turning to the right or the left.

Then you will be successful in everything you do.

Study this book of instruction continually.

Meditate on it day and night so you will be sure to obey everything written in it.

Only then will you prosper and succeed in all you do.

This is my command – be strong and courageous!

Do not be afraid or discouraged.

For the Lord, your God is with you wherever you go."

Mitch's eyes filled with tears as this scripture spoke to his very soul.

"Mitch, do you believe that Jesus Christ is the Son of God, that He died upon the cross to save you and is resurrected?" asked Jed.

Mitch could barely speak for the lump in his throat. "I do," he swallowed.

"Then I baptise you in the name of the Father, the Son and the Holy Spirit," he said, plunging him under the water with the help of Joel.

When he surfaced, the change in him was visible. He had gone in a boy and come out a man. Jed and Joel exchanged glances. The anointing of God upon Mitch was palpable. They knew to expect great things from this young man. Tom and his family and the congregation cheered and clapped, delighting in his dedication.

Stanford was startled when suddenly he felt a very wet nose shoved into the palm of his hand! "What the?!" he yelped quietly. Hughes was standing next to him, grinning stupidly. And sitting at his feet was a huge great Saint Bernard!

"What have you got there?!" Stanford asked in surprise.

"I found him in a cage at the back of the Phillips brothers' garage, when we arrested them this morning." He beamed, very pleased with himself.

"It's not?!" asked Stanford incredulously.

"Yep! I just had his chip scanned! Seems Kenny gave him to the brothers, so I thought I'd return him to his rightful owner!" he chuckled.

Next up was Jess, helped forward by his dad. This time Lee stepped up with the scripture for Jess. "Jess, at first, I found it hard to pick a scripture for you, because I was trying to find something inspirational. But the minute I stopped trying and asked God to give me your scripture, it all became clear; Your scripture *is* inspiring because it's a confirmation of what the Lord has already done in you and a promise of what he will continue to do. He gave me Psalm 25: 8-10."

"The Lord is good and does what is right;
He shows the proper path to those who go astray.
He leads the humble in doing right,
Teaching them His way.
The Lord leads with unfailing love and faithfulness
all who keep His covenant and obey His commands."

"Jess, do you believe that Jesus Christ is the Son of God, that He died upon the cross to save you and is resurrected?" asked Joel.

"YES, I do," he declared loudly.

"Then I baptise you in the name of the Father, the Son and the Holy Spirit," he said, plunging him under the water with the help of Jed.

Jess surfaced. Only to be dunked straight back under as a large furry blur splashed in on top of him, taking both Joel and Jed by surprise! Jess resurfaced, blowing water out of his mouth. "DUKE!" he gasped, "DUKE! where did you come from boy?!" he laughed, hugging him close. Duke, however, was in rescue mode and began dragging Jess up the steps out of the baptismal pool. Jed and Joel were both dripping wet, the congregation was in uproar – laughing, clapping, and cheering!

The worship team spontaneously played 'All things bright and beautiful all creatures great and small!'

"Somebody get that dog a towel!" howled Jed with laughter, as Duke shook himself dry, spraying everyone in the first three rows! The joy of their reunion was shared by all, that day.

Luckily, order was finally restored, and the rest of the baptisms were celebrated. But it would be a baptismal service that no one would ever forget!

Later, sitting in the church gardens, soaking up the sunshine, surrounded by all the happy smiling faces of his flock, celebrating the baptisms, the family unity, the love, and the food! Jed thanked God.

"Thank you Father for Your abundance,
For Your blessings,
For Your mercy,
 For Your grace,
And for the strength of Your joy.
AMEN"

"You are welcome, my son.
'Behold, I am doing a new thing.'
This is but the beginning…"

THE END

If you have enjoyed this story, and feel led to find out more or perhaps even visit a church near you, where you can meet faithful Christians, check out
https://www.findachurch.co.uk

God, for everything: His inspiration, His patience, and His unending love.

Pastors Tony and Su Williams for always remaining true to God's Word; for your steadfast leadership, teaching, theological guidance, encouragement, and love for your flock; truly loyal shepherds.

Mary and Roly Harris for listening to the first chapter and excitedly pleading for more. You will never know how much that meant to me.

Natalie Townsend for your friendship, unwavering prayers and spiritual support.

Phil and Tracey Colley for your law enforcement advice, kindness, and reassurance.

Dan Marsden for your beautiful artwork, renewed friendship and advice.

Sally and Lydia for picking up the editorial torch with such willingness – for shining it upon my many mistakes and illuminating the correct path I should 'literary' walk if I want to be taken seriously as a writer!

Jo Matthews for being the dear sister I never had; for your calm, loving, loyal friendship, wisdom, encouragement, and undeniable eccentricity! A beautiful, creative soul who willingly shares her mum Shirley and sister Sally with me – you have all kept me sane and treasured over the years.

Chris Mitchell for being the brother I needed and the loyal friend I cherish.

Lydia Sweet my other dear sister friend who always brings to life whatever I ask, with love, patience, and a good dollop of creativity! Your artwork is beautiful. Another undeniable eccentric! And her genial husband Dave for bringing her great happiness and joining our 'Framily' with such courageous aplomb!

Gemma Nickells for your warm-hearted friendship and love of books! And her brother Tommy, whose artistry and help, made everything clearer!

Nicola Berry whose soft sassy heart listened and believed...

And finally my dear son Jordan who, as a boy, made the telling of a bedtime story the highlight of my day. This one is for you sweetheart.

APPENDICES

Glossary
(in alphabetical order)

Adam and Eve – Chapter 4 Page 43
Created by God on the sixth day during His act
of 'creation'. God created Adam – the male –
from 'dust' or the earth. Eve – the female – was
created by God from one of Adam's ribs.
Referenced in Genesis 1 onwards.

Altar call – Chapter 11 Page 201
An altar call is a tradition in Christian churches
where those who wish to make a commitment to
Jesus Christ do so by gathering at the altar,
located at the front of the church. Usually in
response to an invitation given by the Pastor. It is
still referred to as an 'altar call' even when
people gather in a different location or remain in
their seats. It is the call, the invitation, that is
most important. It is also for surrendering
yourself or a situation to God, or allowing God to
change you.

Amen – Chapter 4 Page 39
Means 'So be it' in Hebrew. Used at the end of a
prayer, or when you want to agree with
something someone has just said about God or
His works. Referenced in 1 Chronicles 16:36,
Nehemiah 8:6, Psalms 41:13, to name a few.

Angels – Chapter 4 Page 39

Created by God to be His servants and messengers. To do His will. Referenced in Psalm 148:2-5, Colossians 1: 16.

There are Seraphim, Cherubim, Powers, Principalities, Rulers, Archangels, Angels. They can take the form of enormous, glowing beings with wings or they can look exactly like us. It says in Scripture, "Don't forget to show hospitality to strangers, for some who have done this have entertained angels without realizing it." Referenced in Hebrews 13:2.

Angels guard us – Chapter 5 Page 65

This is a promise from God as Referenced in Psalm 91:11-12.

Anointing – Chapter 12 Page 272

Having an anointing means you have been chosen to fulfil a calling or mission God has appointed for you. It can also mean the application of holy oil.

A. O. G. – Assemblies of God – Chapter 11 Page 193

A Christian denomination of Pentecostal churches.

Authority bestowed – Chapter 1 Page 7

Jesus Christ gave authority to His followers to do the things He could. He said, "And these signs will accompany those who believe: In my name they will cast out demons; speak in new tongues; they will lay their hands on the sick, and they will recover." He also said, "Very truly I tell you, whoever believes in me will do the works I have been doing, and they will do even greater things than these, because I am going to the Father." (Author's paraphrase) Referenced in Mark 16:17, John 14:12.

Backslidden – Chapter 7 Page 94
A Christian term used to describe another Christian who no longer walks with God, who has turned away from God.

Baptism – Chapter 8 Page 125
A Christian rite, symbolising purification or rebirth and full admission to the Christian faith/Church. Usually performed by full immersion in water. Referenced in 1 Peter 3:21, Colossians 2:12, Luke 3:16.

Baptism of Christ – Chapter 12 Page 264
Referenced in Matthew 3:13-17.

Baptismal vows – Chapter 12 Page 270
These are the promises and declarations made during the baptismal ceremony – the full immersion in water, symbolising death of the old life and the birth of the new. The pastor will ask you if you believe in the birth, death, and resurrection of Jesus Christ, who was born and died to save you. You must agree in order for

your baptism to proceed and for you to become 'adopted' into God's family.

(The) Bible – Chapter 2 Page 17
Is a collection of sacred texts and scriptures. Considered to be a product of divine inspiration and a record of the relationship between God and mankind. God's words. God's word.

Blessings – Chapter 6 Page 84
Throughout the Bible, God pours His blessings upon us "Exceedingly abundantly above all we could ask or imagine". Referenced in Ephesians 3:20.

Calling – Chapter 11 Page 195
A 'calling' in Christian terms means the vocation, job, task, role, or ministry, (professional or voluntary) that God has 'called' you to fulfil or perform in your life. He always equips you with the natural gifts and abilities required for your 'calling'. Even when you don't feel you are capable, be encouraged, because you were created for your 'calling'.

Christian – Chapter 4 Page 42
A belief in Jesus Christ as the Son of God and the Messiah – Christ – who was anointed by God as the Saviour of humanity as prophesied in the messianic scriptures of the Old Testament. Being a Christian is not about keeping rules and regulations, performing rituals, or even going to

church. It's about a friendship, a relationship with Jesus Christ.

Church – Chapter 3 Page 33
A Christian group of people who share the same faith or denomination within a community. Can also refer to the building used for religious services. The church of God believes in the existence of one God existing as a Trinity. It believes that Jesus Christ is the Son of God, He was conceived by the Holy Spirit and born of the virgin Mary. It also believes in Christ's death, resurrection, and ascension. The original church began in people's own homes. First referenced in Matthew 16:18, Ephesians 5:25-26, James 5:14-15, to name a few.

Congregation – Chapter 11 Page 192
A gathering, or group of people assembled for religious worship.

Creation – Chapter 4 Page 43
God's act of bringing the universe into being. Simply put:
In the beginning God started 'creating' the Universe.
On the first day God created light.
On the second day God created the sky.
On the third day God created dry land, seas, plants and trees.
On the fourth day God created the Sun, Moon and stars.

On the fifth day God created creatures that live in the sea and creatures that fly.
On the sixth day God created animals that live on the land and the very first two humans – one male, one female – Adam and Eve.
On the seventh day God rested, making it an incredibly special day, a Holy day.
Referenced in Genesis 1-2.

Deliverance – Chapter 11 Page 197

In the Christian faith, 'Deliverance Ministry' refers to liberating and cleansing a person of any demons and evil spirits that may be oppressing or negatively influencing them or those around them. Referenced in Psalm 3:8.

Demons – Chapter 4 Page 46

Are the name given to those angels associated with Lucifer's rebellion against God and his subsequent banishment from Heaven, taking them with him – a third of all angels. Referenced in Revelation 12:7-9, 2 Peter 2:4.

Disciple – Chapter 4 Page 43

A personal follower of Jesus Christ. In His earthly lifetime, Jesus had many followers but there were twelve who were particularly prominent. However, even today if you follow Jesus Christ, YOU are a disciple of His. Amen!

(The) Ecclesia – the called-out ones – Chapter 11 Page 200

Referenced in Matthew 16:18.

(The) Enemy – Chapter 1 Page 7

Christians refer to Lucifer (the fallen angel, cast out of heaven for rebelling against God) as 'The Enemy'. He is also known as Satan, Beelzebub, the Devil, the Serpent, or the Dragon. Because of his rebellion against God, he became God's enemy and therefore the enemy of all God's followers. In his wrath he roams the earth seeking to lie, steal and kill. Jesus also calls him 'The Father of Lies'. He is no match for God. He has already been defeated. But he will try to cause as much chaos, pain, and destruction before his final punishment/destruction. Referenced in Ezekiel 28:12-17, 1 Peter 5:8, John 8:44, Revelation 12:9.

Faith – Chapter 4 Page 43

A strong belief in the doctrines of a religion, based on a spiritual conviction rather than 'proof'. Christian Faith means having a relationship with God, Jesus Christ, and the Holy Spirit.

Faith versus religion – Chapter 4 Page 43

The difference between religion and faith can be confusing, because on the surface they appear to be the same. However, it is my understanding that Religion puts its emphasis on living by the rules laid out by the God of that belief. Whereas Faith puts its emphasis on having a personal relationship with the God of that belief.

(The) Fall – Chapter 4 Page 45
The term often used to describe Adam and Eve's 'fall' from God's grace when they rebelled against His instructions and ate the fruit from the forbidden Tree of Knowledge after Eve was tempted by Lucifer in the guise of a serpent. This was the first sin to be committed. God banished them from The Garden of Eden as punishment. This 'First Sin' is said to be the beginning of the fall from God's grace for all mankind, and because of it, ever since, we are all born as sinners. Referenced in Genesis 3.

Family of God – Chapter 8 Page 128
In the Christian faith, God is our Father. Once you have been baptised you become part of God's family, a brother or sister to all other Christians. God has the heart of a Father and because He loves all of His creation, He wants to draw us back to Himself so that He can be our Father and we can be His children. Referenced in Galatians 3:26, 2 Corinthians 6:18, John 1:12, to name a few.

The Father – Chapter 1 Page 7
'God The Father' is a title given to God within the Christian Faith;
'God The Son- Jesus Christ', and 'God The Holy Spirit' are all equal facets of the Trinity. Referenced in 2 Corinthians 13:14, Matthew 28:19, Luke 3:21-22, to name a few.

Feed the five thousand – Chapter 8 Page 135
Is an expression used when referring to feeding a
great number of people or the presence of an
abundance of food. Inspired by the miracle
performed by Jesus when he prayed two fishes
and five loaves of bread into enough to feed five
thousand people, with twelve baskets of
leftovers. Referenced in Matthew 14:13-21,
Mark 6:31-44, Luke 9:12-17, John 6:1-14.

Feeling in your spirit – Chapter 5 Page 65
The Holy Spirit lives within us and therefore
communicates with us, so when we 'feel
something in our spirit' it is usually the Holy
Spirit working within us and it is important to
take note. Referenced in Mark 13:11.

Fervent prayers – Chapter 12 Page 256
Referenced in James 5:16.

Forgiveness – Chapter 12 Page 260
Referenced in Mark 11:25.

Free will – Chapter 4 Page 45
God created us with the will to make our own
choices. God is often blamed for situations that
are of our own making due to our own poor
choices. Equally there is such a joy and Godly
order when we make the right choices in our
lives. Referenced in Galatians 5:13, Joshua
24:15, Revelation 3:20, Deuteronomy 30:19-20.

The Garden of Eden – Chapter 4 Page 45
Created by God and the home of Adam and Eve until they went against God's will and instructions and ate the fruit from The Tree of Knowledge, which led to them being cast out of the garden. Referenced in Genesis 8-9.

Gates of Hades – Chapter 8 Page 132
The gates of Hades is another name for the entrance to hell. Referenced in Matthew 16:18.

God's Book of Life – Chapter 4 Page 44
Also known as The Lamb's Book of Life (referring to Jesus Christ as the Lamb.) It is the book in which God records the names of all those who will enjoy eternity with Him. It is said that this book contains the knowledge of the birth and death and the plans and purposes of each individual's life. As a Christian we want to be in God's Book of Life. Referenced in Philippians 4:3, Psalms 69:27-28, Revelation 3:5, to name a few.

God's love – Chapter 8 Page 128
God loves us very much – ALL of us. He loves us so much that He gave His only Son, Jesus Christ, to save us. Referenced in John 3:16.

Gods peace – Chapter 2 Page 15 & 19
Christians pray for God to pour His 'peace' into every situation, especially conflict, referring to God's peace which surpasses understanding and will guard your heart and mind. God values

peace and Jesus states: "Blessed are the peacemakers, for they will be called the children of God." Jesus left us His peace. Referenced in Matthew 5:9, Philippians 4:7, John 14:27, to name a few.

Gone to Glory – Chapter 12 Page 221
Christians often refer to the death of their loved ones as 'Gone to Glory' – gone to be with God in His glorious kingdom. Referenced in Psalm 108:5, Psalm 8:1, Psalm 26:8, Colossians 3:4, to name a few.

(The) Good Book – Chapter 6 Page 90
The Bible is often referred to as 'The Good Book'.

(The) Grace prayer – Chapter 6 Page 84
"For what we are about to receive may the Lord make us truly thankful. Amen." Often prayed before a meal.
Joshua added another scripture to his prayer to make it relevant to the occurrences of that day in particular: "Give thanks to the Lord for His unfailing love and His wonderful deeds for me, for he satisfies the thirsty and fills the hungry with good things. Referenced in Psalm 107:8-9.

Healing in Jesus' name – Chapter 1 Page 7
Referring to the ability given to us to heal in His name. In Jesus' name. Referenced in Mark 16:17-18.

Hearing the Lord – Chapter 4 Page 45
People hear God communicating with them in various ways; anything from actually hearing God speak, to relevant scriptural words, thoughts, actions, and other people passing on a 'word' to you from God. Referenced in John 10:27, Romans 10:17, Jeremiah 33:3, John 8: 47, to name a few.

Heaven – Chapter 4 Page 43
Heaven, the realm where God lives. Referenced in Genesis 1:1-2, Psalm 124:8, Amos 9:6, John 14:2-4, to name a few.

A hedge of protection – Chapter 1 Page 6
Christians pray for 'a hedge of protection' to surround them, their families, their lives, jobs, properties etc., to keep them protected and safe. Referenced in Job 1:10.

(The) Holy Spirit – Chapter 4 Pages 44 and 48, and Chapter 11 Page 195
The dove is regarded as a symbol of the Holy Spirit. Referenced in Matthew 3:16-17, Luke 3:22.
Also called 'The Spirit of Truth', He is the Spirit of God, God's own spirit, sent to us by God at Jesus Christ's request to come and live in us. He

is our protector, comforter, guide, teacher, and so much more. Also referenced in John 14:16, John 14:26, Acts 2:3-4, 1 Corinthians 3:16, Romans 15:13, to name a few.

Intercession – Chapter 7 Page 99
The act of intervening or helping on behalf of another. Christians will often intercede with prayers for another person/s, nation/s, and the World.
Intercessor – Someone who intervenes on behalf of others. Intercessory prayers are very much a part of Christian life. Referenced in Ephesians 6:18, Acts 7:60, 1 Kings 13:6 to name a few.

Joseph – Chapter 2 Page 17
Son of Jacob. Referenced in Genesis 37.

Joseph – Chapter 2 Page 17
Earthly father of Jesus Christ and husband of Mary the earthly mother of Jesus Christ. Referenced in Matthew 1:18-25, Luke 2:1-7, Luke 2:16-20, to name a few.

Kingdom – Chapter 4 Page 55
The name given to the place that God inhabits – Heaven – The Kingdom of Heaven. The spiritual realm over which God reigns as King. Also, the fulfilment on Earth of God's will. Referenced in Matthew 6:33, Luke 9:2, John 3:3-5, to name a few.

Lectern – Chapter 11 Page 192
A tall stand with a sloping top to hold a book or notes from which someone, a preacher, pastor, teacher, or speaker can read while standing up. Usually placed at the front of the church.

(The) Lord's Prayer – Chapter 5 Page 71
The prayer Jesus taught his disciples, and frequently used by Christians as part of their prayers.
Referenced in Matthew 6:9-13, Luke 11:2

Our Father, who art in Heaven
Hallowed be Thy name
Thy Kingdom come
Thy will be done
On Earth as it is in Heaven
Give us this day our daily bread
Forgive us our trespasses
As we forgive those who trespass against us
Lead us not into temptation
But deliver us from evil
For thine is the Kingdom
The Power and the Glory
Forever and ever
AMEN

Mattersey Hall Bible College – Chapter 6 Page 85
In Doncaster, England. A Pentecostal Bible college for theological training.

Meet and greet team – Chapter 12 Page 264
In a Christian church this is a group of friendly members of the congregation whose purpose is to welcome you, to make you feel at home and comfortable when you arrive at the church. They are there to answer any questions you might have, to introduce you to other members of the church, provide you with beverages and generally put you at your ease in any way they can.

Pastoral care team – Chapter 11 Page 196
This is a team of Christians within the church congregation or family that help others by supporting, guiding, sustaining, nurturing, reconciling, and healing. This could simply be listening and praying with someone, visiting sick members in hospital, having a cuppa and a chat, being a friend in time of need. They come under the authority and guidance of the pastor.

Persecution of Christians – Chapter 5 Page 67 and Chapter 8 Page 134
This is happening throughout the world and has been since Jesus' time. He warned His disciples that if they followed Him, it would be so. Referenced in Matthew 5:10, 2 Corinthians 12:10, 2 Timothy 3:12, Acts 14:22, to name a few.

Petition and persistent prayer – Chapter 7 Page 113
We are taught to pray without ceasing.
Referenced in Ephesians 6:18.

Post ascension – Chapter 4 Page 47
Jesus didn't leave us alone. He asked His Father
– God, to send us a 'Helper', so we wouldn't be
on our own ever again. Referenced in John
14:16.

Prayer Burst – Chapter 4 Page 38
A term for sending out prayer requests within a
community of 'Pray-ers' – Intercessors or Prayer
Warriors. Similar ways of sharing prayer needs
may be called a Prayer chain, Prayer circle,
Prayer links and so on. A Prayer Burst suggests a
rapid response.

Prayer team – Chapter 11 Page 196
The prayer team offers much the same support as
the pastoral team but through the practice of
prayer. Interceding, supporting, and helping
where necessary.

Praying – Chapter 1 Page 6
To enter into spiritual communion with God the
Father, Jesus Christ the Son and the Holy Spirit.
A 'spiritual conversation'. Whether internally
(silently) or externally (speaking out). Presenting
your requests and petitions to them, as well as
praising and thanking them for what you have
been given, and the whole of creation.

Referenced in Psalm 145:8-19, John 16:24, Romans 8:26, 1 Thessalonians 5:17, Luke 18:1, to name a few.

Purpose – Chapter 4 Page 38
The Lord has a plan and purpose for each and every one of us. Referenced in Jeremiah 29: 11

R.E. or Religious Education – Chapter 4 Page 46
The study of all religions. Often on a school curriculum.

Religion – Chapter 4 Page 43
The belief in and the worship of a superhuman controlling power. A particular system of practices pursued with great devotion and conviction.

Religious book – Chapter 3 Page 22
The Bible is a collection of sacred texts and scriptures. Considered to be a product of divine inspiration and a record of the relationship between God and mankind. God's words. God's word.

Reminding the Enemy of his future – Chapter 11 Page 200
Refers to the Enemy's defeat. Referenced in Revelation 20:7-10.

Retreat – Christian Retreat – Chapter 6 Page 89

Defined as a definite time spent away from one's normal life for the purpose of reconnecting, usually in prayer, with God. It can also be a place to stay at – away from normal life – for the same purpose.

Righteous anger – Chapter 5 Page 70 and Chapter 12 Page 242

There is a time and a place for what God terms 'righteous anger'. Anger that is justified and expressed appropriately, as demonstrated by Jesus when He cleared out His father's Temple by overturning the tables and driving out the money changers and merchants. But we are also warned not to allow the sun to go down on our anger.

Referenced in Matthew 21:12-13, Mark 11:15-19, Luke 19:45-48, Ephesians 4:26-27, to name a few.

Secret Place – Chapter 1 Page 6

Christians refer to the quiet secluded place where they regularly go to pray, as a Secret Place. It can be anywhere, a room, a cupboard, a lonely hilltop, a walk, as long as it is secluded and not deliberately 'public'. It is somewhere they can pray, read their Bible, praise, worship, and commune with God, without being seen, without a 'public display' of their time spent with God. Some even refer to it as their 'War Room'. It is a special place where they can go and privately do battle with the enemy and engage with God. Christians are encouraged to have a 'Secret Place' by Jesus Himself as referenced in Matthew 6:6-7. It is also a place of refuge, a place of safety as Referenced in Psalm 91:1 ('Secret Place' has been replaced with 'Shelter' in some translations.)

Seeing in spirit – Chapter 12 Page 256
Can refer to the supernatural ability to 'see' the revelation that God has shown you. Not in the physical realm, but in the spiritual.

Shekinah Glory – Chapter 5 Page 70
Shekinah means 'God's divine presence' His dwelling place. Glory means 'God's importance, the weight of His presence, the respect, the honour and the majesty'.

Signs and wonders – Chapter 1 Page 9
Refers to miracles seen and performed and promised by God. Referenced in Acts 2:22, Hebrews 2:4, 2 Corinthians 12:12, Romans 15:18-19, to name a few.

Slain in the spirit – Chapter 11 Page 196
Is a Pentecostal term used to describe a form of prostration in which the individual falls to the floor, overcome by the power of the Holy Spirit, who is ministering to them. This can be with healing, deliverance, or revelation.

Speaking in tongues – Chapter 6 Page 79, Chapter 8 Page 124
Speaking in the language of God. Available to us when the Holy Spirit comes to live in us. Referenced in Acts 2:4, 1 Corinthians 1:5, Acts 19: 6, to name a few.

Spiritual influence – Chapter 1 Page 7
Relating to or affecting the human spirit or soul as opposed to material or physical things. Also relates to a religious/faith belief. Angels and demons operate within the unseen 'spiritual realm' and their presence can have an influence on us. Referenced in Colossians 1:16, Ephesians 6:12

Spiritual Realm – Chapter 4 Page 46
Is the additional existence of a realm or realms outside the physical existence of Earth. Heaven is one such realm; in between is another such realm, where there is a constant battle raging between God's Angels and The Fallen Angels (Lucifer's followers – the ones who rebelled against God and were thrown out of Heaven). This realm can affect us here on Earth, as can God's Heavenly Realm. BUT in Christ we ALWAYS have the victory – no question! The Enemy is NOT equal to God – ever! Referenced in Colossians 1:16, Ephesians 6:12, Revelation 20:1-15, 1 Peter 3:22, to name a few.

Spiritual warfare – Chapter 7 Page 102
Battling with supernatural forces within the
'Spiritual Realm' that influence us within the
'Physical Realm'. The Enemy does not want us
to achieve God's plans and purposes for our
lives, so he will do everything within his power
to stop us; he will lie, steal, and kill to do so.
BUT in Christ we ALWAYS have the victory –
no question. The Enemy is NOT an equal force
to God – ever! Referenced in 2 Corinthians 10:3-
5, 1 John 4:4, 1 Peter 5:8-9, to name a few.

**(The) Ten Commandments – God's
commandments – Chapter 4 Page 49 and
Chapter 11 Page 192**
**I am the Lord your God. You shall have no
other gods before me.**
Do not bow down and worship idols
Do not use the Lord's name in vain
Observe the Sabbath day, keeping it Holy
Honour your father and mother
You shall not murder
You shall not commit adultery
You shall not steal
You shall not give false testimony
You shall not covet
Referenced in Exodus 20:1-17

Testimony – Chapter 12 Page 264
In Christian terms to 'testify' or give a
'testimony' means to tell the story of how you
became a Christian. It can also mean to share

with others, something of importance or relevance that God did for you or in your life. Testimony is used in the Bible. Referenced in Matthew 24:14, John 4:39, John 3:11, to name a few.

(The) Tree of Knowledge of good and evil – Chapter 4 Page 45

God created Adam and Eve with free will and gave them permission to eat of any fruit within The Garden of Eden except from The Tree of Knowledge of good and evil. Referenced in Genesis 2:16-17.

(The) Trinity – Chapter 4 Page 48

Father God, Jesus Christ and the Holy Spirit. Referenced in 2 Corinthians 13:14.

Vision – Chapter 11 Page 195

A vision in Christian terms is a supernatural revelation from God. It can come in the form of a sleeping or waking dream. It can be detailed, in depth, or can be a sudden 'flash' or 'burst' of visual and spiritual insight. God reveals what He needs you to know/see. Referenced in Numbers 12:6, Acts 18:9-10, Daniel 7:13-14, to name a few.

Worship – Chapter 2 Page 18

In Christianity, worship is the act of attributing reverent honour and homage to God. It involves praising God in music and speech, readings from Scripture, prayers, sermons, and holy ceremonies. Referenced in Psalm 5:7, Psalm 22:27, Psalm 29:2, John 4:24, Romans 12:1 to name a few.

Worship and praise – Chapter 5 Page 72
Referenced in 1 Chronicles 16:23-31, Jeremiah 20:13, Psalm 75:1, to name a few.

The worship team/band Chapter 11 Page 194
A group of singers and musicians who lead the congregation in song and musical worship, singing thanks and praise to God, Jesus Christ, and the Holy Spirit. Referenced in Ephesians 5:19, Psalm 150:1-5, Psalm 98:1-7, to name a few.

Bible verses
Indirect quotes and references (in order of appearance)

You may want to look up these verses, or any others in a physical Bible, or online. The way they are presented is like this: John 3:16. The 'John' refers to the Book; the first number refers to the Chapter in that book; the second number refers to the Verse in that chapter. In a physical Bible a list of the 'Books' is found at the beginning and will give you the page number to find the book you need. In that book, look for the chapter, a big bold number, then the verse number, small and next to a word. In an online Bible, you should be able to put the whole reference in a search box, and it will find it for you. Remember that different translations of the Bible may use different words, but they all have the same meaning.

We are in this world but not of it – Chapter 1 Page 12
"They are not of the world, even as I am not of the world." Referenced in John 15:19.

Flesh and blood – Chapter 4 Page 46
'We do not wrestle against flesh and blood, but against principalities, against powers, against the rulers of the darkness of this age,

against spiritual hosts of wickedness in the heavenly places'.
Referenced in Ephesians 6:12.

When Jesus died, our sin died with Him – Chapter 4 Page 47
Referenced in 1 Peter 3:18, Romans 5:8, Mark 10:45, to name a few.

Jesus rose again. Jesus is alive. He is as alive today as He was back then and will be tomorrow. Chapter 4 Page 47
Referenced in Revelation 1:18

Jesus ascended into Heaven – Chapter 4 Page 47
Referenced in Acts 1:9-12

Jesus' commandment – Chapter 4 Page 49
Love thy neighbour as thyself, or in modern language: Love your neighbour as you love yourself. Referenced in Matthew 22:37-39.

God's grace and mercy – Chapter 4 Page 49
Referenced in Ephesians 2:4-5, Hebrews 4:16, Numbers 6:24-26, to name a few.

Defeated Enemy – Chapter 4 Page 50
He is trampled beneath our feet. Referenced in Romans 16:20, Psalm 91:13

Keep your eyes on the Lord – Chapter 4 Page 50

Referenced in Colossians 3:2

Armour of God – Chapter 4 Page 50

We are instructed to put on 'The Whole Armour Of God' to protect us against the lies and deceits of the enemy.

It is a 'Spiritual Armour' Each piece depicts elements of our faith that gird us and strengthen us, so that we can safely stand and 'fight' against the enemy and still remain standing once the battle is over.

The Belt Of Honesty (The truth)

The Breastplate Of Righteousness (The righteousness of God)

The Shoes Of Peace (The Gospel)

The Shield Of Faith (The covering of God because we believe)

The Helmet of Salvation (The Lord Jesus)

The Sword Of The Spirit (The word of God)

Referenced in Ephesians 6:10-18.

Standing on God's Word – Chapter 5 Page 62

Referenced in 2 Corinthians 1:20-22, Psalm 33:11-12, Luke 21:19, to name a few.

Plugs from ears and scales from eyes – Chapter 5 Page 63

It is asking God to open our eyes and ears to His truth. Referenced in Acts 9:18, Isaiah 55:3, Job: 42:5, to name a few.

Power in the name of Jesus – Chapter 6 Page 76
His name is above all names. Referenced in
Philippians 2:9-11, Matthew 28:18-20, 1 Peter
3:22, to name a few.

Pray in tongues – Chapter 6 Page 79
Referenced in Acts 2:4, 1 Corinthians 1:5, Acts
19:6, to name a few.

Parable of the Lost Sheep – Chapter 7 Page 94
Referenced in Matthew 18:12-14, Luke 15:3-7.

Chapter 7 Page 103
For the Lord your God goes with you, He will
never forsake or leave you.
Deuteronomy 31:6
This an absolute promise from God.

**The Lord always forgives – Chapter 7 Page
116**
Referenced in Daniel 9:9, Micah 7:18-19,
Matthew 26:28, to name a few.

The Prodigal Son Chapter 7 Page 116
This is a story Jesus told in the Bible, meaning
that no matter what we do, we will always be
welcomed back by God.
Referenced in Luke 15:11-32

The Enemy's time is nearly up – Chapter 8 Page 134

It is written that the Enemy (Satan) roams the earth roaring like a lion seeking someone to devour. He wishes to destroy everything that God has created; and he will do this until his demise, which is prophesied. The nearer to his demise he gets the more he will try to destroy. Referenced in 1 Peter 5:8, Revelation 20.

Holding Jed's arms – Chapter 11 Page 197

This is a direct reference to when Moses fought in a spiritual battle against the Amalekites, holding his arms aloft over them. As long as he held his arms aloft over the battle, the Israelite army were winning the physical battle below, but as soon as he lowered his arms, the Amalekite army would begin to win. After a time, he became tired, so Aaron his brother and Hur his nephew, sat him upon a stone and held his arms aloft for him. Referenced in Exodus 17:11-12.

King of Kings – Chapter 11 Page 198

Refers to Jesus Christ. Referenced in Revelation 19:16, 1 Timothy 6:15 Revelation 7:14 to name a few.

He sits at the right hand of His father God, interceding on our behalf – Chapter 11 Page 198

Referenced in Mark 16:19, Luke 22:69, Hebrews 12:2, to name a few.

Making ready for the day we join Him at the heavenly banquet – Chapter 11 Page 198
Jesus has promised that we will join him at the heavenly banquet to celebrate His victory. Referenced in Isaiah 25:6, Psalm 23:5.

Celebrating His return, His victory, and our own coronations – Chapter 11 Page 198
Referenced in Luke 21:25-28, 1 Thessalonians 4:16-17, 2 Timothy 4:8, James 1:12 to name a few.

His princes and princesses. He has prepared a crown for each and every one of us – Chapter 11 Page 198
Referenced in Revelation 2:10, 1 Peter 5:4, Revelation 3:11, to name a few.

The Enemy has been defeated. He is beneath our feet – Chapter 11 Page 199
Referenced in Romans 16:20.

He has plans to prosper you and to do you no harm – Chapter 11 Page 199
Referenced in Jeremiah 29:11.

He gives you victory wherever you go – Chapter 11 Page 199
Referenced in 1 John 5:4, Deuteronomy 20:4.

He prepares a table for you in the presence of your enemies – Chapter 11 Page 199
Referenced in Psalm 23:5

He offers you the keys to His kingdom – Chapter 11 Page 199
Referenced in Matthew 16:19.

He has promised never to leave you or forsake you – Chapter 11 Page 199
Referenced in Deuteronomy 31:6.

Nothing you do could make Him love you any more or any less than He already does – Chapter 11 Page 199
Referenced in Romans 8:38-39, Jeremiah 31:3, Psalm 86:15, to name a few.

Your King died to save you – Chapter 11 Page 199
Refers to the crucifixion of Jesus Christ – His death upon the cross. Referenced in 1 Corinthians 15:3, 1 Peter 3:18, 1 Thessalonians 5:10, to name a few.

In His name He has given us the power and authority to drive out demons, to speak in new languages, we can lay hands on the sick and they recover – Chapter 11 Page 199
There is more to this verse, however, it must be used with care – talk to an adult who holds a position of responsibility in a church BEFORE

you act on any of these verses. Some things in the Bible are so powerful that they should NOT be used without fully understanding. They should NEVER be used lightly or experimented with, and certainly NEVER without a responsible and knowledgeable ADULT present.

Referenced in Mark 16:17-18.

Chosen for such a time as this – Chapter 11 Page 200

This references Queen Esther and how she was born "for such a time as this", describing how she could use her position to influence and prevent a tragedy for her people. Referenced in Esther 4:14.

Get thee behind me Satan – Chapter 11 Page 200

Refers to what Jesus said to His disciple Peter – suggesting that Peter's thoughts and ideas were not Godly at that moment. Referenced in Matthew 16:23.

You are more than a conqueror through Christ who loves you – Chapter 11 Page 200

Referenced in Romans 8:37.

Walk in victory – Chapter 12 Page 241

Referenced in 1 Corinthians 15:57, Deuteronomy 20:4, 1 John 5:4, to name a few.

Kicking the dust off his sandals – Chapter 12 Page 242

Refers to what Jesus told His disciples to do if they were not welcomed in a particular place. Referenced in Matthew 10:14.

Not to laugh at the downfall of another person – Chapter 12 Page 244

Referenced in Proverbs 24:17.

What the Enemy intended for bad, God will use for good – Chapter 12 Page 267

Referenced in Genesis 50:20.

Bible Verses
Direct quotes (in order of appearance)
Taken from various Bible translations.

Chapter 4 Page 44
If God is for us, who can be against us?
Romans 8:31
This is a declaration and a promise from God to us.

Chapter 4 Page 44
No harm will overtake you; no disaster will come near your tent. For He will command His angels concerning you, to guard you in all your ways; they will lift you up in their hands, so that you will not strike your foot against a stone.
Psalm 91:9-12
This is a promise made to us by God.

Chapter 4 Page 45
Faith comes by hearing about God, and hearing about God through His word – the Bible.
Romans 10:17
This is a statement of truth that Faith does come by hearing about God from His 'word', His Bible. (Author's own wording)

Chapter 4 Page 46
Obey God, resist the devil and he will flee. Draw near to God and He will draw near to you.

James 4:7-8
Advice given to all God's followers.

Chapter 4 Page 47
That God, who loved us so much, sacrificed His only son to save us. Jesus Christ was born into this world to be our Saviour. 'He died for us and rose again'. And 'through Him we receive our salvation'- our redemption. And eternal life after death.
John 3:16
(Author's own wording)

Chapter 4 Page 54
Where two or more are gathered in my name I will be with them
Matthew 18:20
Jesus assured His disciples of this.

Chapter 5 Page 68
With His love He will calm all your fears. He will rejoice over you with joyful songs.
Zephaniah 3:17
God will always love us and calm us, and sing over us as demonstrated in this scripture.

Chapter 5 Page 70
Evildoers do not understand what is right, but those who seek the lord understand fully.
Proverbs 28:5

Chapter 5 Page 70
He reveals the deep things of darkness and brings utter darkness into the light.
Job 12:22

Chapter 5 Page 70
Do not take revenge, my dear friends, but leave room for God's wrath, for it is written: "It is mine to avenge; I will repay."
Romans 12:19

Chapter 5 Page 71
Maintain love and justice, and wait for your God always.
Hosea 12:6

Chapter 5 Page 71
We are hard pressed on every side, but not crushed; perplexed but not in despair; persecuted, but not abandoned; struck down, but not destroyed.
2 Corinthians 4:8-9

Chapter 5 Page 71
For the Lord, your God will be with you wherever you go.
Joshua 1:9

Chapter 5 Page 73
The lowly He sets on high, and those who mourn are lifted to safety.
Job 5:11

Chapter 5 Page 73
Weeping may endure for a night but joy comes in the morning.
Psalm 30:5

Chapter 6 Page 76
Whatever you ask in my name, this I will do, that the Father may be glorified in the Son.
John 14:13

Chapter 7 Page 113
He who is in you, is greater than he who is in the world.
1 John 4:4
Meaning that God is greater than the Enemy.

Chapter 7 Page 115
For He is strong in your weakness.
2 Corinthians 12:9-11
Meaning that God's strength is sufficient for us in our weakness.

Chapter 7 Page 116
Cast all your cares upon the Lord. Be strong and courageous. Be not afraid or discouraged, because the Lord your God is with you to help you fight your battles.
Deuteronomy 31:6
This is a promise, an encouragement, and a comfort from God to us.

Chapter 11 Page 195
Through His gates with thanksgiving and into
His courts with praise.
Psalm 100:4

Chapter 11 Page 198
A member of a chosen race, a royal priesthood,
a dedicated nation, God's own, special,
purchased people.
1 Peter 2:9

Chapter 11 Page 198
Run the race in such a way as to get that prize.
1 Corinthians 9:24

Chapter 11 Page 199
He has commanded His angels concerning you,
to guard you in all your ways.
Psalm 91:11

Chapter 11 Page 199
No weapon formed against you will prosper.
Isaiah 54:17.

Chapter 11 Page 200
I have fought the good fight.
2 Timothy 4:7

Chapter 12 Page 243
With God all things are possible.
Matthew 19:26

Chapter 12 Page 244
Do unto others that which you would have done unto yourself.
Matthew 7:12 and Luke 6:31

Chapter 12 Page 269
And I will give you shepherds after my own heart, who will feed you with knowledge and understanding.
Jeremiah 3:15

Chapter 12 Page 269
Therefore, if anyone is in Christ, they are a new creation. The old has passed away; behold, the new has come.
2 Corinthians 5:17

Chapter 12 Page 269
O, Lord, You have examined my heart
And know everything about me.
You know when I sit down or stand up.
You know my thoughts even when I'm far away.
You see me when I travel
And when I rest at home.
You know everything I do.
You know everything I'm going to say
Even before I say it, Lord.
You go before me and follow me.
You place your hand of blessing on my head.

Psalm 139:1-5

Chapter 12 Page 270
Be on guard.
Stand firm in the faith.
Be a man of courage.
Be strong.
And do everything with love.
1 Corinthians 16:13-14

Chapter 12 Page 271
Be strong and courageous, for you are the one to lead these people to possess all the land I swore to their ancestors I would give them.
Be strong and very courageous.
Be careful to obey all the instructions Moses gave you.
Do not deviate from them, turning to the right or the left.
Then you will be successful in everything you do.
Study this book of instruction continually.
Meditate on it day and night so you will be sure to obey everything written in it.
Only then will you prosper and succeed in all you do.
This is my command- be strong and courageous!
Do not be afraid or discouraged.
For the Lord, your God is with you wherever you go.
Joshua 1:6-9

Chapter 12 Page 273

The Lord is good and does what is right;
He shows the proper path to those who go
astray.
He leads the humble in doing right,
Teaching them His way.
The Lord leads with unfailing love and
faithfulness
all who keep His covenant and obey His
commands.
Psalm 25:8-10

Chapter 12 Page 275

Behold, I am doing a new thing.
Isaiah 43:19

Songs

The songs referred to in the story are taken from
the album
'When The King Calls'
Lyrics and melodies by Nicola Samuel-Stevens
Musical arrangement by Steven Barry Jones

This is the song that Jed, later quotes the lyrics
from, during his sermon.
'Sing praises to our King of Kings, The Lord of
all the wondrous things,
Let everything that takes a breath, Praise The
Lord! Praise The Lord!

With the exception of this one, which is a hymn from 1848, found in the public domain.
Written by Cecil Frances Alexander

'All Things Bright And Beautiful' Chapter 12 Page 274

Nicola lives in the beautiful Southwest county of Devon. She is a proud mum of one son, one dog, three cats, two lovebirds and a whole shoal of goldfish!

Nicola first worked within the NHS as a qualified nurse, before pursuing a career in the arts and graduating from Mountview Academy of Performing Arts with a Diploma in Acting & Musical Theatre; later adding a Bachelor of Arts Honours in Theatre & Performance with English.

Nicola has acted, written, and directed throughout her career.

When the King Calls is Nicola's first novel. She feels privileged to share with you, the love, joy, and wonder of her Faith. "May God bless you and keep you and make His face shine upon you and be gracious to you; the Lord turn His face towards you and give you peace. Amen."

'WHEN THE KING CALLS' can be found in Paperback, eBook and Audiobook on *Lulu*, *Amazon* and *Audible*.

The music album 'WHEN THE KING CALLS' can be found on iTunes and the sheet music is available in paperback on *Lulu* and *Amazon*.

Contact Nicola
Visit her at; www.nik-a-nory.co.uk
Email: nik@nik-a-nory.co.uk
Look for her under NIK-A-NORY on *Facebook*